Concrete Roses

Le'Taxione

This is a work of Fiction. The events and characters described Herin are not intended to refer to specific places or living persons. Any similarities between character's herin and living or deceased persons are purely coincidental.

Concrete Roses
Fiction

Cover Art By: Le'Taxione™ For Diamond Culture Art

Le'Taxione™ Publishing
Email: Letaxione@nstepgangology.com

Le'Taxione™ Publishing and the Crown Logo are trademarks belonging to Le'Taxione™.

Dedication

I dedicate this work to the Structural Gang Culture ©. We must undergo a radical reconstruction where in we stop being tyrants in our communities and become examples of socio-economic and political success. Despite what you hear – the game is not chess, its monopoly!

Le'Taxione™

Introduction

The missing gardener – No One thought it through. Ego's hidden, Agenda's created - germination from contaminated soil. It seemed like a good place to plant, hidden behind the fence of the façade of class. The fence was painted with faded crucifixes but economic actuality – a pay check away from poverty. The upper class saved paint - covered the truth with a lie – The community embraced the lie – the man of the house poured concrete around it – covering the rich soil to emulate riches – assimilation, that must have been his dream. I was planted between the cracks in the concrete - watered with bitterness and lies. Gaze upon this rare black rose – protruding thorns for my foes....... I thrive.

- Alafia Medina

Forward

Nobody cries is a novel that takes the reader through a plethora of conditions-circumstances-events and environmental dynamics that affects crimogenic social constructs and the human beings that inhabit them. It gives the reader an evanescent glance into the psyche of those at diametrically opposite realms of society, yet employ the same venal tactics that constitutes one as criminal and the other as politically savvy-titles that refer more to ones class than ones character.

The Character "Lana" represents the trials that every woman in America is faced with, though they may not play out as visceral as her trials does, the aspects of her trials-the broken home-neglect-addiction-abuse-exploitation-misogyny-workplace discrimination etc. has become the norm in a society that marginalizes the feminine principle to its own detriment.

The Character "Kisasi" on the other hand does not represent the Norm as it applies to the youth in general and black youth in particular. He is faced with prevalent circumstances and ills in the black community but he chooses to actively address those crimogenic circumstances instead of becoming part and parcel to the destruction of his community and self.

The morally corrupt depiction of the political ideology and practice exposes to the public the behind scenes tactics that are employed by the people that the population has entrusted their fate to, through the vote –how said trust is trivialized and violated on a continuum. This story documents the challenges of two people to stay true to themselves and the principle that procured their love. It makes evident the attractive pull of money, perceived success and the lengths that one would go to in order to achieve assimilation – even at the cost of true love...

Acknowledgement

I want to breathe eternal life into the memory of my daughter "Special." May she rest in peace – for her transcendence of this plane of existence was the catalyst for my transformation. May you be pleased with me.I love you eternally.

-Le'Taxone™

CHAPTER 1

Lana was born December 9, 1964, at Emmanuel Hospital in Portland Oregon to an interracial couple. Her mother Mona Santiago was a beautiful Puerto Rican woman and her father Cater Xavier was a tall African American man who had been originally from Haiti but had been adopted, as a child by an American couple that had visited Haiti in the summer of 68 and fell in love with the 4 year old child, Carter, who had been orphaned due to the death of his biological parents who fell prey to the aids pandemic rampant in their country.

This being Lana's reality she enjoyed a rich cultural influence in her life yet her parents were not exempt to the social ills that plagued America. For example Mona had become addicted to crack cocaine when Lana was 11 years old. Lana remembered, bitterly, the times when there was no food in the house due to her mother's addiction. One cannot fathom the sway that cocaine has on its host. At one time in her childhood Lana had to wear the same clothing that she wore the previous year for her mother had taken the welfare check from the month of August and purchased cocaine, in an attempt to sell it and make a profit, but as usual she ended up being her best customer.

Lana watched as in the absence of her father, her mother became promiscuous and began using her body to obtain the drug. She watched in horror as men would frequent her two small bedroom apartment at all times of the night and share her mother's bed. No one knew at that moment how this reality would affect Lana's developmental process or the havoc it would wreak on her psyche, but no one cared, or no one had the presence of mind to take into consideration Lana's needs and fears, for they were, for the most part, caught up in their own addiction. Lana's father's absence, though similarly horrific, had become the norm for the black families in blighted community across America. Though he loved his daughter, he was poorly educated in the skills to gain useful employment. Perceived to be excluded from the American dream of success, wealth, and power, Carter allowed himself to become a byproduct of his dire circumstance. He succumbed to the phantasmagorical concept of "get rich quick" and live the life of riley thereafter. He, like most black men in impoverished communities, equated work with slavery and peonage. Because the job market for Black men in his circumstance was so miniscule, his only opportunity for employment lye in mere labor positions, positions that though they would garner a check, were deemed to be exploitive and degrading.

And like some black men in impoverished communities, instead of going back to school or pursuing a trade, he invested himself in socially constructed criminality to his and his families' detriment. This fact brought him face to face with the criminal "just-us" system wherein black men were disproportionately sentenced to prison than any other ethnicity, not because black men committed more crime, Carter would come to realize, but because there was a systemic racism, built into the judicial system, that perpetuated this ubiquitous reality.

Lana was haunted by the fact she had to visit her father at Oregon State Penitentiary (OSP). She remembered the stale smell of the prison visiting room and the disdain in which her mother was treated by the correctional officers(c/o's). Though her father's face beamed with joy at her presence she could see the pain and want behind his eyes. It destroyed him to see his daughter under these circumstances and Carter would later confess the agonizing pain that he experienced when the visit was over.

CHAPTER 2

Lana was 18 years old and poised to graduate from Jefferson high school with a 3. 9 grade point average. In April of 1983 Lana returned home from school with a plan to go straight to her room, lie down and rest before cooking dinner for Mona and herself. As Lana walked up the block she could see what looked like her uncle Carl's 1970 Cadillac parked in front of their house on 13th and Ainesworth.

At that moment Lana experienced a plethora of emotions. Her mother had stopped using drugs and was in recovery. Lana did not like her mother's brother, Carl and for good reason. Carl was a Vietnam veteran that had been introduced to heroin during the war. He began using heroin to cope with the blood and gore that were concomitant with combat but he was developing a habit that he could not easily kick upon arrival back in the states.

He returned home to hostility and a dire economic reality wherein he could not obtain employment. Due to his post traumatic stress disorder, and his subsequent "flashbacks" he was not employable.

Lana hated Carl and everything that he stood for. He was the fleshly manifestation of evil and in her mind, the reason that black men were the subject of negative stereotypes but her antipathy and loathing of Carl was far deeper than anyone outside of Carl and herself knew.

After Lana's father Carter, was sentenced to a 25 to life prison sentence for robbery/murder when she was just 13 years old, Carl came to live with them after being dishonorably discharged from the Army. During that time Carl and Mona would sit in the kitchen and shoot heroin together, each one assisting the other. One day as Lana watched Carl and her mother's drug use in horror, she observed Carl tie what looked like to her, some rubber tubing around the upper part of her mother's left arm, turn her Palm upward, tap the inside of her elbow, injected into her arm, a needle, and push its contents into her arm. Mona would then slump forward, onto her own lap as if she'd died, and lie prone in that position for what seemed to be hours.

After watching this scenario Lana retreated to her room and cried. This scenario became so frequent in the household that Lana became desensitized to its enormity. But this scenario gave birth to another atrocity more horrifying than the sheer magnitude of the unveiled act. Though Lana's room had become her safe haven, her fortress that protected her against the evil that lurked just outside of her door, the security of her fortress would eventually be breached by the resultant manifestation of that evil.

On a Sunday, Easter day 1977, after injecting Mona with heroin, Carl came into Lana's room and molested her. Lana fought against his animalistic impulses but was overpowered by the strength of her uncle. After Carl completed this vicious betrayal of her trust he merely pulled up his pants and left her with his stench lingering in her nostrils. Lana cried out as her mother lay slumped on the kitchen floor but her cries fell on deaf ears.

"Why!?" How could he do this to me? Lana's conscious thoughts screamed in her head but the question went unanswered. Little did Lana know that the betrayal would play itself out in a church setting and though she reasoned that she was consenting to sex she was in all reality manipulated into the act by another form of predator.

Lana never told her mother what Carl had done to her. She feared being taken from her mother and Mona was all that Lana had in the vein of family. Her father was serving what amounted to a life sentence and he had no family in the lower 48 United States. That being the reality she internalized the pain while simultaneously fostering resentment for her mother and nurturing hate for her uncle.

"What the hell is this pedophile doing at my house?" She asked herself as she approached home. Thoughts returning to the present moment. Once she got to the sidewalk in front of her house she could hear her mother frantically screaming her uncle's name," Carl! Carl!" Lana rushed into the house fearing the worst. As she ran into the kitchen she saw Carl lying on the cold tile of the kitchen floor, blood trickling down from the injection point, a needle protruding from his arm. Mona stood over him in hysterics as he lay lifeless on the floor.

Once Mona noticed that Lana was in the kitchen she turned to her and screamed, "Help me get him up." Lana looked directly into her mother's eyes without blinking and stated," let that bastard die." and as she used to do as a child, retreated to the sanctity of her room and slammed the door. Once inside her room Lana sat on her bed, clutched her pillow, and breathed a sigh of relief.

CHAPTER 3

Kisasi was born to parents, that in their youth, were active members of the black liberation Army in Oakland, California who'd fled to Oregon when the FBI began it's cointelpro campaign against what they described as threats against national security but was in all reality the government's attempt to quell the rise of any organization that advocated liberation for black people in the United States and abroad.

Pamela Wright and Alvin Dixon both fled California after members of the black liberation Army stormed a Police Department in San Francisco and killed several police Officers before being killed themselves. As members of the Organization Pamela and Alvin new that they would become targets of the FBI and the fact that Pamela was pregnant made necessary their flight. After arriving in Portland Oregon Alvin and Pamela changed their name to veil their identities and give their child the best chance at having a normal life, wherein both parents are in the home working together to exhibit the upward mobility that many blacks merely dream of.

Pamela gave birth on December 15, 1964 to a son whom they named Kisasi. Kisasi was Swahili for "vengeance" It was Vitani (Alvin) and Malika (Pamela) desire that Kisasi Grow up to champion the rights of black people here in America and they fed him social, economic, and political thought to this end. Something transpired that Vitani and Malika had no idea would transpire, a contingency that they didn't plan for.

The FBI'S cointelpro program effectively dismantled the Black Liberation Army through suppression tactics, propaganda, incarceration, informants, division, drugs, etc. This left a vacancy in the black community and gave birth to street organizations. Kisasi, having a revolutionary spirit and no way to exercise it started an organization called the "Diamonds" in an attempt to feed his revolutionary ambitions and bring a consciousness to the youth in his community that had been subverted by the prevalence of drugs.

One day Kisasi was patrolling Ainesworth, he could hear a woman inside a house screaming Carl! Carl! Kisasi then crossed the street and watched from a distance as an ambulance pulled up to the home. He then watched as the paramedics wheeled a body on the gurney, covered with a white sheet out of the home. As the first responders lifted the gurney and placed it into the ambulance he heard one of the medics state, "we have an overdose" as she closed the Ambulance doors. This was the state of his community. Drugs were claiming the lives of black people at both ends of this pandemic. Whether they sold the drugs or used the drugs lives were forfeited and resulted in a depletion of black men and women, leaving in its wake spiritual vacancy and impaired households, the utter destruction of family and community.

This void was subsequently filled by criminalization, insensate violence, chaos and brigandage. Youth were socialized for failure and incarceration, and as if that wasn't enough the most common form of death between the ages of 16-25 was murder.

Black people were killing each other at a magnificent rate and no one seemed to care.

"This has to change" Kisasi silently reasoned, but how? How could he inject a philosophy into the hood that would supplant this suicidal mentality that was the norm in his community? And even if he could get the youth to invest in a progressive ideology how could he eradicate the ubiquitous drug trade in his community?

Drastic times called for drastic measures and the thoughts that Kisasi were entertaining were nothing less than drastic. One may say that they were extreme.

CHAPTER 4

It was May of 1983 and Lana was walking to Safeway to purchase some Tide to do her laundry. She'd gotten about a block away from the store when she noticed Kisasi walking in her direction. She had seen Kisasi on several occasions in the neighborhood and found him attractive, but she'd not spoken to him due to her perception of him. Lana thought that Kisasi was one of those ignorant brothers that lived to be nothing but a thug. She heard, through the grapevine that Kisasi was a leader of the Diamonds and though she'd never witnessed any of them selling drugs, due to the stereotype she automatically thought he did. As they came closer to one another their eyes met and neither broke eye contact. At that moment Lana felt something deep inside of her that she'd never experienced before.

She felt a spiritual familiarity, a security, a desire that she couldn't explain. As they drew even closer Kisasi spoke Uhali gani ndada." What did you say? Lana asked as she stopped on a dime. Kisasi stopped and repeated himself in English, "How are you doing sistah?" "I'm fine," Lana replied as she smiled at Kisasi coyly. They were now at a standstill facing each other. Lana broke the awkward silence. "What language was that you used?" "It's Swahili." Kisasi replied then introduced himself," my name is Kisasi," he stated and then extended his hand. Lana took his hand and said, "My name is Lana," and flashed a smile.

Kisasi noticed that Lana's eyes were a light Hazel, her lips full and defined, her face as if it was drawn by an artist in perfect dimension. Her voice was feather soft and inviting. She was beautiful though not conceited and her hand was soft and supple." Where are you on your way to?" Kisasi asked. "I'm on my way to the store." Lana replied. "Alright then I'll catch you another time," Kisasi stated, they turned and walked in their own direction hoping to see each other again soon. Lana arrived at the store, purchased a container of Tide and returned home. She sat on the porch the whole day hoping to catch a glance of Kisasi to no avail. Later that night Kisasi was walking through the hood when he heard someone call his name from the porch where the ambulance had brought the dope fiend out on a gurney. "Who is that?" He replied." It's Lana," the voice returned. Kisasi's heart rate increased immediately though he didn't make that fact evident in his demonstration as he walked up the steps from which the voice came. It was night and Lana was even more appealing than she was in the light of day. "Uhali gana."

Lana struggled to repeat the greeting advanced to her earlier that day by Kisasi. He smiled and corrected her," you mean "Uhali gani." "Yeah, Uhali gani," Lana said through her smile.

"I didn't know that you lived here, this is where that dope fiend died at last week," Kisasi stated." Naw they revived that bastard," Lana said with venom. "You sound like you wanted the brother to die," Kisasi said rhetorically but nothing could have informed him of the reply that Lana would publish;" I wish that nigga would have died," Lana vehemently stated.

Kisasi, seeing that this was a very sensitive subject redirected his line of questioning." How old are you sistah?"" I'm 18" Lana replied, "I'm 18 too" Kisasi replied, then continued," my birthday is December 15" "My birthday is December 9th," Lana said excited that their birthday was in so close proximity of each others.

"Sagittarius!" They both said at the same time through smiles of satisfaction." I don't believe in luck or chance. I think that we were meant to meet," Kisasi advanced." Now the question is where do we go from here Kisasi?" Lana asked." We get to know each other and see where that takes us," Kisasi answered as he gazed directly into Lana's beautiful hazel eyes.

At that moment Lana became overwhelmed by her desire to kiss Kisasi but she disciplined her desire fighting off the urge to do so. It was too soon to become intimate or even entertain the thought of intimacy with this guy that she'd just met earlier that day. Why did she feel so strongly for this guy? Lana silently asked herself in the midst of their conversation. Kisasi, marveling at Lana's beauty too felt something deep in his chest for Lana. She was like no other female that he'd ever met. She was sincere, authentic and silently strong but he could see the pain behind her beautiful eyes, a pain that cried out to his sprit. She exhibited a need to be held and secured against whatever it was that caused her pain. She needed to be protected against the ills of society that she may grow unencumbered to reach her full potential.

Kisasi was brought back to the conversation by Lana's sweet voice," did you hear what I said Kisasi?" Lana asked." Yes, I heard you," Kisasi lied. "I have to go Lana," Kisasi stated. He had to remove himself from her presence for she excited passions in him that he'd never experienced and this scared Kisasi." Do I at least get a hug?" She playfully asked. "Without a doubt," Kisasi stated, faced Lana, and wrapped his arms around her.

Time stood still while she was in Kisasi arms. Lana felt his power as her hands traced the contours of his back, wanting to melt into him and hide in his strength. He held her tight and secure. He held her how she needed to be held. Kisasi broke the embrace and as he walked down the steps he stopped, turned and asked, "When can I see you again?" "Anytime, you know where I live." Lana replied. Kisasi walked off into the night and made a mental note of their electrical embrace, then smiled out loud.

CHAPTER 5

Lana lay in her bed unable to sleep. She thought about Kisasi the whole night and came to the conclusion that she was in love. This had to be what love felt like, she reasoned, what other reason would explain why she could not stop thinking about Kisasi?

Morning came without warning, interrupting Lana's reminiscing. Once again it was time to face the world and its challenges. After brushing her teeth, showering, moisturizing, and styling her very long hair, Lana cooked breakfast for her mother and herself. As usual she ate alone her mother was still in the bed. Carl had facilitated her relapse and Lana could only hope that it was just a onetime thing though she knew better.

This drug heroin was so potent that it made women sacrifice the needs of not only themselves but of their children. It takes priority in one's life and every waking moment is spent in pursuit of this drug. It becomes a part of one's biological needs and it refuses to be ignored. As Lana left the house she yelled" I love you mama" over her shoulder and not waiting for the sentiment to be returned, she closed the door behind her. As Lana got to the corner of her block she was pleasantly surprised to see Kisasi standing there she excitedly spoke "Uhali gani Kisasi" "Sijambo ndada," Kisasi replied." Can I walk you to school?" Kisasi asked," Without a doubt," Lana answered as Kisasi had the day before and smiled. As they walked there was an uncomfortable silence. It was like they both were consumed by the sheer magnitude of poverty that they visualize in their community.

They saw drug dealers, drug addicts, prostitutes, and an old black man lying next to a dumpster with a bottle of wild Irish rose stuffed into a brown paper bag clutched in his right hand. This reality tore at Kisasi's essence as he fought back tears at the condition of his people. Lana wore her heartfelt discontent on her face as they traverse the terrain and panned images that constituted their community. "This is crazy," Kisasi broke the silence. "I know, I've seen this every day for the past 18 years and though the individuals change the scene remains the same." Lana said. "This is why we have to go on the offensive and exercise self-determination because if we don't this will remain our reality," Kisasi said. "This will never be my reality," Lana said as they kept walking towards Jefferson high school. When they arrived Kisasi asked Lana when she got out of school,"3:30," Lana replied."Can I come back through and walk you home?" Kisasi asked. "Of course," Lana stated and they parted ways.

Kisasi walked to his Comrade Askari's house three blocks from Jefferson high school. Askari was a 25-year-old brotha that had inherited his parents home after they were killed in a freak car accident that transpired while they were driving back to Amarillo, Texas to visit family. Askari was 21 years old when his parents died and had suffered from depression for a year afterwards. He had been informed that the people that caused the accident that claimed his parents lives were high off of cocaine and in the wake of this tragedy he'd become politically conscious and vowed to fight against the ills that plagued the black community.

Askari greeted Kisasi at the door. As he walked into the house he was escorted into the den where members of the Diamonds had gathered for their daily classes on everything from Math, history, to economics and politics.

"Salutations comrades," Kisasi stated as he entered the room. His greetings were returned by the Diamonds, in unison. "Today, on my way here, I witnessed some of the worst of poverty, addiction, and its resultant transient reality I've seen in a while. What's real is that it's becoming so prevalent that it is now accepted as a normal aspect of our lives and that is far from the truth. There is nothing normal about the disenfranchisement of our people. As a matter of fact it is abnormal for so many to be without shelter one of the basic necessities of sustaining life, while in the richest nation of the world, but we can no longer blame others for the condition that our actions placed us in. It is my opinion that a lack of education is the root cause of our conditions and drugs perpetuate the hopelessness that we see every day in our communities. This means that it has now become our responsibility to end the drug trade in our communities."

"How are we going to do that?" Askari asked. "We are going to divide the Diamonds into two groups that will control sections of the community and you will be responsible for ridding your section of drugs." Kisasi told the group.

"What if the drug dealers refuse to stop selling drugs in the community?" Askari asked "Then we'll force them to stop," Kisasi replied. Kisasi knew that in order to stop drugs from being sold in the community he would have to go to war with the drug dealers and that would take an arsenal. It wasn't Kisasi's desire to perpetuate black on black violence, as a matter of principle he was against genocide, but the fact remained that there were black men that were poisoning the community and people that he loved and, because they made a living doing so they would not give up their ghetto riches without a fight.

This fact brought Kisasi face to face with the reality that blood would run crimson through inner-city streets when a no drug position was advanced. Kisasi cringed at this reality but girded his resolve to change the reality in his community with something that his father Vitani would say to him when he would inquire about those who are deemed to be in the way of advancement." Everybody is not going to make it" He would say. Vitani would then use the natural process of conception to rationalize his curt assertion saying, "Just as you were one of billions of life germ that was injected into the vaginal tract, an hostile environment, struggled and succeeded to be the one to fertilize the egg, becoming the first cell of life, you must struggle to sustain life and just as those that could not overcome you in that struggle to come into life, died off and became nutrition for you, so will it be for those in this hostile environment, they will struggle to sustain life or they will die off and become nutrition for the true vanguards of life." Though Kisasi didn't grasp the totality of what his father was telling him in that moment, his words were now bearing fruit at the time that he needed true counsel.

CHAPTER 6

Graduation was coming up and Lana wanted to visit her father at OSP to share her accomplishments and plans with him but, when the time came, Mona had again spent all day with Carl getting high causing her to miss the visit. After realizing that her mother was again beholden to dog food (heroin) she made plans to visit her father alone.

In May of 83 Lana caught the Greyhound bus to Salem Oregon to visit her father at the Oregon State penitentiary (OSP). As she was being processed she panned the visiting room and saw her father sitting anxiously, they both flashed smiles but she noted that he had lost weight. She quickly dismissed the thought and finished processing. As she approached Carter he stood and she threw herself into his arms. They were always happy to see one another but this time Carter held on extra tight and lingered in their embrace longer than he ever had. Once the embrace was broken and the niceties exchanged they sat down for what would be an emotionally charged visit.

Lana looked deep into her father's eyes and saw all that he attempted to veil. She saw the pain behind his eyes and again realized that he seemed emaciated." What's wrong daddy?" Lana asked. "There is nothing wrong baby girl," Carter answered. Lana looked directly into her father's eyes and said," don't lie to me daddy, please don't lie to me."

Carter took a deep breath and water filled his eyes. He wasn't scared about what he'd learned but he knew how it would affect his daughter and that tore at his very essence. He searched for a palatable manner to describe his illness to his daughter to no avail." I'm going to keep it real with you baby girl, the doctor says I have cancer," Carter said bluntly. Lana's heart felt as though someone had punctured it with an ice pick. She stared at her father in disbelief. Everything began to move in slow motion. She searched her mind for the words to say as her world came crashing down around her. Carter disturbed the silence in an attempt to reassure Lana saying. "I don't believe anything these quacks say baby girl. They are second rate doctors that only work in the prisons because they've been sued in the so call free world for malpractice." Though Carter was correct for the most part, this didn't bring solace to Lana.

"How long daddy?" Lana asked. "They said I only have a year to live baby girl but only God truly knows," Carter replied through a kind of easy smile." This is not funny daddy, you have to take this seriously," Lana stated. "All right baby girl I'll take it seriously." "You promise?" She asked, "I promise baby girl, now let's enjoy our visit," he replied.

Lana and her father talked about everything under the sun. Lana told him of her plans to attend college and become an attorney so she could get him out of prison. Carter smiled and told Lana that whatever she chose to do with her life she should do it for herself and no one else. Lana moved the conversation to politics to avoid any disagreement but the fact was she had already made up her mind and nothing or nobody would deter her. She missed her father and in his absence was subjected to the most horrific atrocities. She knew that if her father was there these things would have never transpired. She would be safe in his presence and Carl would pay for forcing himself upon her. Her mother would stop using drugs and they could be a happy family. These are the things that Lana longed for in the still of the night.

Carter expressed to Lana the importance of the plight of black people as a collective and that the plight must be aided by first individual success that allows one to use their success to assist their community. Before they realized it six hours had passed and the visit was over. They had become so engulfed in the discussion that they lost track of time. They both stood and held on to each other as if they may not see one another again in life. Little did either one of them know this would be their last visit.

CHAPTER 7

Lana's thoughts were plagued with the impending death of her father while returning home on the Greyhound bus. Her eyes filled with salty water that streamed down her face uncontrollably. This pain could only be equated with the pain of her uncles' imposition onto her when she was a little girl. The helplessness that she felt was excruciating, palpable. Who would protect her in her father's absence? Where could she find the security that only the possibility of her father's presence afforded her?

Out of this pain came thoughts of Kisasi. She'd often found that her thoughts of security and solace rested with Kisasi. Though they'd just met, the time that they'd shared was marked by caring and unspoken, genuine desire for one another. Though Kisasi had never expressed, verbally, his love for her his eyes made evident his feelings. There was no doubt in her mind that Kisasi loved her and she too, loved him. "I am not going to let what I feel for him go unsaid," Lana told to herself. It was Lana's plan to confess her love to Kisasi and she prayed that he would return her sentiments without reticence.

Lana arrived home to an empty house. That was cool with her because she wanted to think on the events of the day and clear her head. She needed some time alone but she longed for the presence of Kisasi and silently prayed that he would walk up as she sat on the porch. Just as she finished her silent prayer of sorts Kisasi hit the corner of her block, and she smiled out loud.

Kisasi was on his way to her house to see if she had returned from her visit with her father and when he'd seen that she had, he was filled with joy, though he didn't outwardly express it. As Kisasi approached, Lana ran down off of the porch to meet him. She jumped into his arms wrapping both her arms and legs around him. "What's up baby girl?" Kisasi asked as he returned Lana's embrace.

Lana just held him tightly, not offering a response. Then as if the dam had burst, she began to weep like a little girl, uncontrollably. Kisasi was perplexed but he allowed her to have this moment without question, without interruption.

Only when Lana's tears subsided did Kisasi renew his original question, "What's up baby girl?" he asked. Lana's feet returned to the ground as she relinquished her embrace. She looked Kisasi directly in the eyes and said, "I love you

Kisasi," and without apprehension Kisasi said, "I love you too Lana," then kissed her deeply and passionately as the world continued to rotate unbeknownst to them.

They exchanged tongues for what seemed to be an eternity only breaking the kiss when they heard the loud barking of a neighbor's dog. Lana took Kisasi's hand and said "I need to talk you," then led him up the steps to the privacy of her porch. Kisasi didn't resist and when they reach the porch he sat in a chair next to Lana. "Kisasi," She began, "My father is dying of cancer," Kisasi winced in pain at this reality and asked, "are you all right?"

I'll be all right but daddy was the only man in my life that I could trust," Lana said." You can trust me Lana, I'll always be here for you and I promise to protect you at all times," Kisasi said. Lana smiled and said" you promise?" "Without a doubt," Kisasi answered. "You promise to take care of me Kisasi?" Lana asked. "Till death do us," he answered. "I'm moving in with Askari next month. "He has a five bedroom house that his parents left to him and he's going to put me on the deed," Kisasi said. "Why would he do that for you?" Lana asked. Because he's my, comrade and I saved his life."

Though Lana wanted to pry further into Kisasi's and Askari's relationship she suspended her line of questioning noting that she would again pry at a later time but now it was all about Kisasi and herself.

"I graduate next month then I start college at Oregon State University in September. Can I come and live with you?" She asked. "That's why I mentioned it baby girl but let me explain before you make that decision. Askari and I are going to be actively eliminating drugs from the community and not everyone is going to agree with this move. This means that violence may be on the menu and I don't want you to be subjected to that possibility," he said.

"I agree that someone needs to be active in stopping drugs from being sold in our community but I don't advocate violence. I think that violence only begets violence," she said. "I respect your position baby girl but we've come to a point and time where we need results now and peaceful demonstration takes too long to yield results. Don't get it twisted, I don't seek violence, but I know that these cats will not just lay down and stop selling drugs and when you make that suggestion you have to be ready to demand it," Kisasi said. "And you are ready to demand it Kisasi?" Lana asked. "With my life," Kisasi answered.

Though Lana didn't like Kisasi's answer she respected his determination. Lana knew from watching Kisasi that he believed that drugs were the reason for every ailment of the black community and that he loved black people with a love that was beyond his years. Kisasi wasn't like other brothers his age. He was mature and serious. When he spoke he spoke of the collective rather than the individual.

He was a man-child and she loved him for that reason. "I could just stay in the dorm and visit your house on break," Lana advanced. "My house is your house baby girl, after all you are my Malika," Kisasi said.

CHAPTER 8

Lana and Kisasi were inseparable leading up to the day of her graduation, spending time together conversating, planning, and just getting to know each other as individuals through sharing one another's life experiences. Lana was amazed at how open, candid, and honest Kisasi was about his family and their previous ties to the BLA and the philosophy of that organization.

Of course Lana, being influenced more by the Dr. Martin Luther King's doctrine of peaceful dissent, didn't agree with the methods of the BLA but she could agree with their objective and that was liberation from tyranny and oppression that goes hand in hand with racism and the disenfranchisement of second-class citizenry.

At the same time Lana knew that she was being unfair to Kisasi in the exchanges for she wasn't as open as Kisasi was. How could she be? How could she express the true dysfunctionalism of her family and still enjoy Kisasi's love? Would he even want to share his intrinsic self with her if he knew that she was a rape survivor? Or would that fact taint her in his eyes. She would do it strategically and now wasn't the time she reasoned. The exchanges of discourse were very intimate at times, but Lana noticed that not once had Kisasi ever tried to inappropriately touch her or make any sexual insinuations. She respected and loved him for this reason but simultaneously wondered if he was as attracted to her physically, as he'd expressed that he was intellectually.

When her intrigue became too much for her to bear she asked Kisasi," Are you attracted to me physically? "Kisasi looked at Lana astonished that this beautiful, caramel complexioned woman would ask such a question. How could any man not be physically attracted to such quintessential beauty? Kisasi silently asked himself before asking Lana," Why do you ask that?" "Because you never tried to have sex with me or even hint at the possibility," Lana replied.

Kisasi, in his intellectual manner stated "I respect you as a queen and when the time presents itself you'll let me know. Until then there is no pressure on my end; and to answer your question, Hell yes I am attracted to you physically!" Lana smiled coyly and said," I was beginning to wonder," they both erupted in laughter.

Kisasi looked at his watch and seeing that it was now 5:00pm said" Damn I was supposed to be at our meeting at 4:45, I'm 15 min. late. I have to go baby girl." "Can I go?" Lana asked. "Of course," Kisasi answered, he was elated that Lana was interested in the cause and wanted to share his philosophy in greater detail with her. This would be the perfect opportunity to do so, Kisasi thought. Lana and Kisasi walked, fast paced, to Askari's house for the meeting. When they arrived and knocked at the door it was flung open in anticipation of his arrival. There Askari stood then pushed documents towards Kisasi. "What is that?" Kisasi asked. "It's the deed to the house comrade, read it," Askari excitedly urged.

Kisasi panned the document and smiled inside when he saw his name as part owner of the house that Askari's parents had willed to him. "Welcome home comrade," Askari said as he turned sideways clearing the entrance into the step down living room of the home. Kisasi entered and embraced his comrade, to the applause of the membership. Not wanting the sentimental aspect of this moment to supplant the urgency of the meeting, they broke the embrace "Uhuru!" The Diamond members yelled back in unison, "Sa sa!"

The cry of "freedom now" was the way that Kisasi would call their meeting to order while simultaneously calling their purpose and goals into focus. "This is Lana," Kisasi introduced. "Uhali gani," the group replied in unison "sijambo," Lana returned. They all walked into the den and started the meeting. Lana sat with the other women that were present and listened as Kisasi commanded the undivided attention of the membership. Several issues were discussed at the meeting. Socio-economic and political thought were at the forefront with Kisasi explaining the folly in adopting the philosophy of Marxism. "Why would those of us who seek liberation from oppression attempt to employ the ideology and goals that have historically oppressed?" Kisasi advance.

"Our political thought cannot be anchored in Marxism, our political philosophy must be tolerant and engaging for everyone would not agree with our tactics though our objectives are similar. If we adopt Marxism we alienate ourselves from the masses, making ourselves easy targets. Our political philosophy will be reciprocalism, meaning we will embrace assistance from anyone who shares our objective and we will assist anyone who shares our objective. This is not a race issue, it's an issue of equity," Kisasi said to the applause of the Diamonds.

"What is your position on violence?" Lana asked from the midst of the group." My position on violence is this, by any means mandatory," Kisasi said and the group erupted in applause. "Now we are going to break up into our committees and discuss ways to better serve our communities. I'll be meeting with the patrol group over there," Kisasi said. The membership broke up into four groups, social, economic, political, and patrol to address the needs of the community and create solutions that would address those needs.

After the meeting had ended Askari approached Kisasi and said" I need to speak with you in private." They walked into the kitchen where they could be alone and Kisasi said "What's up comrade?"

"My parents left me a lump sum of money and I want you to know that half of it is yours," Askari said. "Listen Askari, you don't have to do that," Kisasi said, "I know man, but if it wasn't for you I wouldn't be here today and for this cause I'll spend it all. I believe in this comrade and I believe in you," besides you can't turn down $500,000" Askari said and walked away leaving Kisasi standing perplexed.

When Lana saw that Kisasi was alone she seized the opportunity to speak to him concerning the meeting. As she approached she could see a blank stare on Kisasi face "what's wrong," Lana asked. Kisasi smiled and said "nothing at all." "I want to be part of the cause, "Lana blurted. "We would love to have you baby girl," Kisasi said still reeling from the news that his comrade Askari had just sprung on him. "Lets go" Kisasi said taking Lana's hand and walking towards the door.

Before they could get to the door Askari yelled "Kisasi," Kisasi stopped and turned to greet his comrade. "Here's your key comrade," Askari said as he extended the key to Kisasi. Kisasi took the key from Askari's hand and said "I love you comrade," Askari returned the sentiments and retreated back into the den where the group was.

After walking Lana home Kisasi went to his parent's house, went directly into his room and replayed the events of the day. At 18 years young he was part owner of a $375,000 home and had $500,000. From this reality he drew the conclusion that this cause was ordained by the ancestors and at that moment, again pledged his life to the cause, and fell asleep.

CHAPTER 9

Kisasi awakened to the smell of breakfast, as he'd done since he could remember. His mother Malika was cooking and this would be the perfect time to discuss, with his parents his decision to move out.

After brushing his teeth and washing his face Kisasi joined his parents in the kitchen. "Uhali gani?" Kisasi said upon sitting at the table. "Sijambo, asante sana," was his parent's chorussed reply. As they sat and ate the steak, eggs and hash browns, which Malika had prepared, in silence; a rule that his father had instituted when he was five, thoughts raced through his mind.

When they were all done eating Kisasi broke the silence, "I'm moving out," He informed his parents. "Where are you going to live?" Malika inquired. Kisasi had already come to the conclusion that he wouldn't share the finer details of his arrangement with Askari and he maintained that resolve when he simply answered "with Askari" "Isn't that cat 25 years old?" His father Vitani asked, Kisasi nodded his head in the affirmative not wanting to feed his father's opposition to the move. "What do both of you have in common?" Malika stated in the tone of a nurturer. "Mom's I'm not asking for permission, this is something that I have to do for me and to protect you. I'm going to be involved in activity that I don't want to involve you or pops in, and I can't do that living under your roof," Kisasi said.

Malika shifted her glare to Vitani as if to silently ask him for support on this issue. Vitani caught her eyes but stated "He's grown love and we've given him the tools needed to navigate life," and before Malika could comment Vitani said "You have to let him fly love, we raised him for the struggle. And now we must surrender him to the struggle." Kisasi turned to his mother and could see the tears well up in her eyes before she walked out of the kitchen to her room and closed the door behind her. Kisasi rose up from the table to follow her but Vitani stopped him. "Let her work through this son, she'll be all right." Vitani rose from the table and embraced his son. After abruptly breaking the embrace Vitani walked straight to the bedroom to console his wife and veil his own tears. Kisasi went into the restroom to take a shower and get ready to move. After showering he first called Askari to let him know that he was on his way then he called Lana. "Uhali gani, Lana's voice came over the phone, "Sijambo Mimi Nzuri ndada" Kisasi answered."Talk to me She said."

"Are you busy," Kisasi asked." I'm never too busy for you Kisasi," Lana answered in a sultry but playful manner. "I'm on my way through there, are you dressed," Kisasi asked. "Baby its Saturday morning, nobodies dressed but you," Lana replied. "Get dressed I need to talk to you;" Kisasi said and hung up the phone. It was Kisasi's plan to move his clothes to his new home, then go to the bank with Askari and transfer his funds into an account in Lana's name but he had to first discuss it with her. If she was cool with that, they'd then go and purchase transportation.

Though Kisasi had no transportation he had a driver's license. His father had always expressed the need to have ones documents in order because this is what protected ones rights. "If you don't have drivers license, registration, or identification you are placing yourself at the mercy of rogue police that would use that fact to harass you." Vitani would say.

When Kisasi got to Lana's house she was standing on the porch waiting for him. "Let me speak to your mother before we leave," he said as he reached for the door knob. Lana immediately stepped between Kisasi and the door and said" she's sleep." What was real is that Lana's mother had been up all night getting high and now that she had run out of dope she was sitting in the living room going through painful withdrawals and she didn't want Kisasi to see her mother like that. Though Kisasi, for a fleeting moment, thought that Lana was hiding something, that thought quickly submitted to what he'd come over for." Talk to me Kisasi," Lana said. Kisasi took Lana by the hand, stepped down off of the porch and walked out to the sidewalk." You want to go to the bank with Askari and me?" Kisasi asked as he started walking in the direction of MLK Blvd. before Lana could answer.

As they walked towards MLK, Kisasi said" remember when I told you that I saved Askari's life?" "Yeah" but you never told me what happened," Lana answered." Askari's parents had money and were considered upper-middle-class. They both were doctors and were respected members of our community but they were not conscious. They wanted Askari to be a doctor and tried to keep him away from the brothas that they felt was beneath him. They were snobs but loved their son. After they died in a car accident he began using heroin to deal with the pain of his loss. One day I was walking home and I saw this cat lying next to a dumpster, by a liquor store, it was Askari. He had overdosed. I ran into the store, grabbed a bag of ice and ran back over to him. I tore the bag open, undid his pants, pulled his underwear down to his knees, took a hand full of ice placed it under his nuts and held it there," Kisasi said, while Lana stared at him in disbelief.

"What?" Lana asked rhetorically "I learned from my father that, that was how you revive a cat that had overdosed," Kisasi said." Then what?" Lana asked." He came back to life and though I was only 16 at the time he became my closest friend. I was too serious for the guys my age. I was about the struggle and they were about sports. Askari and I would hang out at the library and with his newfound vigor for life we would talk about the crime in our community and the plight of black people, until one day I said "we have to do something." We talked about the Black Panther party, black

36

liberation Army, the nation of Islam, the United Slaves Organization and all the mistakes that they made and how we could create a group that would adopt the principles and objectives of these groups but create our own philosophy. "And that group is the Diamonds?" Lana asked.

"Right, but here is the part that's going to blow your mind, Askari's parents both had $500,000 life insurance policies and last night he told me that half of it was mines," Kisasi said still in disbelief. "What!" Lana stopped and yelled so loud that people driving by broke their necks to see what was going on.

"That's what I wanted to talk to you about. Can I put the money in a bank account in your name? Kisasi asked. "You would trust me with that kind of money?" Lana replied. "I trust you with my life Lana," Kisasi said, took her by the hand and began walking again.

They arrived at the house that Kisasi called headquarters and entered. Askari was sitting in the den reading, "Kisasi?" Askari yelled. "Uhuru." Kisasi yelled back, "Sa Sa!" Askari replied as Kisasi and Lana walked into the den. "You ready?" Askari asked. "Yea," Kisasi replied. "I'm going to put the money in Lana's name so that I won't draw any undesired attention to myself or the cause. I don't want the comrades to know that we have this kind of money. This fact could be used to cause division within the organization," Kisasi replied. "I overstand," Askari stated, because they had spent time at the library studying Black Organizations they overstood the envy that was at the root of dissention within the organizations. It made no difference which Black organization it was or what their ideology was, their destruction could always be traced back to the envy that members fostered and cultivated for their leadership and this envy was born of another's covetousness of a position within the organization that he and his self aggrandizement thought he was better suited to hold. In almost every instance the person seeking the position of leadership bestowed upon another did not possess the qualities or character needed to act in the capacity that he sought and it was out of this selfishness that he would compromise the organization.

Kisasi new well this historical fact and he also knew that money destroyed unity by creating a perceived class separation. He didn't want to be perceived as one of the "haves" in the midst of the "have nots." Lana, Askari and Kisasi walked into Wells Fargo Bank, downtown Portland Oregon, and though they were there to make a legal transaction Kisasi felt himself to be out of place. This was what marginalization and a life of being treated in accord with an oppressive stereotype caused one to experience when placed in close proximity of those who'd benefit from the imposition of these negative stereotypes.

In his studies Kisasi had learned the role of banks during chattel slavery and the "reconstruction period" of the late 1800's wherein Jim Crow laws and black codes were instituted to eradicate any progress that had been made after the emancipation proclamation. It was the banks that not only discriminated against blacks but also played an active role in the disenfranchisement of black businesses.

Kisasi watched as Askari and Lana opened a bank account in her name and transferred $500,000 into that account though the bank manager smiled the whole time as he personally took care of this transaction, Kisasi could see the disdain for black people that lie behind his piercing glare. He could also see that Askari was purposefully flaunting that he was a wealthy, young black man, the bank managers' worst nightmare. After the transaction they all walked out of the bank laughing." Did you see that racist face?" Askari asked." He turned red as hell," Lana stated" Let's go to the car lot," Kisasi suggested. They walked two blocks down and stopped in a BMW dealership.

CHAPTER 10

While at the car lot Kisasi decided that they could purchase two cars, one in Lana's name and the other in Askari's name. "Why are we doing it like that?" Askari asked. "Everyone knows that your parents had money so they expect you to have nice things and that's how I want it to stay. I don't want the Comrades to know what you've done for me because that may cause them to think that you and I have a relationship that is not shared between them and myself, also I don't need the police in my mix, asking questions putting me under a microscope."

"Cool," Askari said. Lana was quiet but she took note of the moves that Kisasi was making and fell deeper in love with him. She marveled at the thought that he placed into every decision that he made. He was far wiser than his age gave him credit for. He was definitely a leader. They bought a two door 1983 BMW, placed it in Lana's name then bought a triple black BMW of the same model and year in Askari's name. It was Kisasi's intentions to purchase five 78 cutlass's for organizational use and he voiced these intentions to Askari while the car salesman was completing the paperwork on both the white and black BMW's. Askari not only agreed with Kisasi's plan but he offered to purchase five additional cutlasses for the organization. Kisasi smiled and said to himself "that's my Comrade."

"Lana, you ride with me. We'll meet you at headquarters." Kisasi said to Askari and they parted ways. On the way back to headquarters Kisasi told Lana that he now needed her to get the beamer (BMW) insured. "Don't get that cheap insurance either; get that A-1 insurance that covers everything," he told Lana.

"I got you covered baby." Lana said. "Don't you graduate in June?" Kisasi asked." Yeah, are you going to come?" She asked.

That's your day Malika, and I'd rather not impose on that," Kisasi answered." You wouldn't be imposing. I want you to come," Lana said." I'd rather not Malika," Kisasi stated in a manner that left no room for discussion.

They didn't speak another word during the drive back to headquarters. When they pulled up to the house Kisasi broke the silence. "Are you all right?" "I'm cool." She replied. Lana, Kisasi and Askari sat in the den while she called different insurance agencies attempting to locate the best insurance coverage available.

"We're going to have to incorporate." Askari said to Kisasi. "How do we do that Kisasi asked. "Simple, we file the necessary forms; pay the filing fees and wa-la. The business name "Diamonds in the rough" becomes a Corporation." Askari said. "It's that easy?" Kisasi asked. "Well it's a little more than that but, that's the concept. I took business law in college, I can make it happen," Askari, said. "How are we going to purchase 10 cars without raising suspicions about why were purchasing so many at the same time?" Kisasi asked, "We purchase these under the Corporation, that they'll be listed as property of the corporation instead of individual property," Askari answered. "So that's how they do it, it's all a shell game," Kisasi reasoned. "A legal shell game," Askari cautioned. "Make it happen comrade."

Kisasi said and, turned to Lana, "How is that insurance thing going?" He asked as she sat quietly with the phone pressed up against her right ear. "They have me on hold, but I think the best one is, "hello." She said, as the lady on the other end returned to their conversation. "Okay, so that's full coverage, roadside assistance, towing, vandalism, burglary, theft, natural disaster, collision?" Lana inquired. "Okay I'm on my way to your office, you're located on Columbia and MLK, thank you, see you soon, goodbye. She stated then hung up the phone.

Lana picked the keys up from the mahogany 10 seat dining room table that sat in the middle of the den and served as a conference table in the absence of an official membership meeting, at which time it would be moved into a spacious kitchen. Before she could leave Askari came back into the room and said, "We're going to need a couple of computers for corporation records and accounting purposes," "I'll get a couple of them while I'm out." Lana said, kissed Kisasi and left.

"If we are going to be a legal corporation, we are going to need an attorney to represent the corporation. My parents had a friend that teaches law at Oregon State," Askari said. "Contact him and let's get some money in his hands as soon as possible," Kisasi replied. Askari picked up the phone, dialed the number and within seconds was talking to his parents' law professor friend Jeff Ellis. Kisasi could hear Askari speaking to the attorney and though he could not hear what the attorney was saying, he could tell the conversation was favorable. "I guarantee that everything is 100% legitimate Jeff, and no, I'm not joining the establishment," Askari said as he laughed. Askari listened for a second then stated, "Okay, I'll get the paperwork to you in a couple of days along with your retainer fee, peace." Then he hung up the phone.

"That's taken care of comrade" Askari said. "What's the grapes on the attorney?" Kisasi asked. "He's one of those liberal attorneys that can't stand the way race is used when determining justice or the fact that blacks are convicted, far more often than whites, though they commit the same crimes." Askari answered. "So he's a civil attorney?" Kisasi asked. "He's the best civil, criminal, and corporate lawyer in the Northwest, hands down." Askari replied.

"Cool." Kisasi said. An hour later Lana walked into the den. "I got everything taken care of, but I'm not carrying those computers in." She said. "I got it," Askari replied and walked out of the house to the car to retrieve the computers.

Before anyone noticed the day had passed them by. And it was now night. "You might as well spend the night here with me." Kisasi suggested to Lana. Which level of the house do you want Kisasi" Askari asked. "It's up to you comrade" Kisasi stated.

Though the house was now half his, he didn't want to seem ungrateful so he left the choice to Askari. "I'll take the first level so that I can make sure that you are secure," Askari said. Kisasi smiled. "Were going to turn in comrade, "I'll catch you in the morning," Kisasi said as he took Lana's hand and led her upstairs. Once they got to the bed room the first thing they noticed was how big it was. "Damn, this room is big." She said as she panned the dimension of the master bedroom. "Yeah, and look how big that bed is. I'm going to sleep good tonight." Kisasi said, then walked over to the bed and flopped down on it, exhausted.

Lana walked over to the bed and joined Him. She too was exhausted and couldn't think of anywhere else she'd rather be at that time, than alone with Kisasi. Kisasi took off all of his clothes except for his sling shot (t-shirt) and his boxers. Lana followed suit and climbed into bed with him, in nothing but her bra and panties. As he lie between the sheets on his back, she snuggled up against him, and then laid her head on his chest. At first she just lie there listening to the palpitations of his heart imagining the possibilities. She

Le'Taxione

began rubbing Kisasi's chest then traced her left hand down the middle of his torso, then down into his boxers.

She took his erection into her hand, lightly squeezed it, and then moved her closed hand up and down its length. Kisasi turned to Lana, their mouths gently met, and they begin to slowly and passionately exchange tongues. She moaned softly as he shifted positions turning her onto her back without breaking their kiss. He then lifted her bra, freeing her large supple breast and began massaging the nipples between his index finger and thumb. Lana's body writhed under Kisasi's touch as she began to kiss him harder.

Kisasi then slowly traced his hand down Lana's torso, returning the favor, placing his hand inside of her panties. Lana, moist from his touch, spread her legs wide giving Him access to her most intimate self. Kisasi, feeling how wet she was, slowly pushed his index finger into her, then two, and began going in and out of her. Lana pushed her lower body upward accommodating and moaning feather soft. He broke the kiss and took off his sling shot and boxers. Lana too relieved herself of her bra, panties, and all inhibitions. Kisasi put on a condom, then climbed between her widespread legs. He began kissing her again. Her tongue was sweet, her mouth hot and wet. Lana reached down between their bodies, between her legs, grabbed his erection and placed the head inside of her. "Take me Kisasi," she demanded through a whispered moan. Kisasi looked into Lana's face as the light of the moon illuminated her features, revealing her passion and unbridled desire. He pushed his erection into her

She gasped and whispered, "Make love to me Kisasi." He began pushing himself in her as she matched every stroke breathing harder and harder, moaning louder and louder, then she whispered, "Let me get on top." He laid on his back and watched by the moonlight as She straddled him, reached down, put his erection inside of her then began gyrating on top of him.

Kisasi pushed his torso up and down meeting Lana's every movement with force and accuracy. Lost In lust and passion she began moaning louder and gyrating faster and faster until all of a sudden her body went into convulsions and she fell forward onto Kisasi, face pressed up against his. They stayed in that position until Lana's body stopped convulsing.

As they lay there he felt her tears on his face. "What's wrong Malika?" He asked. "Nothing, I have to go." She replied, got up went to the restroom clothes in her hand, cleaned up and started for the bedroom door. Seeing that Lana had not grabbed the keys Kisasi stated, "Take the car," She took the keys from the nightstand, "I'll call you in the morning," He said, She walked towards the bedroom door, abruptly stopped then said, "I love you Kisasi over her shoulder without turning around, and walked out.

CHAPTER 11

The next morning, Kisasi called Lana's house. "Hello, Lana answered as if she'd just awakened. "What's going on, baby girl?" Kisasi asked genuinely concerned about Lana's well being. "I'm good, listen I want to apologize about last night. Something came over me and it was unfair to you that I subjected you to that." She said. "You don't have to apologize Malika, but if we're going to be together you can't keep me in the dark about what you're going through." he stated.

"I don't feel like talking about it right now." Lana said. "No pressure, baby girl whenever you are comfortable, but know that we must discuss this sooner than later, right?" Kisasi asked. "Alright" Lana agreed.

She was aware of the fact that they would eventually, have to talk. She hadn't anticipated the effects of the vicious rape her uncle had subjected her to. At the most unexpected moment it played in her mind like a horror film, causing her to cringe, inwardly, and feel ashamed. One thing for sure is she knew it wasn't her fault. She'd done nothing to deserve such a beastly imposition. It was him! He was the animal and she loathed him for what he'd done to her. What would Kisasi think of her after being told what happened? Would this ruin their love? Would he still look at her the way he did? Her silent line of questioning was interrupted by Kisasi," what do you have planned for today?" "I have to get everything ready for my graduation," Lana, said exhaling heavily. "Okay, I'll catch you later" he said. "Wait, what about the car?" she asked, urgently." That's your graduation present." Kisasi said. "What!" Lana screamed into the phone. "As long as you don't start crying, and promise to get back at me after you take care of your business." Kisasi said. "Thank you! Thank you! I promise, I promise, I love you, Kisasi," Lana said, hung up the phone and began to silently cry. What had she done to deserve the kindness of this brotha? She knew that she deserved the best, but to receive the best was sort of unsettling. This was so new to her that she didn't know how to feel about it. But one thing was for sure, she liked it. She sat there for 15 more minutes as if waiting for the other shoe to fall, but when it didn't, she accepted her blessing and got about the business of planning her graduation.

Kisasi on the other hand, didn't think twice about gifting the car to Lana as a graduation gift. There were so many black people that were dropping out of high school that he was honored to assist one that had stayed the course and graduated, though he didn't agree with the Eurocentric curriculum that was being taught in the school system.

Kisasi thought that the curriculum marginalized black people and the contribution that they made through mastering the sciences before any other human on the planet. But that was his issue and he wouldn't let what he thought of the curriculum obscure the fact that one needed an education to navigate life, he just differed on what a true education was versus being trained." Kisasi," Askari yelled upstairs. "Uhali gani," Kisasi yelled back. "Sijambo, Asante sana Comrade. Come down and let's get this day crackin," Askari said. Kisasi took a shower, got dressed and came down the stairs," what's the rumpus," he asked mimicking a character off of his favorite movie," Millers Crossing. "First, we have to get this retainer fee together to give to Jeff on Monday. I'm suggesting that we both put up $150,000 a piece, then go get a cashier's check and, put it in the safe" Askari said. "I'm with that." Kisasi answered.

"Also call the membership and tell them that we have a mandatory meeting tonight so that we can bring them up to speed on where we're at" Kisasi said. "I think that we should wait until we get everything in place before we notify anyone," Askari suggested. "Why is that?" Kisasi asked. "I don't think that telegraphing our position is a good strategy. We can't trust everyone just because they say that they believe. There is going to be cats that infiltrate this organization just like every other black organization and, the less they know about how we demonstrate beforehand, the better opportunity we have to secure our movement," Askari said. "You're right," Kisasi agreed. Kisasi and Askari spent the next month working to get Diamonds In The Rough up and running as a Corporation only having two meetings in the interim. Kisasi had spent very little time with Lana in that period. She continued to come to the meetings, yet they didn't spend any time together until after her graduation, and Diamonds In The Rough® had become a full fledge Corporation with legal representation. Now it was time to purchase the vehicles for the membership.

Askari and Kisasi went to "fast cars" located on MLK to negotiate the purchase of 10, 1978 cutlasses, for the membership of the corporation. They met with a rather tall, medium build, Caucasian car salesman whom, they could tell had dealt more with black people, rather than whites, and the location of the dealership made that evaluation more plausible, since it was located in North East Portland. Kisasi decided that Askari would do the negotiating since he had, not only a well documented, conventional education, but he was also better versed in business law. On the other hand, Kisasi was home schooled by parents who both attended and excelled in college at UC Berkeley. Vitani's major was political science and Malika's was criminal justice. Kisasi remembered what his father told him when he was 15 years old. He had spoken incorrectly about a political issue that they'd been discussing at the dinner table. "You can never be

50

successful if you don't speak grammatically correct," Vitani admonished him. He told Kisasi of the importance of conveying thoughts and ideas clearly that he may garner the desired result. It was in this vein that Kisasi played the background in this business deal. He watched as Askari engaged the car dealer, intriguing him with his business jargon which facilitated not only the deal but also the delivery of the vehicles.

Kisasi smiled out loud at Askari's performance, after all was said and done, Askari had negotiated for 10, 1978 cutlasses at $6,000 a piece.

CHAPTER 12

Lana was excited. She'd just went to OSU to confirm her enrollment and meet her instructors. In an ambivalent moment Lana decided to make criminal justice her major and business her minor.

Lana met with her respective instructors in lieu of attending OSU in the fall. Though she liked them all, for the most part, she was particularly taken by her law professor, Mr. Ellis. Prof. Ellis exuded confidence and he had an aura of righteousness about him. He spoke very deliberatively as he expressed what he expected of his students. During a makeshift orientation, Prof. Ellis, stated, "If it is your only intention to make money from this profession you have chosen the wrong professor." Lana approached Prof. Ellis after his comments and introduced herself before finishing her walk through the college. After locating the general vicinity of all her classes and double checking the signatures on all of her student aid forms, Lana got into the BMW and headed for headquarters to share her career choice with the one person that gave her the support she so desperately needed at this time in her life, Kisasi. As she drove up to headquarters. She saw three, 78 cutlasses parked in front of the house and reasoned that the plan to purchase vehicles for the organization was in full swing. Lana knocked on the door, "Who is it?" came from inside the house in a voice that was not familiar to her. It was a female's voice, and she immediately became concerned. "Lana" she replied, intending to convey her familiarity with the houses occupants. The door came open and there stood this 5'4" tall, dark skinned, 24 year old, shoulder length dreadlocked, curvaceous sistah. "Can I help you sistah?"

The unfamiliar female asked as she stood blocking Lana's entrance into the home. "I'm here to see Kisasi," Lana stated as she walked past the sistah intentionally brushing up against her. "Who in the hell?" "She's with me Myisha," Kisasi stated interrupting the question as he walked towards the front door. Lana walked straight to Kisasi, kissed him full on the lips conveying to this new female that, "This is my man."

Kisasi, assessing the move, returned Lana's kiss, then introduced the two young women. "Lana. This is Myisha, Myisha this is Lana." "Uhali gani" Lana reluctantly stated. "Sijambo" Myisha stated with just as much reluctance, turned on her heels and walked into the den where Askari was sitting in front of a computer, gazing into the monitor, lightly pressing its key.

Myisha took a seat in front of the other computer and began entering data with urgency. "Who is that female?" Lana asked Kisasi out of earshot of Myisha and Askari. Kisasi, noticing the tension and seeking to quell any discord, answered "That's Myisha, she's a comrade." It was summer in Portland, Oregon; Myisha was dressed in shorts that Lana felt was too tight and inappropriate." Why is she dressed like that?" Lana asked. "Don't trip," Kisasi stated, he took Lana's hand and started towards the den." She's the one that's trippin" Lana said sarcastically as they joined Askari and Myisha in the den.

"Where we at?" Kisasi asked Myisha upon entering the den. "I've completed the forms to make the Diamonds in the Rough Organization, a corporation, listed the vehicles as Corporation assets, and insured them under the Corporation's insurance," Myisha answered and shot a look at Lana. "Talk to me Askari," Kisasi said. "All of our files are updated to reflect the vehicles purchased. I'm now creating a roster of our membership and employing codes to replace the names. I've listed you as president, myself as vice president, and Myisha as our secretary. But we're going to need a treasurer to list on our non-profit application, Askari said." What is a nonprofit application?" Kisasi asked. A nonprofit application is the form where you list board members and finances of your nonprofit organizations, in a nutshell," "Well, list Lana as the treasurer and submit the application along with the bylaws and Articles of Incorporation, Askari said."After we're done, do you want me to call a meeting?" Myisha asked. "Are we ready for that?" Kisasi asked Askari" "Yeah," sistah, call a meeting for tonight and make it mandatory. That night Diamonds In The Rough met for the first time as a legal nonprofit organization, and Askari opened the meeting. "Tonight we meet, not as a street organization, but as a legitimate nonprofit organization. This means that our activity, at least in the public eye, must be conducted in accordance with our bylaws that Myisha will be passing out for your inspection and signature.

If you don't think that you can conduct yourselves in accord with our bylaws, this is not the organization for you. Every one of you will be held accountable by these bylaws and if you are in violation, will be subject to the discipline in these bylaws... "On one level" Askari added then flashed a sinister smile. "Our mission is to rid the community of drugs, crime, and ignorance that facilitates these ills. We'll have to exhibit discipline in our mission because we will be under the scrutiny of the public. This means that we can't claim to be working to better our community and taking part in the same criminal behavior that we claim to be against. If you are not prepared to struggle; if you are not prepared to go without, this is not the organization for you. If you are not prepared to love your community, even when they are not showing you love for this work, this is not the organization for you. It is an historical fact that once you rise up and take a stand, on behalf of black people, you become the number one enemy of not only the FBI, CIA, and local law enforcement, but you may also become the number one enemy of ignorant negroes that feed off of the uneducated and impoverished in our communities. The political "toms" that make a living off of your poverty and they will work against your rise. Also, your rise deprives the drug dealer of his income because he gets rich by selling the drugs that allow those hurting in our communities to escape their reality for moments" Askari said then asked Kisasi to speak.

"As Askari said, we must exhibit discipline, but even more, we must exhibit a military discipline. Overstand that business is war! When you start a business you in essence, begin to compete with others for financial gain and this fact enacts, in other businesses, whether legal or illegal, the law of self preservation. We are now a business that will be competing with legal organizations for funding and illegal organizations for the minds and hearts of the people. Any time that you engage in this kind of business, you must have in place, a group that is willing to protect the business in any manner that becomes necessary, and for this reason, I will be forming a group within the organization for that particular purpose. This group has to be fearless and willing to do what is necessary for the betterment of our community, even if the task is violence." "Yes, sometimes violence is prescribed, though it is not the primary activity of the organization. Those who are a part of this group would not be known to the rest of the group. Nor will their activities be known. That being said, I will choose the members of this group, personally," Kisasi said.

He noticed the way that Myisha looked at him as he spoke, and could also see that Lana too noticed. There was no doubt in his mind that Myisha was flirting with the thought of a relationship between her and himself, though she had not expressed this fact. Kisasi also knew that this dynamic of two women competing for the same man has in the past destroyed the integrity of leadership. He must be sure not to lead Myisha on or allow himself to be seduced by her, but this would be easier said than done. Myisha was a strong, very attractive, sistah that loved her people and her qualities appealed to him.

After the meeting convened Myisha approached Kisasi. "Can a sistah be a part of your group or is it just a male thing?" "Sistah, you know that I don't discriminate in this struggle. Sistah's have been on the front line of our struggle as a people from day one," Kisasi replied. "Good, sign me up," Myisha said, batting her eyes, smiling seductively. Lana caught this exchange and immediately walked into the conversation, saying, "That was a good speech baby," shooting daggers at Myisha. Myisha walked away, and joined Askari as he conversed with brothers and sistahs that attended the meeting, Askari had known Myisha for years. They had attended college together in Eugene, Oregon. He'd been interested in Myisha at one time and though they often flirted with one another, nothing ever came of it. He noticed the subtle tension between her and Lana and hoped it would eventually subside. Little did he know.

CHAPTER 13

Fall crept up on Lana and Kisasi without warning. They had both been so engulfed in the furtherance of their individual goals that they spent little time alone together. They would attempt to make up for lost time in the week that they had before she moved into the dorm at OSU. Kisasi promised to give her his full attention for that week, and he intended to keep that promise. He chose to wait until after she had left for college before he would start the military branch of Diamonds in the Rough, but this didn't stop him from putting together their general orders, restrictive laws, rules of conduct, and planning their activities.

Lana and Kisasi spent a lot of quality time together solidifying their position in each other lives that week prior to her moving into the dorm. They spent time together at the park, the library, the movies and dinner, and at times, at headquarters talking about their future together, and the struggle. He enjoyed her company, but couldn't help entertaining thoughts of this one drug dealer that refused to stop selling drugs in the community and the drastic actions that he may have to take to end this guy's reign.

Lana noticed, at times, that Kisasi was distant in thought and asked, "What's wrong?" "Nothing," he would answer. She had learned not to press Kisasi on anything. That would only cause him to rebel, so she abandoned her line of questioning, for the moment. Just like an attorney, Lana always employed strategy when confronting uncomfortable issues, but one she would address before leaving was Myisha. "Kisasi, I see how that girl looks at you," she said. "What girl?" he rhetorically asked as he prepared himself to rationally address this issue. "You know who I'm talking about," Lana said through a forced smile. Kisasi shifted his position on the loveseat turning his knees first, then the rest of his body, at an angle towards her, "Look babygirl we're in this struggle together and the sistah is part of this struggle. She's going to be in my presence." "I understand that she's going to be in your presence, but I can tell that she wants more than that from you," she said. "And I have no control over that. You're going to be in the presence of brothers that want more, but ultimately it's up to us to stay true each other. I've always kept it real with you, I've been up front with you about everything in my life and you've done the same right," he asked. "Of course," she answered. She knew that she had lied as soon as the words left her mouth, But She was planning to, in the near future, tell Kisasi everything, even about her rape, and she employed this fact to rationalize her lie. Another strategy that she deemed necessary. "Then as long as we keep it real between each other we won't have any problems," Kisasi said through a genuine smile. Suddenly the phone rang, interrupting the moment. Then it abruptly stopped, Askari must have answered the phone in the den where he was working on designing brochures. "Kisasi," Askari yelled from the den, noticing the urgency in his comrades voice, Kisasi immediately rose from the couch and walked into the den, followed by Lana on his heels. "What's going on?" Kisasi asked upon entering, "It's Myisha, she's in the County jail for assault," Askari said. "What's her bail?" Kisasi asked. "50,000" Askari answered. "With 10%, that's only $5000. Go bail her out," Kisasi said.

Lana and Kisasi went back into the living room. He turned on the television and they began watching a movie. A few hours passed before they heard Askari coming through the front door. When he came into the living room, to Kisasi's surprise, Myisha was with him. "She needs to speak to you" Askari told Kisasi, then turned to Myisha and urged her to speak, by gesture.

"What's going down Myisha?" Kisasi asked as Lana shifted to the edge of the loveseat as not to miss a word. "I got into it with my landlord and when he put his hands on me, I defended myself." She said. "Why did he put his hands on you, sistah," Kisasi asked." He'd been trying to get at me ever since I moved in. Sometimes he'd just come by out of the blue, under the pretense that he was checking on the property. Then he would make inappropriate comments like," You're too pretty to be living by yourself." And" if you were with me, you wouldn't have to pay rent." It was cool at first, what woman doesn't like being complemented? Then it progressed into blatant attempts to touch my ass and, when I didn't accept his advances he started harassing me. Today he propositioned me, and when I didn't accept he said that I was being evicted. When I refused to leave he tried to grab my arm and pull me out of my apartment, so I defended myself." Myisha stated matter of factly. Did you ever report him?" Kisasi asked, in an attempt to ascertain the veracity of what Myisha was saying. "Of course, I complained to the police on several occasions, but it's my word against his and him being a Caucasian property owner, guess whose word they believed," she said. "So where are you going to live now?" Lana interrupted. "That's what she wanted to speak to you about Kisasi" Askari said. Kisasi turned to Myisha again to hear what she had to say. "I don't have anybody here except my mother, and she's with some man that beats on her. I don't want to be in that environment" Myisha said. "What about your father?" Lana asked in a manner that let Myisha know that she didn't want her there with Kisasi. "The police killed my father in Mississippi when I was five years old, that's why we moved to Oregon" Myisha shot back at Lana, then turned to Kisasi and asked the question that Lana feared she would ask, "Can I have a room here until I get on my feet?"

Kisasi looked first at Askari, then at Lana. He could see the dread on her face, but this was a comrade in the struggle and he couldn't just leave her in the streets. "Absolutely," Kisasi answered, "I'll get some of the brothas and we'll go pickup your things from the apartment tomorrow. But, tonight we all need to get some rest." Askari said. "Asante sana brotha"

Myisha said. Kisasi and Lana went upstairs to his room and Askari showed Myisha to her room on the first level of the house. Tomorrow, Lana would have to report to the dorm to start the School year. She needed to get some rest. They fell asleep as soon as their heads hit the pillow.

CHAPTER 14

Kisasi, Lana and Askari awoke to the smell of breakfast being cooked. This was a welcomed change from the norm. After everyone went through their normal morning rituals of brushing their teeth, taking a shower and getting dressed, they all met up in the kitchen, where they found Myisha cooking, T-bone steaks, over easy eggs, hash browns, toast, with Smuckers strawberry jam.

"Hotep na Jambo," Myisha greeted them as they came into the kitchen. "Hotep na Jambo," they returned the greeting in perfect unison. About time it smells like a real breakfast in here," Kisasi said through a smile. Askari agreed, as they all sat at the table. "I truly appreciate you guys allowing me to stay here until I get on my feet." Myisha reiterated herself.

"It's nothing, you're our comrade and we can't just leave you out there." Askari said verbalizing both his and Kisasi's position.

The group ate in silence and when the meal was over Lana stated. "I have to go to go the dorm, Kisasi would you walk me to the door?" They both rose from the table, Kisasi said "Asante sana Myisha the meal was excellent." "You're welcome brotha."

Kisasi walked Lana outside to the car, and opened the door for her to get in. Once she was situated she stated. "I don't think that her intentions are pure." "It's not about her Malika, she can't make me do anything that I don't want to do, she has shown me nothing but sincerity, in the cause, it would be counterproductive for me to treat her any other way. The reality is not whether you trust her, but whether you trust me and I've given you no reason not to trust me." Kisasi said. "Of course I trust you Kisasi" Lana said "Then there shouldn't be a problem," Kisasi interrupted, leaned into the car and kissed her. She passionately exchanged tongues with him, in an attempt to convey her love and devotion. It seemed as if they kissed for at least 5 min. She could feel his love for her oozing through his lips, and realized that her insecurities were more about her than Myisha. Lana had experienced the worst, base animalistic exhibition of manhood in her molestation by her uncle, not to mention the abandonment issues she suffered from due to her father's incarceration for most of her life. She unwittingly imposed these issues upon Kisasi. She would have to learn to separate her horrific childhood experiences from her relationship with him, lest she destroy the love they shared.

She made a mental note to actively work on her insecurities while she was away at college. These thoughts accompanied her on her drive and, before she knew it she pulled up into the parking lot of OSU. She took a moment to gather herself. Then she, exuding confidence, walked into the administrative building. Back at headquarters Kisasi, like Lana, prepared for the task at hand. He purchased weaponry for the security group he'd dubbed Almasi, and had chosen a group of 15, three of which were sistahs. Myisha's help was priceless. Not only was she well versed in business management, she was a true soldier in the cause, equally, if not stronger than the brothas of Almasi. There had been several victories for the organization within the first year of its inception.

They had significantly reduced the sale of drugs in the north and north east communities of Portland Oregon and as a result the crime rate was down. The biggest accomplishment was that they did this mainly through educating the community, and very little violence, but that would change soon. There was an influx of California gangs in Portland, which brought a more violent structure and a cohesive group of individuals that employed the sale of drugs as their economic foundation and was prepared to protect that market with their lives. This geographical transmission of lifestyle, ideology, mentality and the culture was attractive to youth that hadn't experienced that lifestyle to such an extreme extent.

The material trappings of that lifestyle were the best recruiting tool that the Californians had and they used it to their benefit. A year after achieving favorable results, in his community, the drug scene again emerged, and with it an insensate violence that Portland had not witnessed before the California gangs geographical transmission.

In June of 84 Lana's father succumbed to cancer. She returned for his funeral. Kisasi made sure he had a proper burial. Lana was shaken and distraught, her father, though absent, was the only man, before Kisasi that she'd felt secure around. "It's going to be alright." Kisasi said as he held her tightly. In November of the same year, Lana's mother Mona, sat all alone in her kitchen, as she held a lighter under a silver spoon heating up the heroin, cotton and water she'd place in the spoon, her mind flooded with thoughts of her life before drugs. She reminisced on the fact that though they were not rich, they shared a genuine love and closeness that got them through tough times. She became flushed with hate for Carl, who brought this poison back into her life. Yet those thoughts were not enough to deter Mona. She'd become physically sick. This would be her last time, she would get help after she get this monkey off her back, she reasoned.

After the heroin and water liquefied into one substance Mona picked up the syringe, placing the tip of the needle directly into the cotton ball, then drawing the heroin up into the syringe. She turned the needle upwards, and using her thumb, shot a light stream into the air, ensuring the needle worked, and eliminating any air bubbles in the syringe, then sat down. Her heart rate increased at the impending injection. She used both her mouth and left hand to tie her right arm at the bicep and began clutching her right fist, releasing and clenching again, causing the vein in the inside of her arm, at the elbow to protrude. She picked up the syringe, pointed the sharp needle at her vein, punctured the skin, then emptied its contents into her blood stream.

Mona felt euphoria as the heroin coursed through her vein, as sweat cascaded down her forehead. She fell out of the chair onto the kitchen floor and lie there experiencing a feeling equal to a thousand orgasms. Oblivious to her pain in the moment, nothing else mattered. It was In that state of euphoria Mona's heart rate became faint, then stopped altogether. She was found three days later by Carl, who had stopped by to get her high. He walked up to the house as always, saw her through the window, lying on the floor in her bra & panties, unresponsive. Carl went in, stood over his sister's body, took the syringe from her arm, sat at the kitchen table, and while Mona's body lay next to his foot on the floor, he injected himself with the remaining heroin she didn't get to inject.

The funeral process was repeated and again Kisasi was at Lana's side.

Lana returned to college determined to graduate and create a new reality for herself. There is no way she would fall prey to the trappings of the hood as her parents had. She would be successful and wealthy, even if she had to kill herself trying. Her resolve was impregnable and the recent deaths in her family served to strengthen that resolve.

"We'd had some success against the drug trade for a while, but now drugs are on the rise again. Overstand this struggle

will not be won in a day and every time you have success, you will suffer setbacks, but you can't allow the setbacks to discourage you from the pursuit of success. We are now dealing with a different kind of threat. The brothas out of California are more violent than Bobby Joe, Pen or Gucci Dan. We can't use the same tactics that we used against them. We can't just rob their dope houses out of existence. We've sent people in to purchase crack in order to get details on how they're set up and believe me these brothas are prepared for any attempt to jack them. Myisha tell them what you saw," Kisasi said. "They have a brotha who answers the door, who's holding a sawed off shot gun and a military .45 in a shoulder strap. He pats you down to make sure you don't have any weapons. Then he sends you into a room with two other brothas, one holds and serves the dope, the other one keeps his heater in his hand, by his side. After the transaction the armed brotha calls to the others at the door. "One coming out," the brotha at the door motions you to him then rushes you out of the door. Any attempts to debate, haggle, start any small talk is met with verbal intimidation. "Get your shit and bounce!" is what they say."
Kisasi stepped in.

"We have to stop their supply before it gets distributed. We are doing recon to find out when and how they get their supply. We have to be patient and disciplined, but when we get this information we're going to have to be ready to be ultra violent because these brothas are going to protect their product with their lives," he said. "How are we going to get this information?" a voice came from the group. Kisasi turned to face the questioner, it was a brotha named Terrance who before joining Almasi was a major drug dealer. Not wanting to reveal any details Kisasi said, "Let me worry about that comrade you just be ready when I do get this information." Askari, before closing the meeting informed Almasi that they now have vehicles that would be issued to those who had drivers licenses, those who didn't were required to get them. "We have to be as legitimate as possible, the tactics that we employ must be veiled by legitimacy. Not having a license could jeopardize an important mission. So everybody in Almasi must have a license." He then asked for the meeting to be adjourned.

Myisha, Askari and Kisasi sat in the den after everyone had left, to compare notes on the meeting. "Why would Terrance ask a question that he knows or should know, would put us at a tactical disadvantage if answered." Myisha asked. She was suspicious of everybody, but what one calls suspicion Kisasi saw as intuition. This is one of the qualities he loved about Myisha. "I don't think that he meant anything by it." Askari said. "I don't either, but it's better to be safe than sorry," Kisasi said letting Myisha know that he fostered the same suspicions while simultaneously agreeing with his comrade Askari. He learned this strategy from his father, who often and sometimes repetitiously told him, "I witnessed the BLA self destruct due to suspicions in the ranks caused by a woman's presence.

Kisasi knew that Myisha's subtle display of affection for him could cause suspicion and envy within the ranks. He'd planned on discussing this reality with her, out of earshot of Askari. Her more active role in Almasi made the discussion that he'd planned not only imperative, but urgent. He would have to choose his words wisely, lest he painted Askari in an unfavorable light, which would in turn give Myisha the impression that he didn't trust Askari, an impression that could be exploited if she was to betray the organization, and though he didn't see her as a saboteur, he had to "Always plan for betrayal." Vitani would warn him.

CHAPTER 15

1984, New Years Eve, after the celebration, the opportunity to discuss with Myisha his position on Almasi's internal functions presented itself. Askari had been excused for the night, leaving Kisasi and Myisha alone at headquarters. They'd both been drinking to celebrate their victory and the two most recent skirmishes against the California gangs, and though they were both tipsy from the celebratory Crystal Champagne, neither was inebriated.

As they sat on the love seat in the den, Kisasi began the discussion. "Peep game Myisha, you and I have the same perspective on many issues. You have a keen intuition like my mother, and I've always listened to a woman's intuition because it's a gift from god, and a blessing to man. That being expressed everyone is not as profound in thought and this fact may cause them to misperceive your intentions, setting up an envy in their hearts that disallows unity and camaraderie," "Are you speaking of anyone in particular?" Myisha interrupted. "No, I'm not referring to anyone in particular, I'm speaking on an organizational level about the dynamics that causes organizations to self-destruct," Kisasi answered. Myisha looked deep into Kisasi's eyes as he spoke. She was enamored and intrigued by both his youth and wisdom. At that moment, she rose in love with Kisasi and as if by an uncontrollable impulse, she leaned in to kiss him. Kisasi return the sentiment. They passionately exchanged tongues, as their hands explored one another's anatomy. Kisasi moved his hand up under Myisha's blouse, and gently passed his hand over her firm breast. He reached around to her back and unsnapped her bra giving him total access, and gently squeezes her nipples one after the other. Myisha arched her back and moaned with pleasure. Kisasi slid his hand down her stomach and unbuttoned her pants. Straightening her body Myisha made it easier for him to unzip them. Kisasi did so and, moved his hand into her panty's as Myisha spread her legs to accommodate him. Just then they heard a car pull up outside. Kisasi broke the kiss, Myisha left the loveseat and went to the restroom to regain her composer.

Askari came in the house and joined Kisasi in the den. "Where's Myisha?" Askari asked. "I think she's in the restroom," Kisasi answered. "You mind if I entertain company tonight?" Askari asked. "As long as she's of good character, you know we have to be careful. Just like we're trying to infiltrate, they're trying to infiltrate," Kisasi said.

"She's from Arkansas comrade. A college transfer," Askari answered, and walked out to the car to bring the woman in. Myisha came out of the restroom, returned to the den and sat on the couch across from the love seat where she'd previously been sitting. Askari came back into the den with his new friend. "Kisasi, Myisha this is Joann." Kisasi stood extended his hand and said, "How are you sistah?" After they exchanged a handshake, Myisha did the same. "I'll catch you guys in the morning," Askari said as he took Joann's hand and led her into his room, leaving Kisasi and Myisha in the den, alone. When Kisasi was sure that Askari was in his room for the night he broke the uncomfortable silence that lie between Myisha and himself. "We need to talk about what happened between us. Sistah I like you more than I thought. But I also have feelings for Lana, and I don't want this to cause any animosity between any of us." He said.

"Hold on Kisasi," Myisha interrupted. "This doesn't have to cause any animosity. There is no doubt that I have feelings for you, I would love for us to be together, but I'm not a little girl. I'm not going to cause any dissention in the organization. I'm here, first of all, because I believe in the cause and your Leadership, if our relationship goes further I'm cool with it and if it doesn't I can deal with that too. It's the struggle that brought us together and everything else is secondary." "I care for you deeply, Myisha I just don't want to lead you to think that I'm going to leave Lana at this time to pursue a relationship with you. Kisasi said. "I don't expect you to leave Lana, at this time." Myisha answered through a smile.

"You are something else," Kisasi said and kissed Myisha good night. As he lay in his bedroom surrounded by the silence of the night, he thought about Lana and Myisha, then smiled out loud. Though he would tell Lana what transpired between Myisha and himself, He was reluctant to do so. He fell asleep imagining what could have happened if Askari had not come home when he did.

275

CHAPTER 16

It was Spring break 1985. Lana had come to spend the break with Kisasi and catch up on the time that they'd spent apart. She had been doing great in school and looked forward to sharing her successes with her man. She arrived at headquarters early one morning only to find Kisasi, Askari, and Myisha preparing to attend Myisha 's trial for assaulting her landlord. Lana knocked on the door and Kisasi answered. As soon as the door opened she flew into Kisasi's arms. They briefly held each other, broke the embrace then kissed, passionately. "Damn brotha, she's just up the street. You act like she's going to school in Europe somewhere." Askari jokingly said.

"How have you doing been sistah?" Kisasi asked. "I've been missing you." Lana said, then asked "Where is everybody going?" "Myisha's trial is today" Kisasi answered, "Were on our way to the justice center." "I'm going with you," Lana said. Before Lana showed up Kisasi had planned to drive the Cutlass. Now he could ride with Lana, which would give them time to catch up with one another.

"Change of plans, "I'm going to ride with Lana." Kisasi said. "We better move out before we are late. One thing, you don't want to do is be late for trial" Askari said. Kisasi and Askari both wore suits made by Le'Taxione. Myisha wore a Le'Taxione Couture business suit and matching black heels with, the Le'Taxione signature blue sole. "You look good," Lana complimented Kisasi as they all walked out to their cars. "He does, doesn't he?" Myisha coquettishly agreed. Lana ignored her. Askari, now alone in the car with Myisha cautioned her, "Sistah quit shooting shots at Lana." "I'm not shooting shots. I just don't like how she just pops in and out of this struggle and expects the same respect that those of us who are here 24/7gets." Myisha answered. "It's not for you to like or dislike. You just stay focused on the task at hand and your position in this struggle and second, this trial. In that order Askari said. "Is that an order," Myisha asked. "That's a direct order sistah," Askari replied.

"I need to get at you about something Lana but I'll wait until we get back to headquarters, "Kisasi said. I need to get at you too," Lana replied. Lana had met a brotha at college that showed interest in her and she was interested in. The brotha's name was Deshawn Williams.

Deshawn was not as serious as Kisasi and the only struggle that he was interested in was the struggle to finish law school at the top of his class, so he could have his own practice, and of course make a lot of money. The fact was that college had redirected Lana's focus. Though she still believed in the principles that Kisasi held dear, she no longer agreed with his methods. Lana believed that she could be more effective in the struggle after being successful in her personal life and Deshawn was more in line with her aspirations than Kisasi, at that moment in time.

Silence fell in the car. Kisasi wondered what it was that Lana needed to get at him about but he wouldn't have to wonder long. "I'm seeing someone else," Lana broke the awkward silence then cringed internally at his anticipated response but it wasn't what she feared. "Do you love him?" Kisasi solemnly asked. "Of course not," she answered not offering any details. Silence again loomed in the car but only for a moment. "On New Year's, after a few too many glasses of champagne, I kissed Myisha" Kisasi said. "Do you love her?" Lana returned Kisasi's question. Kisasi smiled and answered "Absolutely not." Both cars pulled up into the parking lot of the Justice Center, paid for parking, and walked into the building. They went directly to Judge Felnagles Court Room. Judge Felnagle was known to be not only hard on crime but he was known to sentence Afrikan Americans to more lengthy sentences than their Caucasian counterparts for the same crimes. Once they located the court room they sat outside of the court waiting for Myisha's attorney. "This little skank played her way into the house and seduced Kisasi" Lana said to herself.

Myisha caught Lana's daggered looks but ignored her. She had not the time to entertain Lana's insecurities. Myisha's attorney turned the corner and to Lana's surprise it was the Law Professor Jeff Ellis. Mr. Ellis too was surprised to see one of his star students in the courthouse, "Ms. Xavier, I didn't know that you knew my client." "Yes I've known Ms. Littleton for a few years now," Lana said through a disingenuous smile. Mr. Ellis then turned to Myisha and began prepping her for the court appearance "This judge is a racist Mrs. Littleton so we must be careful to not show any overt emotions in our speech, just stay calm and let me litigate.

Myisha nodded her head in the affirmative. "I've been able to locate other Afrikan American Women who have had similar experiences with Mr. Slesser and they are willing to testify under oath, to this fact," Jeff said. At that moment Mr. Ladenburg, the prosecutor, turned the Corner and motioned Mr. Ellis over to him. Myisha, Askari, Lana and Kisasi curiously watched as Jeff quietly spoke to the prosecutor.

After their brief conversation Jeff returned to his client and excitedly said, "Mr. Slesser wants to drop the charges, apparently he doesn't want the fact that he's a pervert to be exposed but I'm willing to go forward with the trial, if that's what you want?" Myisha looked at Askari, who then looked at Kisasi. Give him the back door," Kisasi said.

All parties walked into Judge Felnagles courtroom and stood as the judge walked in and took his seat on the bench. "You may all be seated." The bailiff said. "This is the case of Oregon vs. Littleton, are the representatives of both parties present?" Judge Felnagle asked. "Mr. Ladengurg for the prosecution your honor." "Mr. Ellis for the defense your honor. Your honor the prosecution is requesting that the charges against Ms. Littleton be dismissed due to deficiencies in our ability to effectively prosecute this case." Ladenburg said. "Does the defense have any objections to this unusual request for dismissal?" Judge Felnagle asked. "No your honor, the defense has no objections," Jeff said. "In that case the charges against Ms. Littleton are dismissed." Judge Felnagle said and tapped his gavel.

"Thank you Mr. Ellis," Myisha said. "I'm just doing my job," Jeff said, then turned to Lana, "Don't wear yourself out during the break. We still have a lot of ground to cover." They both smiled. "Kisasi, Askari, it's always good to see you. Stay in contact my friends," Jeff said, shook both their hands and egressed the courthouse. Back at headquarters it was time to address the pressing issues between Lana and Kisasi. As they sat alone in Kisasi's room, neither wanting to be the first to start the conversation, they listened to music until they couldn't stand the empty air between them.

"So you let this brotha play in your panties," Kisasi interrupted the silence. "I didn't plan on having sex with him. I got lonely and being in an unfamiliar environment I sought comfort." she replied. "I can overstand the need for comfort but that shouldn't have rose to sex," Kisasi said. "And you were not wrong in what you did?" Lana defensively asked. "Of course I was wrong. I should have never kissed the sistah but I didn't give myself to her as you did. I don't want to point fingers we both betrayed one another's trust. The question becomes, where do we go from here?" Kisasi asked. "That's the point Kisasi, we don't go anywhere There's no need for what we share for each other to die, we just have to give each other some space and time to figure out what we are going to do" she replied. "I agree," he said as he sat down on the bed next to Lana. "Do you want the car back," She asked. "Malika, "I still love and trust you. That part of our relationship doesn't have to change, not unless my money starts coming up missing" Kisasi said playfully. "You know I wouldn't do that," she said as they fell back onto the bed, with her on top.

CHAPTER 17

Myisha lie in her room all alone. She was tired of this reality and came to the conclusion that she too deserved to be loved by a man and pledged, that she would no longer sit idly by while the man that she felt so strongly for slipped through her hands. She wanted Kisasi and decided that she would pursue him regardless of what anybody thought about it. The female Lana, now would have to compete for Kisasi, Myisha thought to herself.

She awoke early the next morning and again cooked breakfast for the house. The way to a man's heart is through his stomach, her mother always said and she would now employ that logic in her bid to be his woman. Askari first came into the kitchen followed by Kisasi and Lana, though she didn't sit at the table, "I have to get going, Kisasi will you walk me out?" Lana said and extended her hand to Kisasi who took it, as they walked to the front door. Lana turned to Kisasi before egressing the front door stopped, and wrapped her arms around his neck. "I love you Kisasi, and I want you to be careful." "Don't worry about me sistah. This is the path that I've consciously chosen. I embrace all that comes with it." Kisasi replied.

Lana kissed him, passionately, in an attempt to convey the sincerity of love that she'd confessed but all Kisasi could think about was her kissing Deshawn with the same fervor and even expressing her undying love to him. At that moment, though Kisasi still loved Lana, he began the process of murdering his intimate emotions for her. This was a self defense mechanism that he had learned in order to protect his heart and defuse feelings of disappointment when people did not live up to their potential or his expectations. Kisasi returned her kiss but without the same passion. He'd started the disengaging process the night before and any display of emotions or intimacy threatened that process. Lana noticed the chill in Kisasi's kiss. She knew that the fact that she'd had sex with Deshawn wreaked havoc on his heart but it was better that she told him rather than he found out from someone else, or even worse, she held it from him. She smiled at Kisasi acknowledging that she overstood the fact that he had to detach. She pressed her palm against his face as if she was trying to inculcate the contours for her own personal memories, turned, walked out the door, and began to cry.

Kisasi returned to the kitchen, sat and ate in silence. After the breakfast consisting of his favorites, T-bone steak and eggs, the dishes were placed in the dishwasher, Kisasi, Askari and Myisha went into the den and began their morning session of planning. Time was of the essence. The California gangs were tightening their hold on the Portland urban communities and the minds of the youth that inhabited them.

Confrontation was inevitable and would ignite a war. Kisasi had to construct a plan that would limit the casualties but to think that there would be none, was illogical. This was what politicians described as collateral damage which both sides would soon experience. Myisha informed Kisasi that the sistah that had infiltrated the California street organization had learned of their supply lines but it was more complicated than they had imagined.

"Call the sistah and get her here so that she can explain to me what she's found out." Kisasi said. I spoke with her last night and told her to be here at 9:00am" Myisha said. "After we meet with the sistah, I'll have Almasi meet us here to discuss tactics and strategy," Askari said. "What about the weapons?" Kisasi asked. "They're ready, all I have to do is retrieve them," Askari answered.

An hour later a knock came at the door. Myisha looked at her watch, "right on time," she said and walked towards the door. When she came back into the den she was trailed by a thin, Very light complexioned sistah who looked as if she was of mixed race with long flowing, naturally curly hair and emerald green eyes. "This is Chantel," Myisha said.

"Uhali gani" both Askari and Kisasi said in unison. Chantel looked puzzled at their reply but said "hello,"

"Have a seat sistah," Askari said pleasantly surprised at the beauty of Chantel. Kisasi noticed the coruscation in Askari's eyes and thought "he just had a female here last night." Myisha also saw Askari's play on Chantel but dismissed it. She'd been knowing Askari for years and he had always been somewhat of a womanizer. He'd even shown interest in her and she might have gave him action if he had not already been with a friend of hers. "So what's the grapes on these California cats," Kisasi asked, moving past the pleasantries "Well, I not only found out where and when they deliver the drugs but I also found out that though they are enemies in California, the Crips and the bloods, for the most part, do business with each other when they are out of state. They use one supplier that delivers for both gangs once every four months. These cats are bringing in forty birds every delivery and splitting it, twenty for the Crips and twenty for the bloods," Chantel explained.

"So if we move on the bloods we're moving on the Crip's?" Kisasi asked rhetorically. "Yep," Chantel answered. "Can we engage the Crips and the bloods at the same time?" Askari asked. "Mao tse Tung and che guevera would use no more than fifteen guerilla fighters to engage armies that numbered in the thousands. Of course we can engage them, and with the right strategy and tactics, beat them," Kisasi said. "Well we know that their structure is flawed because if it wasn't they wouldn't have allowed Chantel, a female that they don't know from eve, to know where and when they pick up their supply," Myisha said. "You're right but that fact is balanced by the ultra violence that they engage in. They figure no one, knowing their propensity for violence, will cross them," Askari replied.

"And that's the very reason why we can't underestimate their intelligence, these cats are operating in states across America, somebody is doing the planning." "Unless..." Kisasi began to smile. "Unless what?" Askari asked, his curiosity peaked by Kisasi's smile. "Unless their moving independent of one another out of necessity, not an orchestrated plan" Kisasi said. "What do you mean?" Myisha asked. "I mean, what if instead of the whole set coming together and saying let's move like this?" They are moving independent." Kisasi said. "What are you basing this premise on?" Askari asked. "I've noticed that there's a California gang here called the Diamond Boys that don't sell drugs and if there are groups from California that don't sell drugs then, they are not moving based on an agreed plan to relocate and set up the drug trade in other states. This means that there is no unified mission and if the mission is not unified disunity can always be exploited," Kisasi said.

"According to Chantel 's information their next delivery will be in January, this gives us four months to come up with an effective strategy." Myisha advanced. "We need you to stay inside their organization Chantel, and let us know if Ricky Ru changes dates to pick up the supply, can you do that," Askari asked. "I got you," Chantel answered coquettishly. It seemed as if she was interested in Askari as much as he was interested in her but, Kisasi knew how complicated this interest could make the mission. He would discuss his concerns with Askari at a later date, he reasoned.

CHAPTER 18

Lana returned to the OSU dorm. She felt bad about the fact that she had betrayed Kisasi's trust by having sex with Deshawn but Kisasi had also betrayed her trust by kissing Myisha, she reasoned. This fact, though not substantive, offered relief of guilt for Lana. The fact that she had started spending time with Deshawn at his off campus apartment long before the kiss between Kisasi and Myisha, was suppressed, and not revealed to Kisasi.

Lana noticed, in the Oregonian Newspaper, that there had been a rash of violence in its urban communities. One story read; "Law enforcement attributes the escalated violence in north and northeast Portland to the influx of California gangs and their drug trade," the story went on to describe several instances that correlated with the ideology of Kisasi's organization, an organization that she had supported. The Oregonian reported; "Witnesses have recounted stories of a group of men, acting similar to a special tactics team, have been involved in force entries into drug houses, and reportedly tying up its occupants and only taking their drugs. Problem is, as the drug dealers employ violence to protect their trade this group must reciprocate the violence in order to retrieve the drugs and this perpetuates an escalation of violence." As Lana read and listened to those stories in the news she became convinced that it was Kisasi who was responsible for the drug house invasions and knew that the outcome of this war that Kisasi was waging, would not end favorably.

Lana began spending more time with Deshawn in light of the mutual agreement to give one another time and space, that Kisasi and herself had come to. She spent so much time with Deshawn that it seemed as though she had taken up residence at his off campus Apartment. Her feelings for Deshawn had grown exponentially but she didn't know whether to attribute it to emotions or the loneliness she experienced in the absence of Kisasi or, to proximity and convenience.

One thing that became painfully perspicuous was that Deshawn's feelings for her were not as intense. Of course he'd professed his love for her and, in various ways showed that he cared about her but she'd begun to doubt that he was in love with her. The sex had always been marked by lust and in the beginning that was enough for Lana but Deshawn's un-attentiveness to her implicit needs, outside of the bedroom, had become an issue. Though their aspirations for financial security were the same and the path that they'd both chosen to make that aspiration a reality was compatible, they could not be farther apart, intimately and emotionally, yet she chose to stay in the relationship, as a crutch if nothing else. One night, after spending the whole day together, Lana and Deshawn returned to the apartment to relax. As they sat on the couch watching a movie, he stated "Why don't you move in with me?" She turned to him in surprise. In her mind his request meant that he wanted a more serious relationship, a sentiment that she shared. Lana's heart raced. Did Deshawn finally feel for her as she felt for him?" she silently asked herself. She truly hoped so. "Are you sure that's what you want?" she asked. "Of course that's what I want," he replied.

She smiled broadly on the inside. Little did she know that Deshawn's request was not based on his profound love for her. It was more about convenience and in house sex. Deshawn, though not of moral rectitude, believed in having only one sex partner. He was paranoid about having his career cut short by contracting AIDS/HIV or some other STD that carried with it a social stigma that would prohibit him from realizing his goals. Deshawn knew for sure that Lana was not promiscuous but he would be even more comfortable knowing that they shared the same residence, Lana agreed to move in with Deshawn and for the most part their cohabitation was great but instead of Deshawn becoming more attentive, as Lana hoped that he would be, he, ironically became even less attentive. They spent less quality time together and the sex became more of a chore for her than a fulfilling pleasure. Deshawn was no longer able to bring Lana to orgasm nor did he attempt to. He became very selfish in the bed, and the fact that he neurotically obsessed over contracting an STD caused him to religiously use condoms, made Lana uncomfortable. She'd never had consensual sex with someone that she cared for without a condom and she wanted to experience the sensuality of doing so. Lana planned to discuss this with Deshawn at a later date, in the interim they continued to cohabitate and have sex.

Lana learned how to bring herself to orgasm while with Deshawn. She mastered the art of using his physical while simultaneously thinking of Kisasi and though this technique procured the desired result, it placed even more distance between Deshawn and herself. One day, in late November, on the way to Emmanuel Hospital for a routine physical and check up, Lana decided to ask Kisasi if he'd go with her and of course, he did. While they sat in the waiting room Lana began asking Kisasi about the Diamonds and their activities. How is the struggle going?" Lana asked through an uncomfortable smile. She hoped that this question wouldn't garner Kisasi's antipathy. She knew that her newly acquired position on the struggle didn't bode well with Kisasi and she didn't want this small talk to result in a debate concerning ideology. He was curt in his answer, "We're staying down for the come up," She recognized his lack of interest in discussing this topic and reluctantly refrained from any other questions that she may have entertained on this subject, but only for that moment, she reasoned.

What had happened to them," She silently asked herself. There was a time when Kisasi would discuss any and everything with her. Now he seemed to be a little distant and guarded. "Ms. Xavier, the doctor is ready to see you," the nurse said as she approached Lana, file in hand, breaking the awkward silence. "I'll be back, ok?" she said to Kisasi and followed the nurse down the hall. When Lana disappeared Kisasi processed what he was experiencing in the presence of Lana. He still loved her but felt that she abandoned the struggle like so many people do when they are trained in Eurocentric curriculum. Though Lana was unaware of it, Kisasi knew that she no longer lived in the dorm on campus. He had attempted to contact her and a female that lived in the dorm, assuming that he was a family member, told him that she'd moved in with a roommate off campus. Kisasi, putting one and one together, came to the conclusion that she had in fact moved in with the brotha Deshawn that she had told him about. He'd decided not to ask her about this and why should he?

It wasn't his business and to keep it real, he had more important matters to attend to in the community. Regardless of how she chooses to live her life, his life would be spent in the struggle, with or without her, he reasoned. Though this fact didn't ameliorate the pain that he experienced upon finding out that she had moved in with Deshawn, it facilitated the necessary desire needed to fuel the will to stay on task. Lana got a full physical, including blood test, and then was examined. The gynecologist questioned her concerning what seemed to him to be a cluster of blisters on a bright red base in her vaginal area; which Lana attributed to the frequent sex that Deshawn and herself were engaging in. After her lengthy exam Lana emerged from the hallway that led back to the examination rooms. She didn't think twice about the gynecologists concerns about the cluster of bumps in her vaginal area. Why should she? She wasn't promiscuous nor was she engaging in unprotected sex, to her dismay. It had to be due to how frequently she was having sex. She would stop having sex so frequently, she mused.

"You ready to go," she asked Kisasi. "Everything cool?" Kisasi asked. "I'm in tip top condition," Lana replied and they egressed. He told her that he had to get back to headquarters. "I wanted to spend some time with you and bring you up to speed on how I've been doing in school," she said disappointedly. "What about you moving in with the brotha, were you going to tell me about that?" he pointedly asked. She fell silent. She didn't know that Kisasi knew. "Yes, that was one of the things that I was going to bring you up to speed on" She answered.

It's too late for that Malika." Lana had not been called Malika in so long that she was taken aback but in that moment she was reminded of all that Kisasi had been and was to her. "I'm sorry Kisasi," she offered. 'I'm not trippin baby girl but I wish you would have told me instead of me finding out from some random female, but we're good. How have you been doing in school?" he changed the subject. "I'm doing very well. I'm holding a 4.0 g.p.a" she said more than willing to allow the subject to be changed. She'd never felt the distance that she now felt between Kisasi and herself and she didn't like it. She wanted what they shared back. Lana pulled up to headquarters and Kisasi opened the door to get out. "It's like that?" she asked. "What do you mean, like that?" he asked. "You're just going to get out of the car and not say anything?" Lana asked.

He pulled his leg back into the car and closed the door, "Look Malika, you're in a relationship with someone else and I'm going to respect that because I would want the same respect if you were in a relationship with me. There's no need for us to pretend that's not real. You know how I feel about you and that's till death do us, but until you're truly ready, it would be counterproductive for us to act on that," Kisasi said. "At the same time you can't just act like you don't know who I am." she said angrily, "I'll always be here for you Malika but, at the same time you abandoned the cause and it's not about me not knowing who you are, it's about you knowing who you are and where you came from," Kisasi said, opened the car door and got out.

Lana watched through the windshield as he walked around the front of the car. On his way into the house Kisasi over his shoulder, without looking back said "I love you Malika," then ingressed the house. She sat there for a minute, gathering her thoughts, then she pulled off into traffic.

Myisha watched the whole exchange from the window of her bedroom and smiled out loud.

CHAPTER 19

Myisha closed her curtains and sat down on her bed. She'd witnessed the exchange between Lana and Kisasi and though she didn't know exactly what had transpired she could see that there was some tension between them. It was obvious that their interaction was changing but Kisasi never discussed his relationship with Lana so it would be circumspect of her not to attempt to engage Kisasi in discourse as it related to Lana. This would only cause him to withdraw and she'd now been in his presence enough to know that, Kisasi was suspicious of anyone that superimposed discourse. She would have to be patient and wait until he initiated that conversation if it ever was to take place, but in the interim, she would convey her interest in him full throttle.

Kisasi walked upstairs, ingressed his room, sat on the bed and reevaluated what had just transpired. He was deep in thought when a knock on the door brought him back to the present. "Come in," Kisasi said. The door opened and there stood Myisha in spandex shorts that complimented every curve of her anatomy, and a little girl t-shirt. Without a doubt she was sexy as hell and her jet black, smooth skin was titillating. For a moment he fell silent while evanescent thoughts of the possibilities plagued his mind but they were quickly replaced by a silent loyalty to his feelings for Lana. "What's going down?" He asked. "Nothing, I just wanted to get at you about our plans after New Years, can I come in?" she asked. "Absolutely," he answered. He needed to talk about something to take his mind off of Lana, and organizational structure and strategy always worked, though he made a mental note that he was doing this a lot lately. She came in and with her hand motioned toward the bed as if to ask if she could sit there. Kisasi with his left hand patted a spot on the bed next to himself giving her permission. Myisha sat next to Kisasi with her thigh touching his. Kisasi didn't move and she made a mental note of that fact. "Talk to me sistah," he said. "I spoke with Chantel and the California delivery has been pushed up. Their supplier is going to make the delivery in December rather than January, They want to be in pocket for the holidays." "Does she know where the delivery will take place?" He asked. "The delivery is now at this little duplex on Killingsworth and 33rd. I've already went to the duplex and mapped the ins and outs. It faces Killingsworth but it has a back entrance on 33rd. The apartment next door to it is empty," Myisha explained. "Is there anyone living in the unit where they'll make the exchange?" Kisasi asked. "No, these cats never rent a unit to do an exchange, they just break in when the sun goes down on the day of the exchange, about 1:00 am then vacate" she said.

"That's smart. They pick an empty duplex, wait until the sun goes down ensuring that the property owner isn't making any rounds checking on the property, going in and making the exchange under the cloak of darkness, then moving out before the community awakens, but they've made one mistake. Though the duplex is separated by a wall, they share the same attic and if we can get a squad in before they break in we'll have the jump on them," Kisasi said. Myisha just sat there, silent, as Kisasi evaluated the scenario and prescribed the most effective strategy. She loved the way Kisasi thought and reasoned. He had a beautiful mind and this was one of the things that attracted her to him and his organization. After Kisasi finished his evaluation Myisha coquettishly said, "What do you want me to do now general?" Kisasi smiled and replied, "Make an appointment with the property owner as a prospective renter, have her show you the unit and gather all of the information on the layout that you can but don't stay long, we don't want her to remember anything about you after this goes down. "Kisasi said. "I'm on it," Myisha stated as she rose from the bed and left the room, provocatively swinging her hips as she egressed. Prurient thoughts immediately came to Kisasi's mind as he watched Myisha walk away. Myisha got to the door and quickly turned back to Kisasi as if she'd forgotten to say something to him, when in reality she wanted to see if Kisasi was looking at her ass as she walked away and, he was, she smiled out loud.

Though Myisha was five years older than Kisasi she found herself rising in love with him as the days went on. Her close proximity to him facilitated her love for him and she would lay her life down to perpetuate his, she reasoned. This was definitely true love, a love that she would nurture, cultivate, and eventually share with him. Myisha went to the den to use the phone. "Hello this is gheri Alexander and I'm trying to contact Mrs. Baines, oh, this is Mrs. Baines? Great I am interested in renting a unit from you and I would like to schedule a walk through with you. Yes, today would be fine." Myisha said to the voice on the on the other end of the phone."Thank you, goodbye," Myisha hung up the phone, "Myisha," Askari called out. "What's going down" she answered. "Will you call a Plummer and have them come out? The shower drain downstairs is clogged." "I'm on it." Myisha answered. After making the call to the Plummer, Myisha looked at the clock on the den wall and realized that she only had about 45 min. to get prepared for her meeting with Mrs. Bains for her walk through at the duplex. She would have to use the shower adjoined to Kisasi's master bedroom. As she walked up the stairs to ask permission to do so she could see that Kisasi's door was closed. She knocked at the door but got no response. She knocked again as she gently opened his door. She heard the shower running and hoped that Kisasi was in the shower. She walked into the restroom calling his name. "I'm in the shower," Kisasi stated. "I spoke to the property owner and scheduled a walk through. I got 45 min, to make the appointment," Myisha said, "What are you waiting for sistah?" Kisasi asked. "I have to take a shower and the drain down stairs is clogged, can I get in with you?" Myisha asked and tentatively awaited his reply. "Without a doubt," Kisasi answered. Now was his opportunity to see what that chocolate body looked like unveiled. Myisha relieved herself of all her clothing, pulled the shower curtain back, and got in. Kisasi, not wanting to seem anxious had his back turned with his head under the cascading water. He then traded places with Myisha so that she could get wet and lather up and she did just that. Her body was all that Kisasi thought it would be. She was muscular in a feminine way and even toned all over, not a blemish. Myisha could feel Kisasi gazing at her and decided to exacerbate the sexual tension.

"Will you wash my back for me?" Myisha asked rhetorically as she pushed the bar of soap backwards, without turning to face Kisasi, who took the soap from her hand and began washing her and watching as the lather ran down her back to her ass. He immediately became erect as Myisha reached back between his legs and fondled his manhood. Feeling that he was erect Myisha turned to him, pressed her naked body up against his and kissed him slow and deep. Kisasi returned the sentiments while tracing his right hand down her back and cupped her ass. Myisha pulled him in close as if to merge their bodies together as one. Kisasi moved his right hand around from Myisha's ass and down between her legs. He gently rubbed her clit and when he felt Myisha's body quiver and her legs spread he penetrated her with two fingers. Myisha gasped then let out a throaty moan. Lost in prurient thought, Myisha began pushing her hips forward to meet the in an out penetration of Kisasi's fingers. She wanted so desperately to feel Kisasi pulsating erection inside of her but at that moment she remembered the task at hand and whispered through her

moans, "Can I get a rain check?" I have to meet Mrs. Bains."
"Without a doubt," Kisasi said. Even in the heat of passion
Myisha remembered the mission.

This procured an even deeper respect for her from Kisasi.
Myisha got out of the shower wrapped a towel around her
naked body covering her most intimate parts and descended
the stairwell to her room. Kisasi then turned off the hot
water, employing the cold to manage his erection. Again he
thought about Lana but quickly pushed the thought from his
mind.

CHAPTER 20

It was December 24th, Christmas Eve, and the California delivery was to happen on Christmas day. Myisha 's report on the layout of the property was lucid and thorough. Kisasi had decided to position three members of Almasi in the duplex next door to the delivery and use the attic as one of the points of entry. They would also enter from the front as well as the back door. There would be approximately five people doing the exchange on the California end and to use more than three Almasi members would only enhance the potential for disaster. Kisasi had decided to send Terrance in with Kwame and Antoine to test his mettle. He'd become suspicious of Terrance ever since he'd asked "How are we going to get this information?" during an Almasi meeting. Terrance being a former drug dealer, must have his loyalty tested that there'd be no compromise of the integrity of Almasi, Later on down the line. What Kisasi didn't know was that his suspicions were valid. Terrence had been selling drugs on the side and using his position in Almasi to veil his activity. Kisasi had given strict orders to confiscate the money used to purchase the drugs, an estimated $600,000 and leave the drugs, but Terrance had a plan of his own. Since he would be the one to enter through the attic, this put him in a position to take at least a couple of kilos for himself.

Everybody was in position. Terrance could hear the California cats talking as the heavy weed smoke wafted up into the attic. He could hear Riky Ru and BK blue talking over sporadic, intense coughing. "Where the hell they at cuzz?" BK Blue asked. "They'll be here in a minute blood." Riky Ru answered. At that moment a coded knock came at the door and, three cats with two duffle bags came in. "West up homie," one of the men said. "The same ole grind different time," BK Blue stated. Kwame moved to the front door and Antoine to the back, once the suppliers were inside. The plan was to then count to ten, kick both doors in while Terrence simultaneously dropped down into the bedroom through the attic and enter the front room from the back, pinning the group between them, alleviating the gun play, but Terrance thought that if he entered first, gun drawn, he could get a couple of keys and stuff them on his person before Kwame and Antoine would come in. At the count of three Terrance dropped down into the back bedroom through the attic, came into the front room, gun drawn, startling the California crew but these cats were gangsters and gangtas didn't get robbed. Both Rick Ru and BK Blue turned their heat on Terrance and fired multiple rounds into his face and anatomy, simultaneously, with semi-automatic 9mm's. Kwame and Antoine, hearing this eruption of gunfire, kicked the doors open and the most brutal gunfight that Portland, Oregon had ever experienced ensued.

Upon coming through the front door Kwame drew the Attention of both BK Blue and Riky Ru but before they could get off any rounds, Kwame had hit both of them with his snub nose .44 bulldog revolver. Both hit the floor screaming in agony. Antoine, with his modified, fully automatic Mac 11, sprayed the three suppliers that remained standing transfixed, laying all three of them down, never to stand erect again. When the smoke cleared, only Kwame and Antoine were left standing. Kwame stepped over the bodies of Ricky Ru and BK Blue then kneeled over Terrance placing the tips of his two fingers to his neck to check for a pulse, but found none. "He's dead." "Kwame informed Antoine. "Let's get this paper and bounce," Antoine said. Kwame checked both duffle bags as Antoine peaked out of the front window, re-zipped the duffle bag with the money, picked it up and got ghost. Little did they know BK Blue was only pretending to be dead. After they were gone he got up, grabbed his shoulder wound and left the duplex.

As Kisasi, Askari and Myisha sat in the den watching television, waiting on the report from Terrance, Kwame and Antoine. The scheduled program was interrupted by a newsbreak; "Police and emergency personnel are at the scene of the most, gruesome shoot out that Portland, Oregon has ever seen," The camera then panned the duplex showing the scene taped off with yellow tape. "Inside lay the bodies of five unidentified black males who were gunned down in what law enforcement suspects was a drug deal gone bad," the reporter said. Kisasi looked at Askari and Myisha in bewilderment, then the phone rang breaking the silence. Kisasi immediately answered. "They smoked Terrance," Kwame's voice came from the other end of the pay phone. "Follow the plan and come see me tomorrow umefahamu?" Kisasi said. "Ndio," Kwame answered then hung up the phone. He put the receiver down and said, "Terrence didn't make it." "There shouldn't have been any gun play," Askari said. Kisasi looked into his eyes searching for a fear that could compromise the organization. It wasn't there. "Either these Cali cats had a death wish or somebody didn't follow the plan," Myisha said. "We'll see in the morning Kisasi said, walked out of the den, and ascended the stairs to his room. Myisha and Askari followed suit. There was nothing that could be done about that which had already transpired. They would rest and address the issue when Kwame and Antoine got there.

The next morning Kisasi, Askari and Myisha all awakened earlier than normal. Kisasi was the first to shower and though the Plummer had come and unplugged the drain in the downstairs restroom, Myisha came upstairs to shower. Kisasi didn't mind, because he was anxiously awaiting the arrival of Kwame and Antoine he didn't entertain any prurient thoughts about Myisha. A knock came at the door while Myisha was still in the shower. Askari answered the door as Kisasi waited in the den. Both Kwame and Antoine walked in, Kwame carrying the duffle bag. "Uhali gani comrade," Kisasi said. "Sijambo," both Kwame and Antoine replied in unison. "What happened?" Askari asked getting directly to the point. "Everything was going as planned. We were all in position, counting to ten, but at about three we heard gunfire erupt so we had to go in," Kwame said. "I could hear Terrance saying put your hands up, from the back door. He moved too fast," Antoine said.

At that moment Myisha came into the den. "What he say?" she asked. "Terrance moved too fast," Askari answered giving her the concise version. "You know they've dubbed this Christmas Day Murders," Kisasi asked. "That means that they are going to make this case a priority," Myisha added. "Make reservations for these brothas to fly to Fresno. I have family there that will put them up until this situation cools off," Kisasi told Myisha, who immediately got on the phone with the airline. "What are they going to do about money?" Askari asked. "Once they land we'll have $200,000 sent to my people and they'll get it to them" Kisasi answered and shot a glance at Askari to end the subject. Askari caught the look and abandoned the issue. Myisha got off of the phone and stated "We have a flight for two coach seats on Southwest air from PDX to Oakland and, they'll board a plane in Oakland going To Fresno, Yosemite International airport and, arrive there the same day. "What time does the flight depart from PDX?" Kwame asked. "At 1:00 pm," Myisha replied. "That gives us a few hours to rotate before you leave. Call "The No" and let Blue Bear know the comrades are on the way so that someone will be there to scoop them up,"

Kisasi told Askari. "I might as well make sure that the money is there when they get off of the flight." Askari said. "Do that," Kisasi agreed. Askari made a bank transfer,

Kwame and Antoine boarded their flight, while Kisasi planned for the fallout from the Christmas Day Murders.

CHAPTER 21

Lana sat alone in the off campus apartment Deshawn and herself shared. She re-evaluated her life as it stood at that moment. Deshawn and herself were experiencing difficulties in their relationship, difficulties that caused her to suspect that he'd been cheating. He had become aloof and frequently absent in the apartment. There had been rumors circulating of his trysts with a Caucasian female named Amber and though he'd vehemently denied the allegations when questioned by Lana, she believed the rumors to be true.

Her world was crumbling around her as it related to the man she'd chosen to give herself to and if that wasn't enough, Kisasi, the man that had admired, supported and trusted her, was now distancing himself, emotionally, from her. Disheartened by her thoughts of the direction in which her love life was traveling, Lana turned on the television in hopes of escaping reality, if only for a moment. Breaking news: "One of the men killed in the Christmas Day Murders has been identified as Terrance Hall of Portland Oregon the other four men were California natives. Law enforcement states that a preliminary investigation suggests that this was a drug deal gone bad and the fact that 40 kilos were recovered but no money was found, indicates that robbery was the motive. Law enforcement found a trail of blood that extended as far as a block away from the scene of the crime suggesting that someone that was injured in the crime escaped the massacre. There is a $20,000 reward for any information leading to arrests in this case. "Kisasi!" Lana's mind screamed to her. She'd remembered that Kisasi was planning to jack the California gangs in an attempt to stop the influx of drugs into the community. She called Kisasi. "Hello" the feminine and sultry voice of Myisha came over the phone.

"This bitch is answering the phone now," Lana's mind suggested before she asked to speak to Kisasi. "He's busy at this moment can I have him call you back?" Myisha said sarcastically. Lana quickly realized that Myisha was holding all of the cards at this moment and the show of any attitude would only defeat the purpose. She needed to speak with Kisasi and if that meant that she had to bite her tongue and show some humility at this point she would. "Is this Myisha?" Sistah I just need a minute of his time could you please make that happen for me?" Lana humbly asked. "Just a minute," Myisha said and when Lana heard her lay down the phone to go and get Kisasi she called her a variety of bitches, under her breath. "Talk to me'" Kisasi's voice came over the phone. "Hey baby, you good?" Lana asked. "I'm strait sistah, how are you?" Kisasi replied, "I was watching the news and this Christmas day murder thing concerns me," Lana said. "I wouldn't concern myself with it if I were you. These things have become the norm in our communities and since all of the victims were black it will process through the 72 hour news cycle and become void, as black issues always do," Kisasi reasoned. "The news said that they found a trail of blood that led from the crime scene as far as a block away," Lana said. Kisasi had not heard that reported on the station that he was watching. His mind began to race. He knew that both Kwame and Antoine came out of the gunfight unscathed. Damn! His mind screamed. This meant that one of the Cali cats had escaped and would surely want revenge for the robbery massacre. "It's under control," Kisasi said playing down the significance of the situation. "When can I see you Kisasi?" Lana asked. "Things are moving fast at this time, as you can imagine., give me a few days then get at me," Kisasi said. They exchanged pleasantries and hang up the phone.

For the first time in their relationship Lana didn't feel the warmth from Kisasi that she had always felt. She sat back on the love seat, in an empty apartment, and her heart began to cry. Lana ached for Kisasi and the love that they once shared and she wondered if she could recapture that euphoric interaction. It was Christmas day and while she sat in the apartment all alone, Myisha enjoyed the presence of the man she loved. As always, Lana poured herself into her scholastic endeavors in order to mitigate her loneliness and though this tactic caused her to excel in college, it did nothing to mend her heart, yet she pressed on.

When Lana heard keys in the door she immediately looked at the clock. It was 11:00 pm. She'd been so engulfed in her work that she completely lost track of time. The door opened and Deshawn ingressed, closed the door, threw his keys on the coffee table and walked directly to the bedroom without speaking to Lana. She returned to her research but when she heard the shower running she became violently angry. "This punk think that he's going to keep playing me like this," she thought. No longer able to contain her anger Lana stormed into the restroom to confront Deshawn. "What in the hell is going on Deshawn?" Lana yelled. "What are you talking about?" he asked in an attempt to give himself enough time to formulate a response. "You know exactly what I'm talking about. I know that you've been with that little white bitch Amber," Lana said. Deshawn knew he was busted and, the attempt to muster a reasonable response was replaced by anger and indignation. "This is the reason why I don't like being with you black bitches. You're loud, disrespectful, and don't know your place.

I don't have the time or the energy to keep going through this bullshit with you." He yelled from behind the shower curtain. "What's real is that you can't deal with a strong woman, that's why you mess with the white girl. You can run that weak ass game on her but I see through that raggedy shit. If she's so much better than me you why aren't you living with her?" She asked in an attempt to add insult to injury but she didn't expect Deshawn's response. "I do live with her, haven't you noticed?" "He turned off the shower, got out and while drying off said "I can't do this anymore Lana, you abandoned this relationship emotionally, a long time ago. We haven't had sex in months, hell we don't even share the same bed. How long did you think I would be cool with that? I'm a man, I have needs, needs that you weren't fulfilling." "So cheating is the way you address these issues?" Lana asked. "You came into this relationship cheating. You were with me physically but emotionally you were always somewhere else. It didn't bother me at first, I figured that in due time you'd come around but you didn't." Then without any emotion Deshawn said what Lana dreaded…"I'm leaving," He wrapped his towel around his waist walked past her into the bedroom and began getting dressed, packed the rest of his clothing and left as she helplessly watched. It was over.

CHAPTER 22

It was March of 86 and just as Kisasi had reasoned, the Christmas day murders were no longer in the headlines but little did he know that it remained fresh on the mind of BK Blue like a fingerprint by impress. He didn't give a damn about the murders, that came with the territory. He'd long ago learned to embrace the reality of death in California where he'd attended more funerals for fallen comrades than birthdays but what he could not accept was being robbed, somebody has to pay for that. Though Lana took over the payments on the apartment she had not been spending much time there. At times the memories were unbearable but to move out would alert Kisasi to the fact that she'd mistakenly invested in someone that really didn't give a damn about her and though she suspected Kisasi knew that Deshawn's motives were not pure, she didn't want to submit to this fact. One day Lana returned to the apartment after staying in a motel for three days and noticed that there was an envelope affixed to her front door. She removed the envelope without looking at it and ingressed the apartment. Lana sat down on the couch, took off her shoes and opened the envelope to read its contents. The first thing that she noticed was the words "Health Department." The Letter went on to read, "The results of your blood tests are in and you must contact us as soon as possible." It went on to give a contact person Mrs. Barbara Waters, along with a phone number extension #224.

Why do I have to call the health department instead of my doctor, Lana thought as she dialed the number. "Yes, this is Ms. Xavier and I need to speak with a Barbara Waters," Lana said to the voice on the other end of the phone. "Mrs. Waters?" This is Ms. Xavier and I'm calling concerning a letter that was taped to my door by your office," Lana said. "Yes we've been trying to contact you for the past week Ms. Xavier. I have some bad news your blood test show that you have contracted herpes," Mrs. Waters, said matter of factly. Lana fell silent.

She could not believe what she was hearing. Her first thought was that of disbelief. Maybe they got the wrong person, this had to be a mistake, I'm only 22 years old. Those doubts were erased by Mrs. Waters recount of the visit that she had just several weeks prior with her doctor and the question concerning what seemed to be abrasions in her vaginal area. Lana then became anxious, searching her mind for the culprit that had given her this disease. "Mrs. Xavier, are you there?" Mrs. Waters asked. "Yes I'm here," Lana replied. "Do you know who could have given you this disease?" Mrs. Waters asked. "I've never had sex without a condom," Lana answered, and at that moment she relived the rape by her uncle. Lana's anxiousness was immediately replaced by anger. "I know this is a lot for you to process at this time but you have to think about and remember the people that you've had sex with and from this day forward, you are obligated to inform any sex partner that you have herpes." Mrs. Waters said in an accusatory tone.

Lana could hear the accusations and condemnation in Mrs. Waters voice. She spoke as if Lana was some kind of little whore who's promiscuous lifestyle was to blame for her contracting herpes. This is a stigma attached to the disease that she would have to endure for the rest of her life. Lana hung up the phone and consumed by grief, wept for what seemed to be hours. After gathering herself, Lana went to see her doctor. She informed him of the fact that she'd been raped by her uncle when she was 13 or 14 years old. "Those that you've engaged in copulation with must still be tested for their own safety Ms. Xavier." Dr. Richardson said. Lana had only had sex with three people outside of the rape, Kisasi, Deshawn and a guy at the church, who was, at the time three years older than her. She'd almost forgotten about the encounter at the church until this tragedy. They'd attended the Sunday school bible classes together and one day when the adults had let him teach the class he'd talked Lana into having sex with him, but even then he used a condom. He'd told Lana not to tell anyone because he was sixteen and she was thirteen and he might have gotten in trouble.

Lana never told anyone because she liked the guy. She didn't realize that she was too young to consent to sex and that being the reality, the guy had in fact manipulated and violated her sexually. It had to be her uncle Carl that gave her herpes and for that he had to pay with his life. Lana first notified Deshawn who's test came back negative, now she must notify Kisasi.

CHAPTER 23

Myisha noticed that Kisasi had softened his position as it related to the possibility of a relationship between them. Of course he had made pellucid his sexual interest in her. Who could deny the electricity between them but he was now open to the cutaneous simulation that procures the emotional bond that undergirds long time relationships. He'd began to share aspects of his life with her in dialogue and was candid about his upbringing and family structure, something that he'd been guarded about in previous discourse. It was time for Myisha to offer herself, exclusively, to Kisasi in hopes of garnering the same level of commensalism from him and the only way to do this was to state, unequivocally, to him, her desire for an exclusive relationship with him. Askari called a meeting with Almasi. They needed to be informed of new developments that may affect the organization and to be prepared to advance guerilla tactics if necessary to ensure the security of the organization. Kisasi's task was more intricate. He must express the same sentiments as Askari without divulging the fact that Almasi had carried out the Christmas day murders. He'd learned from his father Vitani that "You never disclose in totality, a mission to those in the group that are not taking part in the mission." This tactic insulated the group and protected the integrity, not only of the mission, but also the identity of those who partake in very different aspects of the mission, in very different capacities. He would not lie to the group, overtly, but he would employ the strategy of omission. He would question the absence of Kwame and Antoine publicly to suggest that their whereabouts were unbeknownst to Askari and himself. This would work as a deterrent to any question that the group would otherwise pose to them.

Kisasi started the meeting, "Does anyone know where Kwame and Antoine is? When he received no answer he directed Myisha to mark their absence as unexcused, then he Continued. "As you know there was a massacre a few months ago that the police has called the Christmas day murders. It's only logical that our organization will come under scrutiny because we have been openly vociferous against the sell of drugs in our communities. This means that eventually you may be questioned by the police department or even targeted by drug dealers. It is imperative that you continue to state our organizations position to the authorities and stand on our principles if confronted by drug dealers but we have no information or knowledge concerning the Christmas day murders. Stay hypervigilant, always protect yourself but if it is possible don't engage in public violence. The police department will be looking for any display of violence by our organization to implicate us in the murders. Don't give them the opportunity. Travel in three's and obey all traffic laws. We don't need any criminal publicity," Kisasi said before allowing Askari to address the group.

"I don't have much to add to what Kisasi said. This is a very sensitive time and we must protect the larger organization. They must continue to fundraise and work with businesses and other organizations to continue to serve the populace. We need you to patrol the community while the public face of the organization does it's work, to make sure that they are not hindered in their service. You have your orders, execute them." Askari said ending the meeting. Members of Almasi stayed, ate bar-b-que Myisha had prepared, and slowly egressed three at a time. After the last group left Myisha, Kisasi and Askari cleaned up the kitchen then sat in the den to relax and discuss aspects of the organization. "I think that you covered that well Kisasi, It gave them the language to use if interrogated, the posture to take if confronted, and implied that we had nothing to do with the murders but most of all it insulated the organization as a whole," Myisha said. "It also relieved us of any culpability in the murders without having to lie to our comrades." Askari added. "The only issue now becomes, where does BK Blue stand? Will he eventually seek retribution," and if so, how do we address that problem?" Kisasi asked. "Lets cross that bridge when we get to it," Askari said. Askari got up aggressively leaving Myisha and Kisasi alone in the den. Myisha chose this moment to express to Kisasi her love for him and her desire to have an exclusive relationship with him but as she began to speak the phone rang. Damn! Her mind screamed as Kisasi answered the phone. "Alright, I'll see you in a minute," Kisasi said then hung up the phone. "Who was that?" Myisha asked innocently. "That was Lana she said that she had something to discuss with me. It's probably about the crime," Kisasi said. "I have something important that I want to talk to you about too but, I'll wait until you're finished with the sistah," Myisha said. 10 minutes later there was a knock on the door. "She must have called from a phone booth." Myisha reasoned as she went to answer the door. "Uhali gani ndada?" Myisha asked Lana after opening the door. "Sijambo ndada, Asante sana, Uhali gani?" Lana replied. "Sijambo," Myisha answered and turned sideways gesturing Lana in. She was sure being nice, Myisha thought to herself as Kisasi appeared from the den to meet Lana.

"I'll catch you later Myisha. Let Askari know I'm with Lana and please check on those new mobile phones for me, if it's feasible purchase five of them for organizational use," Kisasi said as he and Lana egressed. As they got into the car He could tell that something weighed heavily on her. She was not her extrovert self. She was guarded and avoided eye contact with him. "What's going down?" he asked apprehensively. "I don't know how to say this," she said. "Just say it," Kisasi stated impatiently. "I have herpes," Lana said bluntly.

He immediately searched his memory. He'd only had sex with Lana once, and was certain he used a condom and stated this fact. "I know, but the doctor still wants you to be tested," Lana said. "What about Deshawn?" Kisasi asked.

"He's been tested and the test came back negative. They can test you now and give you the results before you leave the hospital," Lana said. "Let's make it happen," Kisasi replied. Lana and Kisasi sat at the hospital from 1:00 pm to 5:00 pm that night. Finally the doctor called Kisasi and Lana back into the exam room to notify them that Kisasi's test results were negative. As they sat in the car prepared to return to headquarters Lana began crying uncontrollably. "When I was 13 my uncle Carl raped me," Lana said between the tears. Kisasi's mind immediately returned to the time when Lana's uncle had been wheeled out of her house on a gurney. He also remembered her reply after they'd become acquainted and he'd asked her about the incident, "I wish that nigga would have died," she vehemently said. Now Kisasi knew why there was so much vitriol in her response. He had violated her. Robbed her of her innocence and self worth, distorting her self-concept and as if that wasn't enough, his savage behavior has shackled her with a disease that there is no cure for.

Kisasi held her close in an attempt to comfort her. He wiped the tears from her eyes but the pain could not be as easily administered to and he could only imagine what she experienced, emotionally. "He's going to pay for this Malika," he said. She had not heard him call her Malika in a while. It was comforting and, informed her that he was not judging her at a time she needed so desperately to know that she was not being judged.

CHAPTER 24

Myisha could see the despair on Kisasi's face as he ingressed the den. "What's wrong brotha?" she asked. "Nothing," Kisasi said curtly. Though it was obvious to Myisha that he was in fact perturbed but this wasn't the time or the forum to push him for answers. She would give him space on this issue, at this time. But would revisit the subject later, she reasoned. "What's on the menu?" He asked changing the subject. "Well they've offered me a position at Kaiser Hospital as a Physician assistant," she said. "I didn't know that you were in the medical field," he said. "That's because I'd been waiting for this position to open. There was no logic in me working beneath my pay grade. I've struggled hard to get my credentials and I refuse to take just any position especially if it didn't allow me to work in the capacity in which I was trained," Myisha replied. "I feel you sistah. If you need transportation you can access any one of the Cutlass's that you want. There's no need for you to be subjected to public transit," Kisasi offered. She interpreted this gesture to mean that he truly cared for her and in that vein didn't want her to be subjected to an unsafe public transit system that could possibly threaten her personal safety. She was correct in her reasoning. Kisasi had, through proximity, and shared methodology and purpose, developed sincere feelings for her.

"I want the black one" she said like a child during Christmas time. "What would you like to have for dinner tonight?" Kisasi asked to Myisha's surprise. She had cooked all of the meals since she'd been in the house, not because she was required to, but because she felt that it was a way of showing her gratitude for the support that she received from both Kisasi and Askari. "What's the occasion she asked. "Were celebrating your new job opportunity and the financial liberation that it gives you." he said. "In that case I want steak, lobster and a salad." She said. Kisasi didn't eat seafood often and didn't eat crustaceans like lobster, crab or anything with a segmented body and paired limbs.

He remembered his mother saying "You are what you eat so if you eat scavengers you'll exhibit the characteristics of a scavenger." This, she reasoned, was one of the reasons that black people in America exhibit such vile behavior at times. One cannot separate behavior, quality of life, mentality or intellect from diet, his mother reasoned. "I don't eat scavengers but the steak and salad sounds good," he said. "I would like to spend some one on one time with you Kisasi so let's get some Champaign and set aside some time after dinner," she suggested. "I'm with that. Also I want to invite Askari and Chantel to celebrate with us. It's obvious that he likes the sistah and I need you to orientate her and make sure that she overstand our position from a woman's perspective he said. "I'm with that but I don't want to celebrate with them all night. There are things that I want to explore with you,"

Myisha said, her words laced with sexual innuendo. "Oh yea, before I forget, I purchased those mobile phones that you wanted. They are in my room," she said, before picking up the phone to call Chantel. Kisasi wanted Askari, Myisha, and himself to have the mobile phones so that they could reach each other at all times. He'd figure out who to give the others to after considering the importance of their role in the organization and the trust that he was willing to invest in them. "Thank you sistah," Kisasi replied and egressed. Kisasi went into Myisha's room to retrieve the mobile phones. Upon entering he visually swept the room and noticed that she had hung pictures of Huey P. Newton, Elaine Brown, Herman Bell, Geronimo Pratt, Marcus Garvey, Pam Afrika, Stokely Charmical, Angela Davis, Asata Shakur, Elijah Muhammad, Patrice Lumumba, Nat Turner, Maulana Karenga, Denmark Vessey, and Harriet Tubman. Dr. Martin Luther King and Malcolm X were not featured.

She had a virtual museum of art in her room that featured black leaders and our contributions to the world. This fact aroused Kisasi's curiosity and he made a mental note to address this with Myisha at a later time. She also had a considerable collection of books, Kisasi noted. As Kisasi stood in the middle of her room, in awe, she walked up behind him. "What's wrong," she stated, startling Kisasi who replied, "I didn't know you were so well versed." If she hadn't known him, she would have taken his statement as an insult but knowing the character of the man making the statement she knew that he was complementing her on not only her knowledge but also on her selection of leaders. This meant that they shared the same reverence for the same people. She smiled and tendered to Kisasi the mobile phones.

"Keep one for yourself," he said and egressed her room. He then stopped at Askari's room, gave him one of the mobile phones, and informed him he'd planned a dinner for Myisha to celebrate her new position at Kaiser Hospital. Saving the part that he knew would most Interest Askari for last, Kisasi then said "Chantel is coming too." Askari brimmed with excitement at that bit of information. His interest in Chantel went unexplored due To the fact that Kisasi had expressed to him his concern for complications that may arise out of a relationship between the two. The fact that Chantel had been invited to share dinner with them, at headquarters, informed him that Kisasi's concerns had subsided and that he was, at least, open to the possibility of a relationship between the two but Kisasi was a strategist and as a strategy he thought it prudent to keep Chantel close. He'd heard on a news report that detectives were following a tip given to them by Mrs. Bains, the owner of the duplex where the Christmas day murders took place and that tip led them to a woman named Gheri Alexander who they listed as a "person of interest" in the case.

Though Chantel didn't know the inner workings of Almasi, she was privy to the fact that the California cats movement was of great interest to Kisasi, Askari, and Myisha. Kisasi had to make sure that their interest in the Cali cats movement remained a secret and if this had to be accomplished through dating the sistah, that's what had to transpire. It was his hopes that Chantel would, of her own volition, adopt the ideology of the organization and become active in its public, community work. He could employ the complexion of her skin to open doors that otherwise may be closed.

CHAPTER 25

1986 slid into 1987 without fanfare. Lana had completed her four years undergraduate degree and now would pursue her doctorate in juris prudence. She'd decided to move to Texas to finish her education. There would be less distractions and she would be insulated from the stigma that herpes superimposed on its host. No one there knew her, or knew of her struggles and this would put her in a position to choose the information that she would disseminate about herself. This would give her life semblance of normalcy without the discrimination that was concomitant with this disease. She called Kisasi to inform him of her decision to continue her education in Texas. "Uhali gani ndada? "Kisasi said excitedly when he heard Lana's voice on the other end of the telephone. "Mimi sijambo upendo,"Lana said imparting upon Kisasi her love for him, then continued, "I'm going to finish my education at the University of Texas. I hear they have one of the best law schools in the country," she said. Kisasi, at that moment, went through a myriad of evanescent thoughts of the times that Lana and himself had shared. There was no doubt that he still loved her and the fact that she was leaving the state wore heavy on him.

"Are you sure about this?" Kisasi asked in an attempt to cause Lana to reassess her decision. I've thought about it and I feel it's the best thing for me. There's too many distractions here and I need to be somewhere that I can focus on my education," Lana said. Kisasi knew exactly what Lana was referring to and though he overstood her need to relocate, he hated the fact that she would be so far away. "Whatever you need to do to ensure that you graduate I'm with you. Do you need anything?" Kisasi asked. "As a matter of fact I'm going to need help with my travel expenses. I'll live in the dorm and work part time to earn money for my food and clothing." Lana said. "Anything you need, don't hesitate to ask. Regardless of what has transpired you know I got your back," Kisasi said informing Lana once again that the fact that she had contracted this disease hadn't changed how he felt about her and that he still held her in the highest of esteem. "Asante sana Mimi upendo. I want to spend some time with you before I leave," Lana said. "Without a doubt Malika," Kisasi replied, exchanged pleasantries and then hung up the phone. After the brief conversation with Lana, Kisasi sat in his room reminiscing on the time that he'd shared with Lana and when he recounted how they met, he smiled out loud. A soft knock came at the door, "Come in," Kisasi said. Myisha slowly ingressed, peeking her head in from around the contour of the door, eyes coruscating, "What's up brotha?" she asked. "Nothing, what's going on with you?" Kisasi returned the question. She sat on the bed next to Kisasi. At last, she had him alone and she would take advantage of this rare opportunity to inform him of the feelings she experienced for him.

"Lets just keep it real, I want to have an exclusive relationship with you" she said. Kisasi sat silently for a moment. He too wanted to share an exclusive relationship with her but he still entertained feelings for Lana and that fact prohibited him from giving himself, totally to anyone. "I'm interested in you Myisha and I would like to see where this interest will lead us. I have to keep it real with you, I still have feelings for Lana. If you can deal with that then we can explore what we feel for each other." He said. "A little competition never hurt anyone, may the best woman prevail," Myisha said confidently. There was no doubt in her mind that she was the better woman between the two and she would prove that fact now that she was afforded the opportunity to do so. It was only a matter of time, she thought to herself. She would employ all of the wiles of a woman to convince him that she was the woman for him and in the end he would belong to her, exclusively.

"Kisasi," Askari yelled up the stairs interrupting the discourse between Myisha and Kisasi. "Ndio?" He answered. "Meet me in the den, we need to talk," Askari said. Myisha leaned in and kissed Kisasi full on the lips before they egressed his room to meet Askari in the den. As they descended the stairs she stated. "I want to spend some time with you Kisasi, we were suppose to have dinner with Askari and Chantel but I had to go to work, remember?" Myisha said. "I'm looking forward to it," he replied as they reached the bottom of the stairs and ingressed the den where Askari was sitting.

"What's on the menu brotha?" Kisasi asked. "I've located BK Blue and the streets are reporting that he is looking for some get back," Askari said. "Can he be touched?" Kisasi inquired. "Not by anyone that is not a Crip," Askari answered. "Does he have any enemies that are Crips?" Kisasi asked. "BK Blue is a Los Angels five duce Broadway. They have a beef with the Fresno Diamond Boys that started in 1978 in California Youth Authorities (CYA)," Myisha said. Isn't there some Diamond Boys in P.O right now?" Askari asked. "Yea there's a cat named Snip Snap that runs their car and from what I've heard they've been beefin here in P.O." Kisasi said. "All we have to do is add fuel to the fire," Myisha added. "Here's what we'll do, slide Chantel up under Snip Snap. He doesn't sell drugs so he has to be getting his money by other means. Have Chantel introduce the fact that she knows someone that is willing to pay for BK Blue's head on a platter and that she would act as an agent between the two so that no one knows the other one." Kisasi said "What if he doesn't bite?" Askari asked. "Then we'll have to lay him down ourselves. We can't allow him to continue to plot on us without taking action," Kisasi said. "I have a better idea, being a physician's assistant, I have access to a drug called succinylcholine. If someone is injected with it, it will cause muscular relaxation and if the dose is large enough it will cause their whole system to shut down and induce death," Myisha suggested. "What about when they do an autopsy?" Askari asked in a manner that relayed the fact that he didn't think her idea was a good one. "That's the good thing about this drug succinylcholine, it makes the death look like a heart attack," she said then shot a piercing look at Askari.

"When can you get the drug?" Kisasi asked Myisha. "When I go back to work tomorrow." "Get the drug and we'll go from there." He said decisively. He noticed the looks passed between Askari and Myisha and the verbal barbs that they exchanged so he used a tone and verbal inflection that conveyed to both of them that he would have the final word on the issue. Myisha smiled in compliance. Askari, with furrowed brow, egressed the den where they were sitting, went into the kitchen, and began making lunch. "You guys hungry?" he asked after becoming aware of his behavior. "Yea, Kisasi said and joined Askari in the kitchen. "I'm good," Myisha said, went into her room and closed the door. She sat on her bed and replayed what had just taken place. It was obvious that Askari didn't value her opinion but, given his tendency to objectify women she wasn't surprised. What was encouraging was that Kisasi saw the significance of her plan. It would cause too much of a risk to use Chantel again this soon and though the sistah showed courage she wasn't crafty enough to pull this one off. In fact she may place the organization in jeopardy. Lost in thought Myisha was startled when a knock came at her door. "Who is it?" she asked not wanting to speak to Askari at this time. "Kisasi" the voice came from the other side of the door. "Come in," she said. He ingressed the room, sat on the bed beside her and said, "I don't want you to feel that you are obligated to do what you volunteered to do concerning this BK Blue

128

issue. I trust that you're with the struggle and that trust is not based upon, if you do this" He assured her. "I don't just believe in the cause Kisasi, I'm an active agent of the cause and plan to be by your side in the cause," she said.

"I'm going to set up a meeting with Snip Snap, though we won't need him on this BK Blue issue, because I think that we have similar enemies, we can form an alliance that might prove to be beneficial down the line," he informed Myisha. "You know we can't keep just getting rid of those who stand in opposition of the cause. At some point were going to have to win the hearts of the community through ideology," she said. "You're right, but first we have to get rid of this loose end, then we can wage the war of ideology," he said. "Let me change clothes, I want to go with you to meet up with Snip Snap," she said and began undressing in front of him. No longer able to control his desires to have her right then and there, he egressed her room. Myisha, knowing the effect that she had on him smiled out loud.

CHAPTER 26

As Kisasi and Myisha traveled up MLK Blvd., made a left on Killinsworth, a right on 9th st. and went all the way down to Sumner they encountered Snip Snap standing on the corner, surrounded by his homeboys and home girls.

She pulled the Cutlass to the curb. They both got out of the car and slowly approached the group. When they got approximately five yards from the group one of the Diamond boys placed himself in their path denying them access to Snip Snap. "West up cuzz?" The soldier asked. "I would like to speak to Snip Snap," Kisasi answered. Hearing Kisasi's request to speak with him Snip Snap emerged from the midst of the crowd, "What that Diamond like?" he asked. "What's up Snip Snap? Can I speak with you?" he humbly asked. It was imperative that he didn't give the impression that he had beef with the Diamond Boys lest he subject Myisha and himself to a hail of gunfire.

"Who is you cuzz?" Snip Snap asked. "My name is Kisasi," "Revenge huh?," Snip Snap interrupted. When Snip Snap was doing time in California it was mandatory that he learned to speak Swahili and whoever was caught conveying sensitive information about the Crip car in English was severely disciplined.

"Can I speak to you in private?" Kisasi asked. "Anybody speaking Swahili has the right to bend my ear for a minute," Snip Snap said as Kisasi turned and they walked towards the Cutlass. Myisha also walked towards the Cutlass with them, and upon seeing this Snip Snap yelled over his shoulder "Tut!" come hold me down." Tut was a female who was obviously trusted by Snip Snap and as she walked in their direction Kisasi could plainly see that she was armed.

Both Kisasi and Myisha was, too, armed and Myisha too, positioned herself to "hold Kisasi down." As they reached the car Kisasi motioned for Snip Snap to sit in the driver's seat, then he walked around to the passenger's seat, opened the car door and got in. Snip Snap may have gleaned from Kisasi's gesture an inordinate respect but in reality Kisasi was merely giving himself a tactical advantage in case the conversation went awry. If so, he would not be encumbered by the steering wheel. Both Myisha and Tut stood on the driver's side of the Cutlass facing the group. Both making it evident that they were armed yet neither showing hostility.

Sitting in the car Kisasi broke the silence. "As I said I'm Kisasi and I'm the head of the non-profit organization Diamonds In The Rough. My position is that the selling of crack in our communities destroys the moral fabric of our families and hinders the upward mobility of our people." "I've heard about your organization and though I agree with you on the crack being sold in our communities, I'm not petitioning the government for anything," Snip Snap expressed. "Neither do I but we'll get the chance to discuss the ideology of my organization another time, what I want to talk to you about is an alliance based on the things that we do agree on. Neither one of us wants drugs to be sold in our Communities and between us we should be able to put brakes on these cats that continue to poison our communities. I was thinking that we could give your group access to some of our resources and in return you can supply the manpower, when needed, to move against the cats out of L.A. who refuse to respect our mandate, which will ensure that our demonstration won't turn into a California and Oregon war," Kisasi said.

"You're not from here are you?" Snip Snap asked. "I'm originally from Frisco," Kisasi said. "I knew it, I got some people in Frisco," Snip Snap replied. "I got some people from Fresno," Kisasi said. "So you've done some recon on me huh?" Snip Snap asked but before Kisasi could answer, he continued, "I've done some reconnaissance on you too and the grapevine says that the boy BK Blue blames your organization for the Christmas day murders. Look Kisasi, I can look through muddy water and see dry land. I've peeped your demonstration, and have big respect for how you're gettin down but somebody in your close proximity talks too much. That being said I accept your offer for an alliance. I don't like the boy BK Blue anyway."

Kisasi extended his hand to Snip Snap and they shook. The alliance was formed, numbers exchanged, and after Snip Snap opened the car door he turned to Kisasi and said, "I'll expect loyalty, honor and integrity because from this day forward that's what I'm giving you." "That's what you'll receive from me," Kisasi replied. Snip Snap got out of the car, closed the door, bent at the waist, leaned in the driver side window and said, "Call me Snap cuzz," then walked away. Myisha got into the driver's seat, pulled off from the curb and honked the horn at Snap. Snap raised both his hands, spreading two fingers on each of them, then put the fingers together to form a diamond. His whole click followed suit. Kisasi smiled and they drove away. "How did it go for you?" She asked. "We have an alliance but we also have someone within the ranks leaking information," Kisasi said.

Kisasi sat in deep thought as Myisha drove back to headquarters. He had to plug this leak but he also had some loose ends that he wanted to tie up concerning Lana's uncle and now that he'd secured the alliance, the time to tie up those loose ends was at hand, or at least in the foreseeable near future. "You good baby?" Myisha asked breaking her silence. "Without a doubt," Kisasi answered but offered no further discourse. Myisha took notice of the fact that he answered her, after being referred to as baby, without hesitation. He was comfortable with her, and her use of terms of endearment and that fact caused her to feel warm and fuzzy inside. They both sat in silence until they reached the house. Myisha then suggested they rent a movie and use this time alone to explore one another and the possibilities. Kisasi agreed. During the movie Myisha sat so close to Kisasi that she could feel the warmth of his body through the thin layer of his t-shirt. Kisasi, wanting to get comfortable, paused the VCR and removed his t-shirt exposing the muscular build under his sling shot. Myisha took this as an invitation and moved in even closer, placing his arm around her neck and positioning her head to lie on his broad chest. Kisasi accommodated her then re-started the movie "Shaka Zulu." At last, Myisha had Kisasi where she so desperately needed him to be. She ached for his touch and yearned to feel him inside her., his tongue, his fingers, his erection. Overwhelmed by her prurient thoughts, she began lightly tracing her right hand across his chest then down to the buttons on his 501 jeans. One by one she undid the buttons on his jeans exposing his boxer's, reaching into the manufactured opening and pulling his erection through it, to no protest by Kisasi. Now exposed to plain sight, Myisha, first taking in the enormity of his erection, shifted her gaze to his eyes while simultaneously moving her hand up and down his erection.

She leaned in to kiss him, he returned the gesture. As they passionately exchanged tongues Kisasi, with his left hand, began pulling her blouse up over her head, then cast it to the floor. He then reached around the back of her, took the clamps of her bra between his finger tips and unsnapped it. She broke the kiss and pulled her arms through her bra straps exposing her 34DD cup breast, one inch nipples erect. He stood and eagerly removed his clothing down to his boxers, Myisha did the same.

As he marveled at her dimensions accented by her dark chocolate, seemingly flawless complexion, it took all of the control that he could muster to not erupt in pleasure at that very instant. Myisha in nothing but her white, laced panties, walked over to the VCR/Cassette deck, turned off the movie, pushed play on the cassette player, and as Luther Vandross sang, "I'm not meant to live alone, turn this house into a home," she provocatively sashayed back over to the love seat, swinging her hips for effect, and sat back down next to Kisasi. As they re-ignited the passionate exchange of their tongues, Kisasi cupped Myisha's breast then took her erect nipples between his finger and thumb, softly rolling and massaging them. She began writhing in pleasure as he moved his kiss, first to her neck, then down to her breast taking her nipples into his mouth one by one, sucking on them softly, his warm wet tongue driving her crazy. Then he pressed her large breast together and took both of her nipples into his mouth, held them between his lips, and ran his tongue erratically across both of them.

Her body, uncontrollably, convulsed in orgasm as she released a guttural moan of ecstasy. He reached down between her legs into her panties to assess the results of his techniques and found that she was more than moist, she was dripping wet. She spread her thighs as he gently pushed two fingers into her. She pushed her lower body forward to accommodate the penetration. Her breathing became labored, inhaling and exhaling through moans of pleasure and satiety. "Do you have protection?" She asked between labored breaths. He retrieved his 501's reached into the pocket, pulled out a condom, tore it open, put it on and returned, she had removed her panties in anticipation, raised her legs and spread them wide in invitation. He positioned his body between her legs, placed his hands firmly on her thighs and pulled her body to the edge of the love seat. He bent his body at the waist, forward, and again engaged her in a passionate exchange of tongues.

Myisha, wanting to feel his erection against her, grabbed and rubbed it in a circular motion against her clit, slowly, gently. Being no longer able to bridle his lustful desires, He broke the kiss and took control of the situation by placing his erection inside of her. She thrust her hips upward as He buried himself in her then began pushing, then pulling himself out of her at a pace that increased after every stroke. He angled his body every other stroke exploring the inner chamber between hers legs. She could feel him deep inside of her and begged that he go even deeper, "Fill me up Kisasi," she moaned between plummeting strokes. His strokes became stronger, faster and harder in his attempt to satiate her as she matched him, stroke for stroke. "I'm gonna cum, I'm gonna cum," she said repeatedly motivating Kisasi to push harder and deeper "aahhh. I'm cumming," she screamed as he buried himself in her so deep that he could feel her pelvic bone against his. She wrapped her legs around his waist and pulled him so far in her that it felt like his erection was up in her stomach. She came so hard that she could feel it dripping down the crack of her butt.

When the intensity of her orgasm had subsided and she relaxed the grip that she had on him with her legs, he turned her over on her knees, bent her forward onto the love seat, breasts on the cushions, spread her cheeks apart with his hands, and pushed himself in her from the back. Experiencing a little pain with the pleasures of this position, she began pushing her butt backwards into Kisasi's erection as he pounded her and watched as her butt shook with every stroke. "Let me get on top," she suggested between erotic moans. He pulled out and sat up on the love seat, then scooted down to accommodate her as she straddled his lap backwards, placed his erection inside of her, put her hands on his knees and began grinding. When he placed his left hand between her shoulder blades and bent her forward, she spread her cheeks so that he could see his erection going in and out of her as she rode him. Both exploded in ecstasy at the same time. Kisasi could feel her warm juices dripping down between his legs and this fact intensified his ejaculation. Kisasi came for what seemed to be five minutes. "Ooooh, that felt soooo gooood." Myisha purred and lay back against Kisasi while he was still inside of her. The act of coitus complete, Kisasi disposed of the condom then both Myisha and himself went upstairs and showered together.

CHAPTER 27

Upon arrival Lana had found that it was impractical for her to live in the dorm, for this would ultimately present the same issues that she faced while living in the dorm at OSU. She accessed the bank card Kisasi had given her in the formative period of their relationship.

"I'll inform him of my expenditures after I get settled in," She reasoned, also furnishing the apartment from the same account. As she sat in the empty apartment, waiting for the furniture to be delivered, she re-evaluated her journey and where she'd ended up. She silently mouthed profound questions to God. "Why did you let him rape me and give me this disease?" While looking up into the ceiling as if God resided there. Though there was no audible answer that came down from on high, something inside of Lana spoke to her spirit saying, "Every living organism in the universe is accompanied by opposition to its existence but I place not a burden on any human being that they cannot bear." This inner voice brought Lana peace and solace, rejuvenating her will to succeed.

She pulled from rumination back into the present, picked up the phone and dialed the number to Kisasi's mobile phone speaking the numbers out loud as she dialed, "503.287.0902." The phone rang three times before Myisha 's voice appeared on the other end, "Hello," she answered. "Can I speak to Kisasi," Lana demanded. "He's in the shower," Myisha said curtly, "but I'll take the phone to him," imparting upon Lana the access that she now enjoyed. Lana could hear Myisha ascend the stairwell and called her a plethora of bitches in her mind. She could hear the shower running in the background and Myisha saying "You have a phone call Kisasi." "Who is it," Kisasi yelled over the sound of the cascading water. "It's Lana," she answered. Lana was pleased to hear the quickness in which Kisasi pulled back the shower curtain upon hearing that it was her on the phone but that bit of pleasure was soon replaced by anger knowing that Myisha was in his bathroom as he stood naked reaching for the phone. He stepped out of the shower, wrapped a towel around his waist and took the phone from her outstretched hand.

"Hello" Kisasi answered. "Hi baby" Lana stated then continued, "how are you doing?" "I'm fine sistah, how's things going for you?" he asked. "I'm good. I decided to rent my own apartment instead of staying in the dorm and of course I had to furnish the apartment so I went to rent-to-own and got a bedroom and living room set. I used the bank card but I promise I'll pay you back," she said. "You can pay me back by graduating at the top of your class," he said playfully then continued, "How are you holding up Malika?" "I'm good. I'm going to do this Kisasi. I refuse to let events in my life dictate my future," she answered. "That's what I want to hear sistah. Though our experiences have a bearing on our lives it doesn't have to dictate our lives. Take all that has transpired with you and turn it into fuel for your will," he said. "A Knock came at Lana's door, "Just a minute baby," she said, as she sat the phone down on the floor then went to answer the door. She returned to the phone and said, "the rent-to-own people are here with my furniture, can I call you later?" "Of course sistah," he replied. "You won't be too busy will you?" She asked pointedly revealing her antipathy for the interaction between Myisha and him. He caught the shot but chose to ignore it and said "Call me later," and hung up the phone.

The movers of the rent-to-own furniture not only moved the furniture in Lana's apartment but they also arranged the furniture as she wanted it arranged. Now that the apartment was furnished it felt more like home. She sat on the couch for a moment taking it all in. She'd come a long way but in reality the journey had entered into its most intensive phase. This next three years would be grueling and would require tremendous focus to accomplish the lofty goals that she had set for herself but she was determined and would not be denied in her quest to maximize her earning potential. Because life had dealt her such an unfair hand she'd get back at life by being ultra successful, for success is the best revenge.

CHAPTER 28

Myisha awakened Monday morning with a smile on her face. She'd finally completed the act of coitus with Kisasi and during the sensual act she felt a connection that was much deeper, more profound, even spiritual and this fact filled her with joy and security. In the midst of her thoughts Kisasi called her name from the top of the stairs. "Yea," she answered. "Can I see you before you go to work?" he asked. "I'll be up in a minute," she replied. He sat at the foot of his bed waiting for her to ingress his room. A moment later he heard a light tap at his door as it opened slowly he stated "Come in" "Hey baby what's up?" She asked, approached him kissing him full on the lips. He returned her gesture. After breaking the brief but sensual kiss he asked. "Where are we at with getting that succinylcholine?"

"I'm going to try to get it today. I'll be in position to put hands on it when Doctor Zakaria takes his daily 1:00 pm. lunch break," she answered. "Make sure that this doesn't come back to you," he warned. "There are at least 10 nurses and 5 physicians assistants that have access to the succinylcholine and my work ethic is beyond reproach. If anything, one of the nurses would come under scrutiny," she assured Him. Kisasi stood, took her hands and pulled her close to him. Holding her so close that it felt that she was being pulled inside of his figure, he whispered, "I appreciate all that you do for the struggle but even more I appreciate your presence in my demonstration." she melted, emotionally, in his arms and relinquished all reservations as they pertained to their interaction. She belonged, wholly, to Kisasi and trusted him with her life. "Our lives are "inextricably bound Kisasi and I'm willing to die for you," Myisha said. "I'd rather you live for us," he replied. They broke the embrace, Myisha descended the staircase, went out the door, got in her car and headed to Kaiser Hospital. She turned on her radio and listened to her favorite station "K-B00," as she drove, pondering her mission. She arrived at Kaiser Hospital 30 minutes before her shift was to start up as she always did. She took pride in her work and excelled far beyond meager expectations of the disproportionately Caucasian staff. This fact motivated her to strive harder. She remembered as a child, her mother telling her "Because you are Black you have to be two times better in everything that you do because your color places you at a disadvantage in America." As she grew and entered the job market she witnessed the words of her mother play out in occasions wherein she had a far more vast education and work history than her Caucasian counterpart yet she was passed over for the job. Though this was the reality she did not allow this to cause her to become bitter. She merely worked harder and excelled as her mother had advised her to do. Myisha immediately began her duties at the hospital and without warning she was presented with the opportunity to obtain succinylcholine when she heard that Dr. Zakaria had been called to the emergency room to perform an arthorocodomy on an incoming patient. She carefully opened the cabinet where the succinylcholine was stored, removed it from the cabinet, placed the small bottle in her lab coat pocket, closed the cabinet and egressed the room. Walking the corridor at a hurried but measured pace she panned her surroundings keeping her head on a swivel to detect if anyone had saw her. It was not until she reached the elevator, got on, and rode it down to the first floor did she relax.

Myisha emerged from the elevator, traversed the main floor out to the parking lot, placed the bottle in her glove compartment and returned to the hospital to finish her shift. It seemed as though her shift drug on for a year but 5:00 pm had finally came and it couldn't have been a moment too soon. She got into the car, started the engine, and sped out of the parking lot of the hospital relieved that she had gotten away with the caper. She pulled over at Lombard and Columbia at a convenience store and called Kisasi on the mobile phone. After two rings his voice appeared on the other end "Hello," he said. "Hey baby, I'm on my way home, mission accomplished," she stated gleefully through an ear to ear smile. "Touch my hand baby," Kisasi replied. "I'll touch more than that," Myisha said then hung up the phone. Kisasi hung up the phone and smiled out loud, as he sat in the den pondering how he could have the succinylcholine administered to Lana's uncle Carl without him knowing. Askari ingressed the house, with Chantel on his heels and yelled "Habari (hello)?" "Ndani ya hapa," Kisasi replied. Askari entered the den and asked, "Uhali gani comrade?" "Mimi sijambo Asante sana," Kisasi answered then repeated the greetings to Chantel, who was not familiar with the language but smiled out of respect. Askari turned to Chantel and said, "Will you wait for me in my room while I discuss some business with the general?" She smiled and walked out of the den and towards Askari's room. He waited until he heard the door to his room close before he began talking to Kisasi.

"The streets are reporting that BK Blue is talking about his suspicions concerning the Christmas day murders and that he was ready to exact revenge on the cats that done it," Askari reported. "That was his biggest mistake. Now he has to be laid down. Get at Snap and set up a meeting between him and I immediately. I'm not going to let this cat keep breathing after publishing this threat," Kisasi said.

Askari began dialing on his mobile phone and as Snap's voice came over, he walked out of the den to insulate Kisasi from that aspect of the conversation. After a few exchanges he walked back into the den and Kisasi heard him say, "They'll be there," before getting off of the phone. "He'll meet with you and Myisha at 9:00 pm in the Lloyd Center," he told Kisasi

CHAPTER 29

Myisha arrived back at headquarters after a long days work anxious to present Kisasi the succinylcholine. She parked, rushed into the house and found Kisasi in the den. She immediately saw that he had something on his mind as he sat in silence, brow furrowed. "Hey baby," she said garnering his immediate attention. Kisasi, realizing that he had been lost in thought, smiled and replied, "Uhali gani sistah." Myisha reached into her purse, removed the bottle of succinylcholine, extended it to Kisasi and said "Mission accomplished baby."

Kisasi received the bottle, examined it round about, and gave it back to Myisha, "put this in a safe place, we have a meeting with Snap at 9:00 pm at the Lloyd Center." he said.

Myisha, not receiving the expressed gratitude that she expected, turned on her heels and began to walk out of the den. She was almost outside of his presence when she heard him call her name. She turned to hear what he had to say, "You did good baby. I appreciate all that you are," He said. She smiled out loud and said, "Asante sana," left the den and went into her room. Kisasi, now realizing that he'd been aloof when she came in, decided to go to her and ensure that they were on the same page. He'd saw this scenario play itself out between his mother and father and knew, from experience, how a miscommunication, if left unsettled, could take on a life of its own and disrupt harmony in the home. He saw the look on her face when he didn't immediately acknowledge her accomplishments and he needed to remedy that.

Myisha was undressing and getting ready for a shower when a knock came at her door. She knew that Askari was home so she asked "Who is it?" before granting entrance. When she heard that it was Kisasi she excitedly said "Come in," and made no attempt to veil her partial nudity. Kisasi ingressed the room and as always was struck by her physical beauty and, struggled with the prurient thoughts sparked by her. "How was your day sistah," he asked, fighting back his arousal. "It was good. I appreciate you asking," Myisha said coquettishly extending hands to him, inviting his embrace. He took her hands and pulled her close, pressing himself against her. They held each other for a moment then, they sat on the bed, side by side. Myisha in nothing but her panties asked "What's wrong Kisasi?" "We have to lay the boy BK Blue down. He's leaking the fact that he knows who perpetuated the Christmas day murders and that he's ready to exact revenge," Kisasi replied.

"So what's the demonstration?" She asked "Were going to see if we can solicit the services of Snap and his group to eliminate the threat," Kisasi replied. "And if not?" She asked to convey the possibility that Snap may not participate. "If not then I'll personally take Blue's breath, that's the demonstration," Kisasi answered in a matter of fact tone, stood, and walked towards Myisha's bedroom door. Just as he put his hand on the door knob he turned and said, "Lets get together tonight," then egressed. Myisha finished undressing, put on her robe, and headed upstairs to shower in Kisasi's room. Once in the restroom she disrobed and got into the shower wishing that Kisasi would join her. As the water cascaded down her body she lathered herself entertaining prurient thoughts of his hands tracing the contours of her body, down her tight stomach, then between her legs. Her body shuddered at the thought of him touching her, intimately, in her own most private place. "Myisha," Kisasi's voice brought her out of her fantasy, "when you get done meet us in the den." It was about 7:30 pm when she finished moisturizing, getting dressed and ingressed the den where she found Chantel, Askari and Kisasi sitting. "What's the rumpus?" she asked mimicking Kisasi and his love for the movie "Millers Crossing."

"Chantel wants to join Almasi." Askari proudly said. Myisha shot her gaze to Kisasi in search of support for this move. Kisasi, noticing that everyone was waiting for his input said, "This struggle is not a game Chantel and you should not allow your feelings for Askari to influence your decision to be a part of something that you may not totally support. Have Askari explained to you Alamsi's position in the struggle?" As Askari began to speak on Chantel's behalf, Kisasi interrupted him, "I want to hear it from her, comrade."

"He's explained Alamsi's position, totally, and even informed me that I must solidify my allegiance to Almasi with an act that ensures my allegiance for life.," Chantel answered. "And you're ready to do that?" Myisha asked. "I'm ready to do whatever's necessary from marbles to murder," Chantel replied. Askari, Myisha and Kisasi all looked at one another, Kisasi breaking the silence, "I'll take it into consideration." Askari smiled knowing that once Chantel was admitted into the ranks they could further their relationship. At that moment Chantel said something that meant nothing to Askari and Myisha but was of great importance to Kisasi, she said. "Did you know that Lana's uncle Carl, was gay?" "How do know that?" Kisasi asked. "I was downtown and I saw him coming out of the Pink Lantern, off Burnside, hugged up with a man," She answered. Askari and Myisha laughed but Kisasi made a mental note of the information for future use. Neither one of them knew about what had transpired between Lana and her uncle Carl, or about Kisasi's desire to make Carl pay, with his life, for molesting Lana and giving her herpes, he would keep that information to himself.

Don't you have that meeting tonight?," Askari asked Kisasi. "Yes, we'll do that at 9:00 pm," Kisasi answered. "We got about an hour," Myisha said looking at her watch. "Lets leave now so that we can survey the area before anyone else gets there," Kisasi said as he rose from the couch, tossed the car keys to Myisha and left Chantel and Askari in the den.

CHAPTER 30

Kisasi pondered the information concerning Lana's uncle Carl as he and Myisha rode down Fremont St. made a right on 15th and headed towards the Lloyd Center. Upon arriving they found that Snap shared their thought process because he and a couple of his homies were already on site waiting for him to arrive.

Myisha and Kisasi pulled into the parking lot and motioned Snap over to the car. "I need you to go and sit in his car with his homies while he and I talk," Kisasi told Myisha. She opened the car door as Snap got closer which drew his attention to the driver's side of the Cutlass. "She's going to sit in your car with Tut while we talk," Kisasi informed Snap as he now stood outside the driver's side door. Myisha got out of the car and just as she brushed past Snap Kisasi saw him look at her ass. Snap got in and closed the door "What's going down kiwe?" Snap asked. "This issue with the boy BK Blue has become urgent and if it's not handled one of two things are going to happen. Either I'm going to have to kill him in public or, he's going to cause my constituency to be arrested for the Christmas day murders," Kisasi stated candidly. "Without a doubt. I've been hearing that he's been casting his suspicions far and wide. I think he's more so trying to get someone indicted than beefin with them and spreading his suspicions will do just that. If he wanted to funk (go to war) he would have kept the suspicions that he's spreading on the say low," Snap said. "This is what I'm thinking, I want to get rid of this cat but I don't want to start a war between California and Portland. I'm hoping that we can work together, exhibit some operational unity on this issue, whereas both of our goals can be actualized, simultaneously," Kisasi said. "How can I help you?" Snap asked. "I need your group to launch a mock attack on BK Blue and the 52 Broadway's to create a diversion, which in turn will allow me to move against him without suspicion," he explained. Snap sat in silence for a moment pondering Kisasi's suggestion. "We'll get at them when the time is right." Snap said, opened the car door, got out, abruptly turned, bent over, leaned into the car and said "Fix that leak that you got in your organization," then walked towards his car. Within a moments time Myisha appeared at the driver's side of the car, got in, started the car, closed the door, and pulled out of the Lloyd Center parking lot.

Everything good?" She asked. "Ndio." The Diamond boys are going to get at the Broadway's to create a diversion which will enable Almasi to move on BK Blue and hit him without suspicion," Kisasi answered. "Baby I can slide up under BK Blue and hit him with the succinylcholine. It'll look like a heart attack and because he's a known gang banger and drug dealer nobody will scrutinize his death," she suggested. "That would be cool if this cat hadn't openly issued a threat on my life. He has to be made an example of and placed before the street audience as a warning," Kisasi said and fell silent. They arrived back at headquarters. Once Myisha parked and turned off the car Kisasi said, I need you to talk to Chantel. She's already infiltrated the Cali car and we'll need her to get BK out and away from his homeboys so that we can move on him. I know a motel on Lombard St. called the Copper Penny. If she can get him in a room, someone can come in through the restroom window and leave him stretched." "What about evidence?" Myisha asked, "they'll take all necessary precautions including using a revolver so that they don't leave any shell casings," he answered. Satisfied with the foundation of the plan Myisha said, "I'll talk to her tonight." They both got out of the car and ingressed the house where they found Chantel and Askari sitting, side by side in the den. Kisasi sat on the couch across from the love seat where Chantel and Askari were sitting. "I need to talk to you Chantel," Myisha said and walked towards her room. Chantel followed. "BK Blue is spreading rumors that he was preparing to move on the individuals responsible for the Christmas day murders. This constitutes a threat on several levels. First and foremost these rumors can result in the arrest of Almasi members. Secondly it can cause an attempt on the Generals life. Neither option is acceptable, which brings us to a third option….Get rid of the threat all together."

"Where do I come in?" Chantel asked. "First of all, if you come in, overstand that this conversation is between you and I. It's not to be repeated to anyone outside this room," Myisha admonished. "Where does Kisasi stand on this issue?" Chantel asked. "Kisasi knows nothing of the details concerning this conversation for his own protection. He must maintain insulation regarding this issue but I can say that he has entrusted me with the logistics," Myisha responded, then continued, "What I need from you is to get the boy in room 28 at the Copper Penny on Lombard." "And what am I suppose to do once I get him into the room?" Chantel asked. "Whatever he wants you to do. If he wants to drink, do that. If he wants to get high, do that," Chantel interrupted and asked "If he wants to fuck?" "Do that," Myisha stated matter of factly but through a smile to take the sting out of her words, then asked, "Can you handle that?" "Not only can I handle it but it's my job to handle it." Chantel replied. At that moment Myisha knew that Chantel was the right person for this task and as they egressed her room and walked back into the den she smiled out loud. "What's going on?" Askari asked as Myisha and Chantel ingressed the den and sat across from one another next to their respective men. "Just girl talk," Myisha answered before Chantel could get a word out. Askari left the conversation right there and asked if anyone wanted a drink. Chantel joined Askari in the kitchen to fix drinks for everyone. Myisha shot Kisasi a reassuring look in their absence. He felt uncomfortable not informing Askari of his decision to employ Chantel in his plan to move on BK Blue but this strategy allowed him to maintain deniability if things got complicated. "It has to be done like this." He silently assured himself and made peace with this reality.

CHAPTER 31

September 13, 1987, a month after speaking to Snap concerning the role that he needed him and his group to play, Kisasi, Myisha and Askari sat watching television when the story came, Breaking news: "1:30 am, at Cleo's bar and grill there was a gang shootout between rival California gangs. No one was injured but the shootout caused $45,000. in damages to the business." The camera then cut to the owner of the bar and grill, "I'm tired of these gangs shooting my business up. It's time that the Portland Police Department do their jobs and get these gang bangers off the streets." The news reporter came back on and stated a few statistics then moved on to report the weather. Kisasi shot a glance at Myisha then egressed the den, and ascended the staircase. Moments later she met him in his room. "I need you to get

Chantel on the job immediately. The opportunity has presented itself and we have to take full advantage of it," Kisasi told Myisha. "I'm on it," she said and left the room.

Kisasi picked up his mobile phone and dialed Snap's number. "West up?" Snap's voice came over the phone accompanied by a background noise that sounded like a party. "I appreciate that," Kisasi said. "I enjoyed myself," Snap replied, said "Two of um," and hung up the phone. Kisasi laid back on his bed looking at the ceiling. What no one knew is that Kisasi would be the one to take BK'S breath. Myisha came back into the room, interrupting his thoughts. "She'll get him to the Copper Penny, room 28 tonight." Then she asked "Who are you going to send?" Kisasi sat straight up on the bed and stated, "I got that covered," leaving the issue to linger. She pondered the unimaginable. "Is he going to do this himself?" then reluctantly pushed the thoughts from her head. It was 11:00 pm and Kisasi made one of the strangest suggestions to both Myisha and Askari. Without provocation Kisasi stated, "Lets go to the strip club on interstate." Askari, being the womanizer that he was didn't hesitate to agree with the idea. Myisha on the other hand found it odd but didn't object. She'd learned that Kisasi didn't do anything out of spontaneity, everything that he did was the result of strategic thinking. Because the strip club was in the same vicinity as the Copper Penny and Chantel would have BK there, in room 28 that night, her suspicions became real, Kisasi was going to kill BK.

Chantel, in accord with the plan given to her by Myisha, had BK call her once he paid for the room at the Copper

Penny. "I got the room baby, when are you coming through?" BK asked. "Did you get the drink and the weed?" Chantel asked. "I got a pint of Hennessy and a half ounce of that Purple Kush," BK answered. "Good, I'm on my way baby," She said then hung up the phone. Chantel, sitting at the bar in Batman's after hours joint. Ordered herself a triple shot of Hennessy to calm her nerves. She didn't know what was supposed to go down. All she knew was that she had to get the boy BK into room 28 and this is why she was a little unnerved but the triple shot eradicated any inhibitions that she may have entertained. She got in her car and pointed herself towards the Copper Penny.

Kisasi, Myisha and Askari arrived at "Intrigue" and Askari ordered drinks for everyone but when they arrived Kisasi refused and asked the waitress for a blueberry water. Myisha took note of this fact but Askari was focused on the strippers. They sat for at least an hour before Kisasi stood and said, "I'm going to the restroom." Once out of eyesight of both Askari and Myisha, Kisasi walked out of the strip club, retrieved a .22 revolver, gloves and mask from the trunk of the car, then walked towards the alley that led to the back of the Copper Penny.

Under the premise of role playing, Chantel arrived at the Copper Penny clad in a blonde shoulder length wig which along with her very light complexion, created the illusion that she was a Caucasian female. She lightly tapped on the door of room 28 which opened allowing the billowing weed smoke to escape. BK smiled and she quickly, walked into the room. BK mistakenly misinterpreted Chantel 's actions as anxiousness to be with him. She sat on the bed, kicked off her designer heels and said "Can a female get a drink?" He hurried to oblige her, made her a drink and returned to the bed where she was sitting, "Here you go baby," he said as he extended to her a clear plastic cup filled to the rim with Hennessy, turned, lit up a fat joint and choked after inhaling the pungent smoke. She drank the cup of Hennessey and extended it to BK for a refill. He took the cup, simultaneously passed her the joint and after inhaling from it she too began to cough uncontrollably. He refilled her cup, turned on the cassette player, and put a Luther Vandross cassette tape in, to set the mood. Chantel no longer felt anxious. The weed and Hennessy had done their jobs, as a matter of fact she felt kind of horny. Luther was blowing, which along with the alcohol and weed caused her to lose all inhibitions. BK returned to the bed where she sat and sat beside her. They began kissing and groping one another. Kisasi accessed the restroom window of room 28 of the Copper Penny through the alley located in the back of the motel. He slowly opened the unlocked window and was immediately exposed to the weed smoke and the slow music that permeated the motel room. He climbed through the window, undetected, by the rooms occupants. Slowly he walked across the restroom floor and looked out of the cracked door into the motel room where he could see two figures naked, engaged in cunnilingus. One figure, he quickly identified as Chantel lay on her back with her legs open while the other figures head was positioned between her legs as her body writhed in ecstasy. Kisasi used the loud moans of ecstasy to drown out the noises of his footsteps and before anyone was the wiser he stepped up behind BK, placed the .22 at the base of his head, and let off one shot.

BK'S head fell lifeless between her legs as Chantel looked at the masked figure in terror. The figure put its finger up to its masked lips as to signal silence, then turned and went out the same way that it had come in. She pushed BK's lifeless head up from between her legs, got dressed peeped out of the motel door, and when she was sure that no one was looking she left the room, got in her car, and pulled off into traffic, unshaken.

Once outside of the Motel Kisasi placed the .22 revolver in a paper bag and left it in the dumpster. He removed his mask and gloves, stuffed them in the front pocket of his Le'Taxione Urban Couture jeans and walked briskly back to the strip club "Intrigue." Once he arrived back at the club he removed his mask and gloves from his pocket placed them back into the trunk of the car and went back into the club. what did you do in there?" "Damn baby," Myisha asked. "My stomach is bubbling I got to get out of here. Get Askari and lets go home," Kisasi said and walked out of the club to the car and got into the backseat. Soon after She appeared with Askari in tow Myisha got into the driver's side of the car and once everyone was in, started the car and pulled off into traffic. Askari asked, slurring his speech, "Uhali gani comrade?" "I'm good. My stomach is just upset," Kisasi answered then looked into the rear view mirror and saw that Myisha was searching his face. He smiled in acknowledgement. As they pulled up to headquarters they saw that Chantel was sitting in her car in front of the house. "Hey baby girl," Askari said to Chantel as they all got out of the car and walked towards the house. She joined them saying "What's going on baby." Kisasi opened the front door. They all ingressed and walked towards the den.

Myisha instinctively turned on the television and the murder was being described by reporter Nacita Ugalde who was at the scene. The camera first gave a wide lens shot of the Copper Penny Motel then zoomed in on the strikingly beautiful face of Ms. Ugalde who stated. "The murder at the Copper Penny Motel is believed to be the result of an ongoing gang war between two rival California gangs. Jerry Hill aka BK Blue is a member of the California based 52 Broadway Crips and was a "person of interest" in the Christmas day murders. Witnesses state that Jerry Hill was joined at approximately 12:00 am by a 5'6" thin built blond haired Caucasian woman in room 28. No one saw anyone else enter the motel room nor did they see the Caucasian female leave. If you have any information please call the Portland Police Department."

Myisha searched Chantel's face for any sign of fear but found none. Askari still inebriated merely said "Die slow" and walked towards the dens bar to pour himself yet another drink. At that moment it all clicked and Myisha became aware of what had transpired, "Kisasi had slipped over to the Copper Penny and killed the boy." she reasoned but dare not speak aloud. Chantel could see the light in Myisha's head turn on and when she again searched Chantel's face for answers, Chantel smiled coyly. That sinister smile verified, in Myisha 's mind, the conclusion that she had come to.

Kisasi watched as the wheels in Myisha 's head put it all together. When her glance returned to him he looked directly into her eyes without breaking eye contact, then smiled to lighten the moment. All of this took place in a matter of seconds. Askari inebriated was oblivious to the silent interaction.

CHAPTER 32

It was 3:00 am when the phone rang at Lana's apartment in Texas. She rolled over and looked at the alarm clock. Damn! she said out loud. Who could be calling at this time in the morning. She angrily picked up the receiver "Hello!," she yelled into the phone. "Uhali gani Malika," the voice came back from the other end. "Kisasi?" Lana's mind raced. She had begin seeing a guy that she'd met at Starbucks coffee shop in Austin, Texas. His name was Trayvon Gibson. "I wasn't expecting anyone baby, how are you doing?" Lana asked attempting to return her thoughts to Kisasi.

"I'm good Asante sana. I was just calling to see how you were doing," Kisasi said. "I'm doing well. I'm killing them in my class. My g.p.a is 3.8 and I'm editing the law review, a paper that is circulated amongst the student body. I'm also head of the debate team," Lana replied. "That's good Malika, I knew that you had it in you. You just needed a more conducive environment that would allow you to effloresce by honing your inherent talents. It's a trip how environment influences not only ones circumstances but also ones destiny, though it's not the determining factor," Kisasi stated. "What's going on out there?" Lana asked. "You know, the struggle continues on all necessary fronts. We are still engaged in the prohibition of drugs being sold in the community and we still, at times, experience resistance," Kisasi answered.

It was not Kisasi's intentions to expound on the activities of Almasi. Lana would not agree with the strategy that he used to eliminate the threat presented by those who he'd just laid down. As a matter of fact she would vehemently oppose it but Kisasi deemed it mandatory. There was a difference in Lana's greeting that Kisasi immediately noticed but decided not to comment on. She did not return his greeting in Swahili. Kisasi was cognizant of the benefit as well as the detriment of black people being trained in euro centric curriculum and how that training actually draws black people away from the struggle and out of our communities. Their absence, once trained, resulted in black dollars being taken out of black communities leaving an economic void that is capitalized upon by other ethnicities. Kisasi likened this fact to the dynamics that were prevalent during slavery when black women were used as the primary caregivers of their oppressors children. In these times black women who were enslaved nursed, from their breast their oppressors children and those children grew up strong and healthy only to, in most cases, perpetuate the inhumane treatment of the black women who nursed them. Kisasi saw the black community as a breast that other ethnicities nursed from by opening businesses in those communities, grew strong, then perpetuated the inhumane and discriminating treatment of black people.

Yet he didn't blame other ethnicities for taking advantage of the earning power of black people; on the contrary, He blamed black people for not controlling the economics and politics of their own communities. Kisasi, unlike many of his contemporaries and previous black movements, believed in a fair market wherein one could create a product and earn wealth but he overstood that the market was not fair and that the color of his skin far too often separated him from access to the market and therein lied his mission. He exchanged pleasantries with Lana and hung up the phone. There were other things that required his attention. After hanging up he sat in his room alone with his thoughts. Lana laid back in her bed and pondered the exchange between Kisasi and herself. Once again she had kept a secret from him and she felt disgusted.

She immediately admonished herself and promised to inform him of her intimate interest in Trayvon. She too had not informed Trayvon of her medical condition even though she had already kissed him. She didn't think that a kiss would expose him to the herpes virus in her body. Because she was not experiencing an outbreak she didn't think that the kiss was contagious and she so desperately wanted to feel a man's body pressed up against hers. She knew that this was selfish but what was she to do? Why did she have to be without the touch of a man? She was the victim, she reasoned then fell asleep.

CHAPTER 33

Lana awakened the next morning and noticed a tingling in her vaginal area. She went into the restroom, took a makeup mirror and positioned it so that she could see between her legs. She noticed that there was a cluster of bumps on her vagina. She was having an outbreak. She quickly opened the bathroom mirror where she stored the valtrex and took her prescribed dosage. This was the first outbreak that she'd had since being diagnosed with the STD. Her thoughts quickly turned to Trayvon. She wondered if her kiss had exposed him to the STD. She was not willing to tell Trayvon that she has herpes so she had to find a way to get him tested without him knowing that she had possibly exposed him.

While in the shower she came up with the solution. She would tell Trayvon that she was ready to move the relationship further but that in order for her to be comfortable doing so he would have to get tested for STD's before they had sex. Once out of the shower she called Trayvon and introduced the idea to him. Trayvon agreed and assured her that he would, that morning, go get tested and inform her of the results that day.

Lana hung up the phone and prepared for class. She had to gather her thoughts so that this issue would not distract her from her work. Arriving at class, early as usual, Lana sat in her seat and tried to push Trayvon's test out of her mind so that she could concentrate but the fear that he might test positive plagued her every thought.

She'd went the whole day without a word from Trayvon until approximately 2:52 pm she saw him crossing the University of Texas campus. He was coming straight towards her. She tried to read his body language but he was a blank canvas. As he walked towards her it seemed as if he was Moving in slow motion, a fact which excited fear in her. Once they stood in close proximity Trayvon with a sorrowful look said. "I'm positive." Lana's heart began to palpitate uncontrollably. She could hear the loud, rhythmic thumps in her ears. "What!" she exclaimed. Trayvon's expression softened and he flashed a smile, "I was just playing baby, I'm cleaner than fish pussy and that's always in the water," he said as he extended his hand with the test results in it, She quickly took the paper from his hand and read the results. He was right, he had a clean bill of health. She was relieved but now she had to break up with him so that she wouldn't expose him to the STD. "Trayvon it's over between us," Lana said. 'I was just playing baby," Trayvon said in disbelief. "It's not that Tray, I'm not the girl for you and our relationship is causing me to be distracted in class," she lied, then walked away. Trayvon stood and watched as she walked away from him in disbelief. For a moment he struggled with what had just transpired then he said to himself, "Fuck her," spinned and walked in the opposite direction. Relieved that she had actually dodged a bullet Lana told herself that she would forget about men, for now and focus on her education.

She returned to her apartment, started running bath water, lit some candles, got into the bath tub, relaxed and soaked for what seemed to be hours before getting out of the tub. She dried her body off, walked into her bedroom, and laid back on her queen sized bed, alone. As she lay there, naked, she began thinking about the first time that Kisasi and herself engaged in coitus. She became aroused by the explicit thoughts, her nipples becoming erect. Unconsciously she spread her thighs and with her fingers she began to rub her clit in slow circular motions. Then she penetrated the lips of her vagina with two fingers pushing her hips upward to meet the penetration, simulating The act, faster and deeper until she erupted in orgasm "Oooooohhhhhh!," she screamed out loud then said, "take me Kisasi." Pleasure and ecstasy was immediately replaced by sorrow and despair. For the first time Lana realized that she may never have a man to share her life with due to this disease and even deeper, she would never love anyone like she loves Kisasi. Just the thought of him brought her to climax, No other man had ever affected her as he had and she betrayed his trust. If only the opportunity to show him how she really feels about him would present itself. She would not squander that opportunity. Salt water filled her eyes then ran backwards toward her ears staining her pillow case. The only man for her was Kisasi and she'd left him in the care of that bitch Myisha, she admonished herself. She would get her man back in due time she reasoned and fell asleep.

CHAPTER 34

It was 1989 and the insensate gang violence resulted in the communities cry for peace, even if it meant calling in the National Guard and that's just what Governor Blazovich did. A curfew was enacted and the youth were now being subjected to arbitrary and capricious "gang sweeps." Kisasi saw the move for what it was, an occupation. He'd watched this tactic employed in the inner cities across America and he knew that its roots lied in the tactics employed during the civil rights, Black Power movements of the sixties. Only this time the community called for it. He would organize a meeting between rival street organizations to quell the violence and come to some agreement wherein peace could be exercised.

June 2,1989 the first "Peace Summit" in Portland Oregon convened. In attendance was Inglewood Family, West side Piru, Woodlawn Park, L.O.P's, Rollin 20's, 62 Diamond Boy's, 62 East Coast Crips, 47 Kerby Blocc, 37 CVC's, IVC's, Dead end 60's, 357's, Harlem 30's, and the 43 Gangster's. The Summit was held at the A.M.E Church on Dekum St. and sponsored by the Diamonds In The Rough nonprofit Organization. There were various speakers from community organizations such as Mycap, the Redirection House, The House of Emoja, Camp Fire Gang Peace, and local clergy including Bro. Gary X from the nation of Islam. After very insightful speeches by all involved, Kisasi gave the closing remarks saying, "There has been a rash of unprecedented violence here in Portland and across the U.S. attributed to the "Structural Gang Culture," and it's "Doctrine of Retaliation" has been enacted resulting in the loss of lives of our most valuable natural resource.... our youth. I've watched in dismay as news reporters so nonchalantly revealed the ages of those ranging from 15-20 whose right to breathe have been terminated by those in the same age group, whose immature interpretation of manhood denies them the capacity to differentiate between "insult" and "assault" then act in a manner that takes another's right to breathe based on that immature interpretation. The doctrine of retaliation© employed within the structural gang culture, that for the most part, you don't want to engage in, but because you feel that there is loyalty to the hood in the act of retaliation, you grip your 9's, clutch your glocks, and run out into the night looking for a validation that can only be accessed in the light of day. The result of the doctrine of retaliation is more retaliation! The loyalty that you perceive to be made evident in retaliating is not loyalty at all; rather it is disloyalty for it destroys the hood. You have allowed yourself to become "product" that is publicized and advertised to procure or ensure funding for law enforcement and special housing units in the Prison Industrial Complex to validate their existence and transgress yours. "Kisasi ended his spiel to a thunderous applause and standing ovation but he knew that this was only a moment in time. The real test would come after the applause and the standing ovations. The real test will play out in the streets. As He made his rounds through the crowd of street organization members, Chantel approached him and congratulated him on a magnificent speech.

"You really spoke to the hearts of these cats," she said. "Hopefully it makes a difference tomorrow" Kisasi replied. "Well it moved me. I see you in a different light," she said. "What light did you see me in previously?" he asked. "Don't get me wrong I've always saw you in a good light but tonight, I saw something that I had not seen before. Tonight I saw you beyond Portland. I saw you on an international level and that both pleases me and scares me because I know what happens to our leaders," She replied. And what's that? he asked rhetorically. They kill them," she said bluntly, then continued "I dig you, I always have and hopefully I'll get the opportunity to Show you," "Uhali gani baby," Myisha said as she stepped In between Chantel and Kisasi cutting her off purposefully. "Sijambo ndada," Kisasi answered. I'll talk to you later Kisasi," Chantel said conveying her interest In him and walked away. "What was that all about?" Myisha jealously asked. "Who gives a damn," Kisasi replied then said "Lets get out of here," placed his left hand on the small of Myisha's back and guided her through the crowd to the car.

Myisha and Kisasi sat in the den at headquarters and discussed the relevance of the summit over a glass of Hennessy. Askari ingressed the den with Chantel in tow. "Good speech comrade," Askari said then went to the bar to pour Chantel and himself a drink. "Kisasi you were magnificent. You are the best speaker that I've ever heard. You captivated the audience and really made them think. You have everything that it takes to really make a change," Chantel stated. "Damn you act like he's the next great Black Leader," Askari said over his shoulder sarcastically. Kisasi picked up on the jealousy that Askari's comment exuded and looked at Myisha to see if she too caught it. Myisha in a look, that only Kisasi and herself could interpret, confirmed that she'd peeped it but she saw something else. Something even more expedient to her. She saw that Chantel had a thing for Kisasi and both Askari's sarcasm and Chantel's interest in Kisasi was unacceptable.

"Brotha don't tell me that you are catching feelings about her compliment," Kisasi asked. What Kisasi didn't know is that Chantel had, on several occasions, expressed her interest in him to Askari. Askari, realizing that he had allowed his emotions to be revealed, attempted to clean up his comment, "Of course not comrade, we're tighter than that," He answered through a fabricated smile. Myisha shot Kisasi a look that expressed distrust in Askari. She too had saw previous signs of Askari's jealousy but remained silent as to not jeopardize the camaraderie between the two but Askari's intentions were now brought to light and she would not stand by idly and let his jealousy compromise the cause.

Kisasi had studied the dynamic of envy within the organizations and instantly calculated the potential threat. Though Askari had not revealed envy, he had definitely displayed jealousy which, if accompanied by a discontented desire for another's perceived advantages or possessions, will evolve into envy and the fact that Chantel had shown interest in Kisasi would only serve to exacerbate the scenario. A woman's overt interest in a man has always infuriated other men that weren't on the receiving end of her attention. This dynamic even played itself out in the scriptures. In the book of, 1st Samuel, David had fought valiantly for King Saul. So valiantly that Saul had accepted him as his own son. One day when David returned from the slaughter of the Philistines the women came out to meet him and chanted, "Saul has slain his thousands and David his ten thousands. This displeased Saul for the women had raised David above him through their acknowledgement of his accomplishments, above and beyond those of King Saul's, giving David the attention that he felt that only he deserved. At that moment King Saul began to plot the death of David. If this scenario could play itself out amongst the Kings and men of God, we in the hood are placed at a great disadvantage.

Both Kisasi and Myisha made a mental note of the exchanges between Kisasi and Askari but advanced as if the issue was moot. "When the opportunity presents itself I'm going to get at Askari and check his temperature," Kisasi thought to himself. As if the exchange between Kisasi and

Askari wasn't enough, Chantel asked a question that jeopardized the peace. "Kisasi, I know this may not be the best time but things are getting harder for me and I'm unable to maintain the rent that they are charging me for my apartment and I was wondering if I could move into one of you guys spare rooms?" "Of course baby," Askari answered in an attempt to exert his position in the house but, She waited with bated breath for Kisasi's approval. "The comrade said yes," Kisasi said deferring to Askari in an attempt to quell any animus.

A myriad of thoughts raced through Myisha 's mind. Not only did she not want her around Kisasi like that but she knew that the fact that she would be in close proximity to Kisasi would fuel Askari's jealousy. She'd have to get rid of Chantel without compromising the cause. She immediately began devising a plan in the midst of their quasi celebration of the success of the summit.

CHAPTER 35

As Myisha and Kisasi lie in bed together Myisha employed their time alone to express her antipathy for the fact that Chantel had moved into their home. "Baby I don't think it was wise to allow Chantel to move in. I noticed that Askari is not cool with how she pines for your attention, and that could potentially become a significant problem." "I overstand and agree with your concerns but Askari made the decision and if I had disagreed it would have played in his mind that I was disregarding him, making slight of his position and that would only increase the tension between us." He replied. "Lets keep this shit real baby, I don't like the fact that the bitch stays up in your face," Myisha revealed. "Do I sense a twinge of jealousy?" He rhetorically asked through a smile, rolled over on top of Myisha, and looking straight into her eyes stated, "Baby you have no reason to be jealous of the sistah. She can't hold a candle to you," then he kissed her deeply, passionately exchanging tongues.

Chantel spent the night with Askari but her mind ruminated on Kisasi all night long. She had feelings for Askari, at first, but his lack of discipline and expressed angst when she spoke highly of Kisasi deadened her feelings for him. She saw his insecurities play out on the big screen every time she breathed Kisasi's name and though he hadn't explicitly spoke against him his facial expressions, mannerisms and tone in which he discoursed with her at the mention of Kisasi's prowess, spoke volumes. She also believed in Kisasi's work. As a matter of fact that is what made him so appealing to her. At first Chantel felt guilty about entertaining feelings for Kisasi but why should she? She had every right to pursue her interest just as Myisha had in the presence of Lana and she would allow nothing or no one to impose upon that fact, she reasoned.

As night turned into day Myisha awakened to the smell of breakfast being prepared. She inhaled deeply to identify what was being cooked and she immediately came to the conclusion it was T-bone steak and eggs, Kisasi's favorite. This bitch is going all out to get the attention of my man, Myisha said to herself in a whispered tone. She immediately got dressed and descended the staircase, ingressed the kitchen and began to assist Chantel in the preparation of the meal. If you think that you're going to use the same tactic that I used to get Kisasi, bitch you got another thing coming, Myisha said to herself while manufacturing an outward smile to keep Chantel in the blind. Kisasi came into the kitchen, smiled out loud, and said, "That's what I like to see, operational unity," Myisha shot a glance at Chantel and smiled out loud.

Let the games begin, Chantel said to herself. Askari then appeared and quipped, "You got both of them in here cooking now." Kisasi saw no other alternative, he had to address this issue and address it from a position of strength and leadership. "What's the issue with you comrade? Are you harboring some form of discontent towards me?" Kisasi pointedly asked. Both Myisha and Chantel kept moving as if they weren't paying attention to the interaction, but both dialed into what was transpiring. "Why would you assume that brotha?" Askari asked in an attempt to feign surprise and innocence. "I've been catching the little shots that you've been taking in the presence of the sistahs and it's time that we address the issue before it becomes more than it should be." Kisasi said, indignantly. Now the sistahs work came to an abrupt halt. They could no longer pretend that they weren't listening to the exchange. Askari looked over at them as they both seemingly peered into his essence. "Brotha, if it seems as though I've been disrespectful I apologize," Askari said halfheartedly. Though Kisasi saw through Askari's deception, he knew that to pursue the issue, at this moment, in the presence of the sistahs would prove to be counterproductive, and even had the potential to erupt into violence, so he accepted Askari's apology. They shook hands and hugged. It was theatrics but there would be a time and a place to exhaust this Issue, this was neither the time nor place. Kisasi made a mental note to disarm the .40 glock that they kept in the den to protect the home front. Later on that day, after Myisha went to work, both Askari and Kisasi assisted Chantel in moving her things into headquarters.

CHAPTER 36

The year 1990 was pregnant with possibilities. Though Lana had been reading about the gang violence issues in Portland she vowed that no news would deter her from graduating this year and going into practice for herself. She had been through trial after trial on this journey and now she was about to achieve her goal. This reality was like a double edged sword. She had triumphed, against all odds but there was no one there to share in her victory. Though fulfilling, it didn't fill the void in her life caused by experiences that left her bereaved. No mother nor father, or for that fact no family at all, to share her success with. Her mind, as always returned to Kisasi. He was the only semblance of family that she had and she couldn't wait to return to him, degree in hand, and resuscitate the relationship that they once had.

These thoughts were quickly disturbed by the reality that what they had was constructed in the absence of the knowledge that she had contracted herpes through the rape of her uncle.

Could she honestly expect Kisasi to now disregard the fact that she had an ailment? Was it selfish of her to require that he expose himself to herpes? Could love transcend all obstacles? She could only pray. After going through these mental gymnastics Lana returned to the fact that she was graduating soon and regardless of anything else she had, with the financial support of Kisasi, accomplished the goal and this fact rejuvenated her. She decided to call Kisasi and convince him to come to Texas for her graduation. The phone rang several times at headquarters before Chantel answered, "Hello," "Hi, can I speak with Kisasi?" Lana asked. Yes, may I ask who's calling?" Chantel replied. "This is Lana, and who am I speaking to?" Lana asked. "Hey girl this is Chantel. Just a minute I'll get Kisasi for you," she replied. Lana could hear her set the phone down and walk away. What the hell is going on, Lana asked herself as she waited for Kisasi to pick up the receiver. A moment passed and His voice came over the phone, "Uhali gani ndada." Kisasi's voice was like music to her ears and stirred up sentiments in her that had lie dormant in his physical absence. "Mimi sijambo ndugu, how are you doing?" Lana replied. "You know chicken one day feathers the next," Kisasi replied conveying the trials that he'd been experiencing. "Guess what baby?" Lana asked and before Kisasi could answer she exclaimed, "I graduate this year!." Kisasi was ecstatic. "Congratulations sweetheart!," He exclaimed, proud of her accomplishment. "Can you come out and attend my graduation?" Lana asked. "Of course, when is it?" Kisasi answered.

"It's in November of this year," Lana informed him. "I'll be there, if it pleases the ancestors," He said then asked, "How has life been treating you sistah?" "You know, chicken one day feathers the next," She replied in the same fashion that he had and this reminded him of why he chose to love her. Lana continued, "I'm lonely Kisasi. I've been out here with no one to love and no one that loves me for the past three years. I miss you, your strength, your counsel... your touch." Kisasi didn't know how to reply to this confession but he knew that any hesitation in returning Lana's sentiments would crush her. There was no doubt in his mind that he loved her. The fact that she'd contracted herpes did not change that fact and he would give himself to her totally without reticence if, he thought that she and himself would spend the rest of their lives together but, Lana had entertained several different relationships in his absence. That coupled with the fact that they were still young gave him pause. "I miss you too baby." "Okay I'll be expecting you later this year and Kisasi," Lana paused for a moment, "I Love you." "I Love you to sweetheart," He genuinely returned her sentiment, hung up the phone and sat on the love seat reminiscing on intimate moments shared between Lana and himself. Chantel, being privy to the brief conversation between Lana and Kisasi through proximity, stated. "I can see that you love Lana, but are you in love with her?" Kisasi pondered the question for a moment then answered "In all honesty, I don't know." Kisasi stood up to walk out of the den but Chantel stepped into his path. Now face to face inches apart, Chantel said "Don't make any decisions before you give me the chance to plead my case." then kissed him passionately. He returned the sentiment, during which he became erect. Chantel felt his erection as she pressed her body up against his. Kisasi broke the kiss. Chantel reached down and brushed the palm of her hand across the length of his erection, moaned and said "Just give me a chance."

Kisasi egressed the den, ascended the staircase, went into his room and began to process what had just transpired. He pondered the various scenarios that could arise out of the circumstance that he found himself in. He overstood the dangers concomitant with a woman scorned and this fact mandated a delicate and graceful dance between the desires of these sistahs for his affection and his desires for the cause. Lines had become blurred and this fact could jeopardize the cause.

There were now three women, whom he cared about, pining for his affection and all of them, in one instance or another, were privy to sensitive information that could destroy not only him but the cause. Chantel had explicit knowledge of two murders that could implicate Kisasi if she chose to do so. He had to get her hands bloody to ensure that she kept this knowledge confidential and he knew exactly how to do it. He remembered that it was Chantel who'd saw Lana's uncle Carl coming out of the Pink Lantern hugged up with some man and he still had the succinylcholine that Myisha had lifted from the hospital. He'd slide Chantel up under Carl and have her feed him the lethal dose. This would both eliminate Carl and implicate Chantel in one fell swoop.

The only drawback was that Kisasi would have to entertain Chantel's sexual advances. Though he would not inform Myisha of the kiss that he shared with Chantel he would inform her of his stratagem. It was imperative that Myisha not only knew of his plans but that she also overstood his motivations.

CHAPTER 37

In April of "90" Kisasi sat at headquarters alone in anticipation of Myisha's return from work. He had been planning the move on Lana's uncle Carl for the past few months and had not introduced his plan to Myisha. Due to its lack of completion there was no need to breathe an incomplete plan. Incomplete plans were like premature ejaculations; both stemmed from a lack of mental focus and discipline, an inability to master the subject matter and we can all agree a premature ejaculation is detrimental to its host.

Kisasi was deep in thought, aided by the heavy rain that danced against his bedroom window panes as he peered out over the landscape, when Myisha entered the room, instantly bringing his mind back to the present. "Uhali gani daddy," Myisha said as she undressed, removing her work environment, layer by layer. Kisasi turned, walked to her, kissed her lightly, full on the lips, and inquired, "Mambo yako vipi?" "Other than dealing with these racist at this hospital, everything is fine Asante," Myisha answered. "Sit down baby, we need to talk," Kisasi said. Myisha now becoming concerned sat in the recliner as Kisasi sat on the bed. Her mind was racing, what could he need to talk to me about?, she silently asked herself. Kisasi answered her mental question, "I've been thinking and I've come to the conclusion that Chantel has been made privy and part of information and circumstances that if she was to become verbally incontinent could jeopardize the organization, and we have to counter that fact, in other words, she needs to get some blood on her hands so that she can't implement us in anything without implementing herself."

Myisha immediately prepared herself for what she thought that she might hear next. She'd told Kisasi before that they could not keep eliminating people wholesale but she trusted that whatever he thought, was best for the organization and the cause, "What's the demonstration Kisasi?" Myisha asked. "We put her in a position to move on someone herself, without assistance. That way we can maintain deniability, and at the same time get her hands dirty," Kisasi replied. Myisha mulled over the stratagem for a moment, It was brilliant but who? she asked herself then she asked Kisasi, "Who will we have her move on and in what manner?. You know she's not 110 lbs. soaking wet, with boots on," Myisha interjected. "This move will require cunning not physicality and we both know she has mastered that technique," Kisasi said through a smile then continued, "I'll handle the logistics but I need you to overstand that this is what must transpire and don't catch any emotions about how I maneuver It," Kisasi said. Myisha stood clad in nothing but her panties and bra, walked over to Kisasi slowly and stood between his legs as he sat at the foot of the bed, his face at her stomach. She pulled his head into her stomach, as he wrapped his arms around her small waist and looked up into her face she said, in a sultry, sincere tone, "As long as the objective is accomplished I'll tolerate the method."

Kisasi, aroused by her authenticity, leaned back on the bed and pulled her down onto him. Myisha reach under herself, unbuckled and unzipped His Le'Taxione urban couture jeans and freed his erection from the silk boxers that bound it, never breaking her gaze into his grey eyes. She then stood pulled his jeans down, sat on top of him, pulled the silk fabric covering her pussy to the side, placed his erection in her and began to rock back and forth writhing in pleasure. Lost in passion, caught in the throes of lust, they'd forgotten that they had left the door to his room open and the sound of someone entering the house made them aware of that fact. "Damn!" Myisha exclaimed and rolled off of Kisasi who then, hurriedly, put his pants back on, walked over to the entrance of is room, looked down the staircase and saw Chantel walk into Myisha 's old room where she now resided. He then returned, closed the door and said "Rain check?" "Don't think that I won 't be coming to cash it," Myisha coyly said, gathered her clothes and went to take a shower.

CHAPTER 38

Chantel sat in her room staring into her vanity mirror when a knock came at the bedroom door, knock, knock, knock! "Who is it?." she said in the direction of the knocks. "It's Kisasi. Can I speak with you?" The voice on the other side of the door returned. she stood, adjusted the short skirt that she was wearing, sauntered over to the door, opened it, sauntered provocatively, back over to the bed and sat. Kisasi watched then ingressed the room. "Is everything cool?" He asked. "Everything is cool baby," Chantel answered in sultry tone. Kisasi looked around the room, spotted an ottoman, positioned it in front of Chantel, sat down and leaned in to convey the secrecy of what he was about to share with her and said, "Do you remember telling me that Lana's uncle Carl was a homosexual?" "Yea. Why, what's up?" She asked. "Without disclosing the sensitive details. "He needs to disappear," Kisasi said matter of factly. "You now I'll do whatever needs to be done for the cause, just give me the logistics, who I'm going to be assisting and I'm on it," she said. "You'll be on your own on this one sistah but he's a dope fiend and that will facilitate the task at hand. We'll use his addiction and your beauty to get him out of position and simultaneously relinquish his life," Kisasi replied. Chantel shifted her position on the bed and, in the midst of uncrossing her legs then crossing them again, she opened them wide enough that Kisasi could catch a brief glance at the white lace panties she donned underneath her short skirt and the private area that it scantily covered. "So you think I'm beautiful?" she purred through a sinister smile. "Stay focused sistah." he said then continued, "I need you to slide up under Carl and slip him a syringe full of succinylcholine." What is that?" Chantel inquired. "It's a drug that will make his death look natural," Kisasi answered. "Who else knows about this Chantel asked. "No one. This is between you and I." Kisasi answered. He didn't want Chantel to know that he'd conferred with Myisha in this matter. It was just as important that she didn't share any of this information with Askari or anyone else for that matter. It was imperative that he kept certain information confidential to protect not only the organization but also the people closest to him. Everything wasn't for everybody.

Chantel again shifted her position on the bed but this time when she uncrossed her legs she left them slightly agape and asked, "What do I get out of this?" "What do you want sistah?" Kisasi asked. "I want the opportunity to be your woman," she answered. "How can you be my woman when you've already allowed Askari to intimately experience you?" Kisasi asked. "Is that what you think Kisasi? Askari and I have never had sex," Chantel replied. he smiled, looked directly between Chantel's legs then back into her eyes and said "Then who knows what the future holds," Chantel spread her legs wide and leaned back on the bed exposing her lace and coquettishly said, "This is what the future holds." Kisasi leaned forward, kissed Chantel's inner thigh softly, then egressed the room leaving her there, on the bed, in the throes.

He walked into the den and poured himself a glass of cognac. He drank in salute of himself and smiled out loud. Myisha soon joined Kisasi in the den dressed in a shower robe and poured herself a glass of cognac. After taking a drink she asked, "Did you handle that?" "Everything is strait and overstood," Kisasi replied. Chantel ingressed the den and said, "Lets have a toast," then took the bottle of cognac and poured each one of them a glass. She then raised her drink and said; "Long live Almasi," Both Myisha and Kisasi raised their glasses and in unison said "Long live Almasi." They all touched glasses then downed their drinks. Chantel took stock of the interaction between Myisha and Kisasi as they drank more and inhibitions were abandoned. She could see that there was chemistry between them but it was nothing that she could not overcome. The fact is that she wanted Kisasi and refused to be deterred. Whatever it would take to convince him that she was the woman for him, she was willing to do. Askari, returning home, came into the den with Joann in tow. Kisasi immediately looked to Chantel. He gauge her reactions to the fact that Askari had brought another woman home. He searched her face but found not a hint of concern or interest in Askari's indiscretion. Chantel caught Kisasi searching her face and gave him a look that expressed that she could care less.

Myisha caught the exchange between them and made a mental note of it. Askari turned, took Joann by the hand, and proceeded towards his room. Chantel, Myisha and Kisasi all looked at each other, laughed out loud and continued to drink. Chantel walked into the kitchen to refresh the ice in her glass and when she was out of vision Myisha stood directly in front of Kisasi, opened her robe revealing that she was naked underneath, and closed it back before Chantel could return. She returned to the den and resumed drinking. Another hour went by before inhibitions kicked in and they all agreed that they'd better call it a night

CHAPTER 39

Chantel sat in her room pondering what she'd agreed to do on behalf of the organization. then, without provocation, her mind became fixated on the scenario that had taken place between Kisasi and herself. She became aroused as her mind entertained the possibilities, so aroused that she lay back on the bed and imagined Kisasi was on top of her, she masturbated and moaned softly as she erupted in orgasm.

The next morning Chantel retrieved the succinylcholine from Kisasi and headed out to complete her mission. She drove through downtown Portland for a couple of hours and was about to give up her search when she thought to make one more pass. As she drove by the Justice Center she spotted a man fitting Carl's description walking with what seemed to be a teenage runaway through Pioneer Square. She drove down two blocks, parked the car and got out. "If I walk back towards Pioneer

Square in the direction that they were headed in, I'm sure that I will bump into them," Chantel thought out loud.

As Chantel walked back towards the Pioneer Square she wondered "What is this old cat doing with this obviously underage girl?" Her thoughts were interrupted by the fact that Carl and the teenage girl was now standing about a half of a block in front of her. As she walked closer she ran what she would say to him through her mind, "Say brotha, you lookin," Chantel said as she walked up on Carl and the girl. She could see that the teenager had tracks on her neck from injecting herself with heroin but because she was still so young her made evident her youth, though her body seemed to be ravaged by the drug.

"What you got, that black tar?" Carl eagerly asked, sweat beading on his forehead. "Naw, that's garbage. I got that china white," Chantel answered appealing to the dope fiend in him. Carl turned to the teenage female that he was with and asked, "How much did you just make?" Making it obvious that she had been prostituting herself to pay for their drug habit. This fact infuriated Chantel and added venom to the task at hand. This old ass dope fiend was living off of this teenager like a vampire lives off of another's blood. He deserves everything that he's about to experience. "I got $250.00 daddy," the young girl replied, then continued, "But we don't have a needle."

It's your lucky day, I have it already fixed and ready to go," Chantel said as she pulled out the syringe full of the succinylcholine and showed it to them. "Give me a note and this is yours but don't try to shoot all of this at once. It's pure and a couple of my customers have already o.d.'d (overdosed) on it," Chantel explained. It was a known fact that heroin addicts were mentally drawn to dealers that sold the dope that caused fiends to overdose. It was like if it didn't cause an overdose it wasn't good dope.

Chantel watched as Carl began sweating profusely after hearing that some fiends had in fact overdosed off of this dope. The young girl gave Chantel a crisp hundred dollar bill and Chantel gave the syringe to Carl knowing that the dope fiend in him would direct his greed and he would try to shoot the whole syringe in an attempt to experience the ultimate high…... and he would, she prayed.

Chantel walked away from the scene and said a silent prayer, "God let his greed deprive that young girl of that needle and let his death serve as a reason for her to get her life strait," and as she finished her prayer one single tear streamed down her face. She quickly wiped it away, got in the car and drove towards northeast Portland. She pulled up to Irvington park on Prescott, turned the car off and just sat there…thinking.

Circumstances in her life had changed dramatically and now she had rose in love with this extraordinary black man but must compete for his affection. There was no turning back now, blood was on her hands. She was in too deep and refused to be denied. Kisasi would be her man. It was meant to be. The universe had brought them together and she would let no one stand in her way. Chantel left Irvington park and went shopping at the Lloyd Center By the time she returned to headquarters it was approximately 3:00 pm. Askari had left with Joann.

Myisha was still at work and wouldn't return until at least 5:30-6:00pm. That gave her close to two and a half hours alone with Kisasi. She walked into the house, placed the lingerie that she'd purchased from Victoria's Secret in her room, and ascended the stairs towards his room. Once at the top of the stairs she saw Kisasi, through his open door, sitting at the small desk in his room, talking on the phone.

She lightly tapped on the door, he turned to her, motioned her in and continued talking on the phone, "I appreciate the gesture but I don't do this work for awards. I'll tell you what, if you present the award to the Diamonds in the Rough Non-Profit Organization, someone from the organization will be pleased to accept it. No problem, thank you Mamm. Goodbye," Kisasi ended the phone call, turned to Chantel and said, "Uhali gani sistah, have a seat," he motioned to the recliner.

Chantel sat in the recliner and crossed her legs. For the first time Kisasi really looked into her face. She was stunning. Her long, naturally curly hair lay flush against her defined, dimpled cheeks. "Kisasi I've developed deep feelings for you in a short span of time. "I overstand that you have feelings for me sistah but the cause comes first." "I overstand that and I would never jeopardize the cause. I have no issue with your relationship with neither, Lana or Myisha. I guess what I'm trying to say is I'd rather have some of you than none of you because I truly think that in the long run you'll realize that I'm the woman for you but I need to know that I will be given a fair shot at your heart," Chantel said. "I'll keep it real sistah, I can't guarantee that I'll be exclusively with you, just as I couldn't guarantee Myisha that I would be exclusively with her but I can guarantee that I will always respect you and what you bring to this organization. We are all adults and as long as boundaries are respected and honored there should be no problems between us," Kisasi said. Chantel made a mental note of the fact that Kisasi informed Myisha that he couldn't promise her exclusivity and smiled inwardly. She then rose from her seat in the recliner and walked over to Kisasi who was still sitting at his desk. Kisasi stood and, she walked into his embrace, laying her head against his chest, holding him tightly. He returned the affection. She could feel his erection through his jeans, looking up into his eyes she kissed him deeply. He returned the passion. Her desire to feel the fullness of his erection inside of her was overwhelming. She reached into his jeans, grabbed his full erection and explored it's girth and length without breaking her kiss. Kisasi broke the kiss, "Lets go to the den and have a drink." "That sounds like a good idea," Chantel said and removed her hand from Kisasi's jeans.

Once in the den Kisasi turned on the television and poured cognac for Chantel and himself. "To us," Kisasi toasted." To us," Chantel agreed.

CHAPTER 40

Carl and Jennefer moved eagerly to their spot under the Burnside bridge where they could inject the potent heroin that they'd just purchased from Chantel. As they drew closer and closer to their destination they became more and more anxious and the physical results of this anxiety became more and more evident. Carl began to sweat profusely and Jennefer's body began to shake and convulse at the thought of the heroin coursing through her young but tattered veins. Upon reaching their spot under the bridge Carl's greed kicked in. "I'm going to do this one, the next one is yours," he said to Jennefer and as she helplessly protested he took off his belt, plopped down on the ground and tied his belt around his arm, tight, in order to cause his now collapsed veins to protrude. He took the already prepared serum, aimed the needle directly at his defunct vein then pierced the skin.

As he eased the serum into his vein Jennefer, angry that he'd cheated her out of her high, walked away in discuss. Carl, after injecting all of the contents of the needle, knew that something was wrong.

Though he became more and more relaxed he was not experiencing the euphoria that accompanied this ultra relaxation. His breathing became shallow and labored. He tugged at the belt in an attempt to stop the coursing of what he thought was heroin, to no avail. He fell backwards, paralyzed, and as his head hit the ground he knew that something had gone terribly wrong. His whole life flashed before his eyes. His youth, Vietnam, the overdose of his sister Mona and how he callously took the needle from her dead body and shot into his arm the drugs that she didn't get to use then, the rape of his niece Lana. His eyes became big as saucers, his breathing stopped, he expired. Several days had passed and Jennefer had not heard from Carl. In a last ditch attempt to learn of his whereabouts she returned to the spot under the bridge. As she walked closer she saw a human figure lying at the very same location they'd been at several days prior. She drew even closer and as she got even closer the putrescent smell of death assaulted her nostrils. Death was a constant companion of dope fiends so Jennefer harbored no fear for what she might find. As she walked up next to the figure lying motionlessly she saw that the figure was Carl. There he laid, in all of his greed, flies flittering and flirting all around his body. Dope fiends had been walking by and walking over his dead corpse for the past several days in their quest for drugs, no one giving a damn about his condition. Jennefer now stood over Carl's rotting corpse and smiled at his last words, "I'm going to do this one, the next one is yours." She spinned on her heels and as she walked away she said to herself, "Yes, the next one is mine," then smiled out loud.

Myisha, Chantel, Askari and Kisasi all sat in the den watching television and preparing for an event that Kisasi was scheduled to speak at concerning drugs and gang violence in the north and northeast communities when Nacita Ugalde flashed on the screen saying "Today, under the Burnside bridge, the body of Carl Santiago was found in the rubbish. It is believed that he died from an overdose. Drug paraphernalia was found near his body which the coroner suggests had been on the scene for at least three days judging from the extent of rigor mortis and decomposition of his body. This, another senseless death due to illicit drugs underscores the need for effective laws to combat the influx of illicit drugs in our communities." Chantel, Myisha and Kisasi all looked at one another. "Aint that Lana's uncle?" Askari asked. "Who knows," Myisha stated and moved the conversation to the event wherein Kisasi was about to speak. "We only have 45 min. till the function," Myisha continued. "Lets get out of here," but as they all walked towards the front door he turned on his heels and stated, "You guys go ahead I need to speak with Chantel for a minute." Once Myisha and Askari was out of the house Kisasi turned to Chantel, "You did a good job sistah," he said. "I want you to know that I'm in this and whatever the cause needs me to do, I'm with that," she replied and moved closer to Kisasi until they were inches apart. She then grabbed his right hand and placed it up under her short bodyfitting skirt allowing Kisasi to feel the light incontinence of orgasm between her legs. Kisasi kissed her deeply then thanked her for her sacrifice.

"You'll be rewarded," Kisasi stated and they egressed the house to join Myisha and Askari. Chantel got into the car with Askari and Kisasi got into the car with Myisha.

CHAPTER 41

Myisha, Askari, Chantel and Kisasi all arrived at the venue in downtown Portland simultaneously. They were quickly escorted back stage and into a waiting room, Kisasi was informed that he'd be introduced in approximately twenty minutes. They all sat and patiently waited for Kisasi to be notified of his turn to speak. Myisha broke the silence, "Are you ready baby?" she asked and shot a glance at Chantel. "I was born for this sistah and was ready before I came out of my mother's womb," Kisasi replied. At the last summit held at AME Church Kisasi spoke to, for the most part, those who were either members or affiliates of the structural gang culture. This time he would be speaking to youth counselors, social workers, politicians, civic leaders, business owners, clergy and grass roots nonprofit organizations.

His message would have to be delivered from a perspective of the sciences for this is all that they would overstand and be willing to invest in. Though this fact was unsettling to Kisasi, it was real, and if he wanted to eradicate inequality In housing, education and health services, he must deliver a speech that would not only tickle their ears but also raise their consciousness. As he sat pondering this fact, a tap came at the door, a man stuck his head inside and said, "Their getting ready to introduce you." Kisasi approached the rostrum to a thunderous applause and after the applause subsided he began his delivery "Annually, literally millions of taxpayers' dollars are allocated and spent in order to attempt to curb the destructive effects of gangs on American families and communities.

Yet, the growth and negative results of such growth continue to tighten their destructive holds on our communities. In short, those tactics that have been employed in the past have not worked and they have not worked because they do not address both the psychological and sociological negatives that perpetuate gang membership and violence. Gangs are not created in a vacuum, therefore the gang member is not born, he or she is made.

There is a theory developed by Mary Ainesworth called "Avoidant-Insecure Attachment." which in my opinion, is a natural human defense mechanism that causes the youth to minimize his/her interaction with parents, shun parents infrequent attempts to comfort, and ultimately become indifferent to his/her relationship with parents or strangers. This interruption in a youth's psychological developmental process procures resentment for his/her parents, which is then projected onto all adults and cause them to rebel against any perceived authority that resembles their parents, which in turn facilitates, and sometimes perpetuate their matriculation into the structural gang culture. Why do I use the word culture when describing gangs? well, what is a culture? According to the Dictionary of Sociology a sub-culture is "Any system of beliefs, values, and norms which is shared and actively participated in by an appreciable minority of people within a particular culture," so gangs are a culture and cultures are a socially constructed reality, therefore subject to transformation. Attempts to draw lines of distinction between culture and sub-culture, as it relates to gangs, citing the gangs violent behavior, not only prohibits us from overstanding and addressing the gang issue, but it is fundamentally an incorrect assertion for socio-biologists agree that behavior is not genetically driven but socially learned so there is a propensity for aggression in all people. The crowd erupted with applause. When the applause sub sided people began hurling questions at Kisasi. One woman asked, "Are you saying that it's the parents fault that our children are involved in gangs?" Kisasi answered, "It's not that simplistic Mamm, there are both sociological, as well as psychological dynamics that facilitate gang membership, but it all starts with emotional neglect or un-fulfillment in the home." Another person sarcastically asked, "So neglect creates gang members?" "No, neglect does not create gang members but emotional neglect can cause one to be susceptible to the familial structure that gangs offer," Kisasi replied.

Another lady stood and stated, "My name is Naomi Gaston and I am a Council woman who interacts with at risk youth groups daily. I want to know how do we change the violent culture of gangs." "First we must recognize that gangs are in fact a culture. Then we must address the psychological trauma that spurns violence by addressing the thought process out of which violent behavior emanates. Then we must afford the gang member the tools and life skills needed to access the American value system of success, power and wealth for when you have a group that lacks the equal opportunity to access a social orders value system it creates a sub-culture," Kisasi answered. "I say we lock them all up and throw away the key!" a policeman said to applause. It was obvious that not only were local police in attendance but Kisasi had also spotted FBI agents in the crowd.

"You cannot incarcerate your way out of this circumstance. Incarceration only serves to validate the gang member status and influence within the structural gang culture, not to mention adding resentment for law enforcement and the judicial system. The gang member must be reformed and placed back into the community so that his reformation can spark a transformation which will ameliorate the conditions in our communities," Kisasi shot back. The crowd roared for what seemed to be three minutes at which time Kisasi exited the platform. Chantel ran into Kisasi's arms and hugged him. "You were great brotha," she said and relinquished him. Myisha, seeking to upstage Chantel kissed Kisasi on the cheek and said, "you just validated your leadership among our people." "Did you see the FBI out there whispering to each other as you fielded those questions?" Askari asked. "I saw them comrade," Kisasi replied. "You know what that means?" Askari asked rhetorically. "Without a doubt. It means that I've just become a serious threat to the government and the organization will be targeted for disbandment," Kisasi answered.

As Kisasi, Myisha, Chantel and Askari were exiting, the event Council Woman Gaston approached and extended her right hand to Kisasi and stated, "That was an excellent speech." Kisasi shook her hand and said, "Asante Sana, thank you," Sila ya Asante, don't mention it brotha," the Council Woman said flaunting her ability to speak Swahili Naomi Gaston was a tall 5'10" caramel complexion, black woman with a styled short, soft, dyed burgundy afro, strong chiseled facial features and full lips. She was what brothas described as "red bone." "After that speech brotha you're going to need friends and assistance from people within the government structure. I know that you noticed the FBI was in the crowd and that's why I presented the question that I presented. I wanted to give you the opportunity to express your position on gang violence because now the task is to film and record everything that you say and attempt to turn you into a leader of organized rebellion," the Council Woman said. "I appreciate your assistance Council Woman," Kisasi began but was interrupted, "Call me Naomi," the Council woman said, Kisasi nodded in agreement. "Let me give you my number. I want you to call me if you run into any governmental opposition," Naomi said and extended her card to Kisasi. Kisasi took the card from Naomi's hand and recited his number to her. Naomi smiled, Kisasi said, "I will be calling you soon," then she turned and walked away swinging her hips as sistahs do. Kisasi watched as her statuesque figure egressed, and he smiled secretly.

CHAPTER 42

November 1, 1990. Lana's graduation was looming and Kisasi had promised to be there for her, a promise that he would keep. "Sistah I have to fly to Texas for Lana's graduation," he told Myisha the night before his scheduled flight. He'd deliver the news in this fashion for a specific reason. He wanted Chantel to be the one who drove him to PDX to board his flight. "Do you need me to drive you to the airport." Myisha asked in a sultry voice still intoxicated from the love making the night before. "That's all right baby, you go ahead and go to work. I'll have Chantel drive me," Kisasi replied, got out of the bed and ingressed in the bathroom.

As he brushed his teeth and washed his face Myisha ingressed the bathroom in nothing but light blue lace panties and matching bra, "How long are you going to be gone?" She asked in a little girl manner. "For a few days at the most. I'll call and have you pick me up when I get back in," Kisasi answered, rinsed his mouth then turned on the shower, tempered the water, shed his boxers and t-shirt and got in. After brushing her teeth Myisha raised her voice over the cascading water, "Can I come in?." she asked rhetorically while simultaneously opening the shower curtain exposing her nakedness.

They washed each other briefly but tenderly and with affection. Myisha, having to get to work finished first. "I got to go baby, have a nice trip and call me when you reach your destination," she said then kissed him full on the lips. They briefly exchanged tongues expressing, through the kiss, all that was not said. As she egressed the shower and dried her body she remembered a bar to a song that her mother used to listen to "If you want to know if he loves you so it's in his kiss" in their studio apartment every time that she was lonely, aching and inebriated over the murder of her father. Myisha smiled out loud then proceeded to get dressed. Kisasi stayed in the shower a while longer than usual. His neck was stiff as if he'd slept on his pillow wrong and the hot water from the shower, in its own way, helped with the tightness that he was experiencing. His head under the shower head, he didn't hear the shower curtains as they were pulled back but he felt someone's presence. When he opened his eyes from the soothing massage of the water there stood Chantel, naked. "Can I get in?" She asked. though she didn't wait for an answer.

"I waited until Myisha was gone so that we could be alone," Chantel said to ease the concern she read in Kisasi's expression. Kisasi had lathered the wash cloth and began rubbing it across his chest and down his torso in an attempt to mask the fact that he was caught off guard and somewhat uneasy. As he reached his navel Chantel gently placed her hand on top of his and said, "Let me do that." she took the wash cloth from him and started at his shoulders, then his chest, lathering his body. Then she pulled him close in a full frontal embrace and reached around to wash his back. Kisasi turned his back to her to facilitate the cleansing.

She then wrapped her arms around Kisasi from the back as the soap was rinsed away by the cascading water. Kisasi turned to face her, and looked deep into her green eyes becoming fully erect. He picked Chantel up, she wrapped her thighs around his waist, and he carried her, both still wet to his bed and lay her down softly. He stood and surveyed her glistening body from head to toe. Her skin was flawless, her eyes closed, and feeling Kisasi's penetrating glare, she spread her thighs, reached between her legs, and with her fingers spread the lips, moaning in ecstasy. She barely opened her eyes and gazed at Kisasi through the space and her long eye lashes.

He was transfixed on her pleasuring herself and this fact caused her to erupt in uncontrollable orgasms. She screamed softly, body convulsing. After her multiple orgasms had subsided, Kisasi bent at the waist over her, kissed her full on the lips, and said, "Thank you baby, now lets get to the airport before I lose all control and miss my flight." "You're welcome daddy." Chantel moaned, got up and went back into the bathroom to clean herself. They arrived at the airport and Chantel checked Kisasi's Louis Vuitton suit case as he stood in line for his ticket. Twenty minutes later his flight announcement blared over the intercom, "Flight 209 to Texas now boarding at gate 2."

"I booked your flight through Diamonds In The Rough, so you will be seated in first class business section," Chantel said as she straightened Kisasi's tie. "Thank you sistah." When I get back we'll finish that conversation.," Kisasi said through a smile. "I hope so. Have a safe flight," Chantel said, turned and walked away attempting to swing her little hips. Kisasi smiled out loud and boarded the plane.

Kisasi put his Louis Vuitton carryon bag into the compartment over his head and strapped in for the flight. The flight attendant stopped and made sure he was comfortable then went through the script for passengers in case of an emergency. The plane began moving down the runway, speed increasing rapidly, until it began to elevate causing a funny feeling in Kisasi's stomach but before he could really take notice of it the plane was airborne. He took this opportunity to use the planes phone to call Lana and inform her that he was in fact on his way and what time his flight would be arriving. "Hello," Lana's sweet voice came on the line. Uhali gani sistah." Kisasi said,"Sijambo baby." Lana said barely able to contain her excitement. "I'm on my way sistah. I have one layover but I'll be there at about 2:30 am," Kisasi said. "I'll see you in a little while, Mimi upendo we," Kisasi said, "I love you to," Lana replied and hung up the phone.

He ordered a drink and reclined his seat. As he relaxed he replayed the events of the past year in his mind looking for shortcomings and any mistakes that he couldn't afford to make again. In the midst of his psychological wrangling his thoughts were interrupted by the opportunity that had presented itself in the form of Council woman Gaston or Naomi as she implored him to refer to her as. He was now feeling the liberating effect of his cognac and, decided to call Naomi. The phone began to ring and before he could change his mind Naomi's voice appeared on the other end of the phone "Council woman Gaston," how can I help you?" "Ms. Gaston this is Kisasi," "Hello Kisasi, how are you doing," Naomi asked. "I'm fine sistah. I'm just calling to touch basis with you and reiterate that I appreciate all that you said. I look forward to exploring the possibilities that lie before us as it relates to serving our community," Kisasi replied. "So am I brotha, when can we meet privately, I have some ideas that I would like to run by you?" Naomi asked. "Right now I'm on a flight to Texas but I should be back in a week or so, can we meet then?" Kisasi asked. "Privately," Naomi emphasized coquettishly. "Without a doubt," Kisasi replied informing her that he overstood the implication. "O.K., I'll see you later, Naomi said and hung up the phone. Kisasi requested that his drink be refreshed, again reclined, and pondered the possibilities.

CHAPTER 43

Naomi, after hanging up the phone, sat motionless on her couch for a moment. She too pondered the possibilities. What was real to her was that she'd, against her better judgment, had allowed herself to be enticed by this young black man's intelligence-ambition-ingenuity-eloquence and sincere desire to ameliorate conditions in the blighted communities in her district. She'd not had the opportunity to invest in an intimate relationship since she'd caught her husband of 15 years in their house-their bed-with his vastly younger office assistant. Their relationship had already been rocky for it had came to light that after attempting to have a child her husband-Kenneth could not produce children, at least that was the obvious conclusion of deductive reasoning for she'd been to several doctors in order to see if she could have children and all of her tests were good. In a heated discussion she'd informed Kenneth that she had in fact been tested and that they'd found no reason, biologically, that she could not have children.

Kenneth took the news as an indictment of his "manhood" and sought to prove his virility through indiscreet sexual encounters. After the divorce Naomi, though she dated, chose not to become emotionally involved with anyone. She wanted to focus on the youth in blighted communities and found that the only way for her to do that effectively was to become part of the decision making process that affected those youth. At times she longed for the intimate touch of a man but not just any man, a man that overstood her and was compatible intellectually-spiritually-emotionally and sexually. In the midst of reminiscing her mind returned to Kisasi. This brotha's talisman-his demonstration was euphoric and titillating. She was a mature woman, she wasn't contemplating marrying the brotha but she deserved to experience euphoria not to mention the assistance that she could tender to the brotha. "He's going to need me," she attempted to reason –temper her desires, "and fair exchange ain't no robbery," she mused and smiled out loud. After wrangling with the dynamics surrounding this "encounter" Naomi asked herself "why not?"

At that moment she decided to assist the brotha in his endeavors-which were of great importance to her and, if it became intimate, which she'd do everything in her power to effectuate, they were two consenting adults and she would show the young brotha what a woman was. Naomi picked up the phone and dialed. The phone rang a couple of times before a man picked up, "This is Governor Gossett how may I help you?" "Walter?" Naomi asked in disbelief that the governor had answered the phone personally. "Naomi?" Governor Gossett returned, "yes, how are you doing Walter?" Naomi asked, "I'm doing fine Naomi how are you?" The governor asked, "I'm fine how is the wife?" Naomi asked, "She's fine," the governor responded. Naomi immediately went into political mode, "Listen Walter, I've met this young man who is doing phenomenal work with gangs, I wanted to know if I could set up a meeting between you, him and myself that he may familiarize you with the work that he's doing and get some insight from you that would facilitate his work." Though to the naked eye this seemed like an innocent request, Naomi had knew Walter since they were in elementary school and she'd helped him win his governor seat and knew of his secret indiscretions, for she'd been responsible for orchestrating the cover ups. Walter in the public eye was a very conservative republican representative but behind closed doors, He was sexually impulsive and these impulses juxtaposed with the fact that he was into bondage-masochism put him in a position where a young woman who'd requested that he simulate asphyxiation during their tawdry sexual encounter almost died, a fact which intensified orgasm for Walter.

This all transpired at a campaign dinner put on by Naomi at Walter's house, unbeknownst to his wife Madison, who was downstairs entertaining donors and supporters of his campaign. Naomi being familiar with both Walter and Madison went upstairs looking for Walter, walked into his room to find him standing, eyes glazed over with a thousand yard stare, while the young intern lie on the bed lifeless.

"Walter, you selfish bastard! what did you do?" Seeing Walter standing there unresponsive, She leaped into action and began resuscitating the young intern. "Get the hell out." she screamed over her shoulder at Walter who then egressed the room. After she convinced the young intern that she could not cash in on the incident and promising to assist her, she led the intern out the back entrance of the home and rejoined the campaign dinner, no one the wiser. She shot a glance at Walter ensuring him that everything was taken care of, he smiled. In all reality Naomi despised Walter. He was not qualified for the governorship, a position that she well qualified for and coveted, but she was a black woman in a white male dominated arena, so she seized the opportunity to influence legislation from behind the veil, blackmail? Of course not, this was whitemail.

She felt it her duty to attempt to save these youth from the bleak reality that plagued their existence and since she was too inhibited by the same social construct that impeded their dreams she was justified in her strategy to extract any favor, of a political nature, that she needed to at least make an attempt to even the playing field, for those that entered this hostile environ-she reasoned.

Her mind returned to the present upon hearing the governor's response to her request, "Of course Naomi, anything I can do to help," Walter replied. 'I'll get back to you with a date and time, we'll go from there," Naomi suggested. "Talk to you then," Walter stated. They exchanged goodbyes and hung up the phone. Walter, too, fostered antipathy for her, for he envied her intellect and industriousness. He knew that she was a better legislator than himself and that her talent to organize, manage and bring the best out of her subordinates was not only greater than his but she genuinely cared about people. He, on the other hand, only entered politics out of a lust for power and obligation to his father who had, at the time, been a United States Senator. He detested the fact that Naomi not only had the Intel that she had concerning his fetishes but, he also resented the fact that though she never explicitly used it as a bargaining chip, it was implied incentive for him to aid, assist and facilitate her endeavors. Now she wanted to sanction someone who wants to ameliorate the conditions that helped him get elected.

What Naomi didn't know is that the governor was complicit in the proliferation of drugs in urban communities. It was a necessary evil Walter reasoned and, an effective political platform that garnered him political hegemony in an unforgiving, ever changing political climate. He would assist Naomi but this would be the last time. He would free himself from this threat and he would use the corruption within the Portland Police Department and, his political clout to carry out his insidious plan.

CHAPTER 44

When Kisasi finally made it to Texas he was not only tired but tipsy. As soon as he walked off of the plane Lana was there to meet him. She jumped into his arms wrapped her legs around his torso and screamed into his ear so loud that he thought he would become deaf. "I'm so excited to see you baby." She stated. "Hotep na Jambo ndada-Uhali gani?" Kisasi inquired. "Sijambo-utakaa kwa muda gani?" She asked. "Siku mbili." Kisasi replied. "Two days !" Lana exclaimed. "I'm just getting my foot in the door with the organization I don't want to lose traction, he continued, I was invited to speak at this venue in downtown Portland the speech was a success, I drew the parallel between gangs and culture expounding on the need to view gangs in the context of culture that one may reform and transform the resultant behavior." She watched as Kisasi explained what had transpired at the event, the coruscation in his eyes reminding her of the time when he would speak at headquarters to a small group of individuals that believed in him and who sought a drug free community.

She remembered that at one time she too fought that fight side by side with Kisasi, and in that instance she realized that they were growing apart, this tore at her essence. "Let me take you to my apartment Lana suggested but Kisasi, not wanting to be placed in an intimate situation with her stated, "Chantel booked me a room at the Hyatt through the organization, you know the demonstration beautiful, for all intents and purposes this is documented as a business trip." He searched her face for any adverse reaction and when he saw that she was taken aback he shot-"You can stay with me at the hotel and bring me up to speed," flashing a smile. "That's a great idea baby." Lana agreed, and they egressed the terminal, got into the rental car and headed for the Hyatt. "Are you tired or hungry baby." Lana asked. "My room has all the amenities sweetheart, I intend to exploit them," he replied through a smile and sunk into the leather seats in the rented Mercedes. She pulled up to the Hyatt and they were greeted by the valet. "Park the car I'll be spending the night." After checking in at the desk, receiving the room card, they ingressed the elevator and ascended to the penthouse suite on the 7th floor. Upon entering the suite the phone rang. "Hello" Kisasi answered. "This is room service will you be needing anything Mr. Kisasi?" the front desk asked. "As a matter of fact send me up a bottle of your best champagne and some strawberries." Kisasi said looking directly into Lana's eyes. She flashed a smile. This was not a sexual overture, Kisasi merely wanted Lana to feel free from the stigma related to her disease.

Within a moment there came a knock at the door, "room service." A man's voice said from the other side of the door. Kisasi opened the door and instructed the help to place the items on his cart in the living area and tipped him $50.00 as he left the suite. "Join me on the couch," Kisasi suggested and motioned her, arm extended, palm up.

As she took her place on the couch, Kisasi popped the cork on the bottle of Champagne. As the pressure escaped the bottle it made a popping sound then it's contents oozed out of the bottle down its neck, cold and foamy. He first poured Lana a glass then himself. He then raised his glass above his head and stated "A toast to the most beautiful attorney I've ever met." She held up her glass then placed it to her lips and partook of the libation. He then moved to the couch, sat beside Lana and fed her one of the plump sweet strawberries. He watched as she slowly, provocatively devoured the strawberry, moaning for effect. They sat, drank, reminisced, discussed the recent events in their lives and enjoyed one another's company. Kisasi needing to get some rest suggested that Lana sleep in the room and he take the couch, She agreed and retired to the room. As she got to the entrance of the room she looked back over her shoulder and said "I love you Kisasi," He returned the sentiments and continued undressing. As he lay on the couch he began thinking about how she must feel, he wanted so desperately to be with her, she was his first love, friend, confidant, companion and his comrade. He wanted her to know that these facts had not changed though the circumstances had.

He got up from the couch, went into the room and got into bed with Lana and held her as they fell asleep.

Four hours later the phone rang, He rolled over looked at the clock that read 7:00 am, picked up the phone "wake up call." The voice on the other end stated. "Thank you." He replied and hung up the phone. "It's time to get up sistah, he said as he shook her, then went into the bathroom to take a shower. As he lathered himself, Lana came into the bathroom and sat on the toilet. As she urinated she thanked him for making her feel secure.

"I was being selfish baby I needed to hold a familiar body more than you needed to be held," he said. In an attempt to alleviate any feelings of inadequacy that she may be entertaining due to her ailment. "I'm a big girl Kisasi you don't have to manage me." she replied yet she did feel inadequate, less than, and jaded at times. She often found herself questioning her womanhood, her viability, for this reason she poured herself into her craft graduating in the top percentile of her class, yet she longed to be loved and experience that physical connectivity that is shared between a man and a woman, what woman didn't? When Kisasi got out of the shower Lana was gone, on the bed a note, he picked it up and began to read "I know that my ailment changes things between us I'm having problems processing that. It's so unfair! This bastard violates me and I have to pay the price, I have to bear the stigma of a disease that I did nothing to receive. I thank the creator I have a man like you in my life, a man that has supported my dreams and ambitions selflessly. I'll pick you up at 5:00 pm for my graduation. I love you sincerely, Malika." Kisasi noticed she had signed the note with the same name that he'd given her in the formative years of their relationship, he smiled out loud.

CHAPTER 45

Lana and Kisasi sat silently in the Benz as she transported him back to the airport after her graduation ceremony. They'd traveled several miles before Lana pierced the awkward silence, "Are you sure that you can't stay a couple of more days baby?" "I wish that I could sistah but I have to get back and do some follow up on my last speech. Now that I've pierced this circle I have to ensure that the agenda is pushed properly, this issue is too urgent to rely on fortuity. These youth, rather they know it or not are in trouble, legislations being passed, laws are being enacted, in order to capture them and arrest them in the embryonic stages of their developmental process and they have not the foresight to see that they are being socialized for and desensitized to incarceration." Kisasi replied.

They both fell silent again but this time Kisasi spoke, "I am so proud of you sistah. You've come a long way against all odds and made a life, a career for yourself. What you've learned no one can ever take that away from you." "Kisasi," Lana interrupted him mid sentence, "When are you going to realize that you can't change the hood, the hood was there before you and it will be there long after you've expired. Black people don't give a damn about your work! As a matter of fact they are your worst enemy. They are going to oppose you at every turn and, one day you're going to wake up, old and gray wondering what happened to your life. This struggle of yours is going to rob you of your youth and leave you broken." "And that supposed to be the deciding factor of whether I engage this struggle or not, Kisasi asked!?

His voice changed timbre, "How dare you get at me like it wasn't this work and the resultant successes that put you through college and you have the audacity to question its viability? Have you allowed the veiled process of training-perpetuated by these Eurocentric institutions of learning to cause you to abandon the cause that you and I agreed was necessary for our community, for our people to effloresce? Have you forgotten what our reality is while being trained to assimilate into this social construct by doing the bidding of an un-just, justice system wherein the color of my skin becomes the determining factor of my sentence?" "That's not what I'm saying Kisasi, Lana interjected, "What I'm saying is that you will spend your life fighting for a segment of society," A segment of society!" Kisasi asked In disbelief then continued, "It is this segment of societies blood, sweat and tears that built this country and now saturate the streets of inner cities across America. We are far more than a segment of this society, we are the drivers of this economy and because some of us are chained to the slave mentality I'm suppose to abandon my efforts to ameliorate the conditions in our communities? It is that kind of thinking that keeps us on the plantation-mentally,"

Lana fell silent and remained that way until they pulled up at the airport, parked and exited the car. As they were walking to the ticket counter she spoke, "Kisasi I'm sorry for what I said, I know how important the struggle is to you and it was not my intentions to minimize your work or make you think that I don't believe in you," "Don't worry about it sistah" Kisasi said, gave her a big hug and walked through the makeshift corridor to board the plane. As he egressed through, he heard Lana yell "I love you Kisasi" but he pretended not to hear her. She'd revealed an aspect of her character in that exchange. He made a mental note of that fact.

As Kisasi sat, drink in hand, 33,000. miles in the sky, he pondered not only what had transpired between Lana and himself but, also the dynamics that surrounded the work that he'd been doing and would have to do to effectuate change. This was a daunting task but others had come before him and embraced all that came with it. Lost in thought, he barely recognized the man

That had sat directly to his left. Once he did recognize him he took account of his dress and demeanor. There was something suspicious about this man and though he was sure of the fact that he didn't know him, there was something familiar about him. Kisasi searched his mind in an attempt to place the stranger, where did he know this guy from? he asked himself, then it hit him, this cat was on the flight with him from Portland to Texas.

FBI agent Joseph Bolds had been a part of the agency for 25 years. He'd been recruited to infiltrate black organizations and cause dissention from within back in the 60's but when J. Edgar Hoovers cointelpro program successfully dismantled the Black Panther Party, United Slaves Organization (US), Southern Christian Leadership Conference (SNCC) Dr. Kings organization, Black Student Unions etc. Agent Bolds was reassigned to desk work, which he resented. He became disgruntled with the obvious racism within the Bureau and how they'd employed misinformation, disinformation, deception and lies to render Black leaders and their organizations ineffective but his greatest antipathy was for self, for he helped destroy Black leaders that were innocent of the charges levied against them by the Bureau-CIA-House Committee on Un-American Activities etc.

After he'd served the Bureau in their suppurate surreptitious plots, they discarded him like a used, putrescent tampon until recently when he was tapped to gather Intel on this emerging threat whose parents had been tied to the Black Liberation Army, though never indicted for any subversive activity. Yes he would gather Intel. but he would not be used again to destroy Black Leadership or organizations that are sincerely attempting to better the plight of the poor. He remembered what an agent, who was Chief of the Racial Intelligence Section once said "If you have good intelligence, and know what it's going to do, you can seed distrust, sow misinformation." Agent Bolds was only 20 years old when he'd been tapped, due to his youth, to infiltrate the Black Panther Party (BPP). He watched and carried out the orders of his superiors to create distrust within the group and undermine its efforts to work in tandem with the US Organization. One incident played in his mind like a horror movie over and over again. In September 1968 FBI director J. Edgar Hoover described the Panthers as "the greatest threat to the internal security of the country" at which time he launched his terrorist campaign to "stop the rise of a Black Messiah"

By July 1969, the panthers had become the primary focus of the cointelpro program and was the target of 233 tactical attacks. The bureau was cognizant of a power struggle on the west coast between the BPP and US and chose to employ tactics to exacerbate these tensions. This effort included mailing anonymous letters and caricatures to BPP members ridiculing the local and national BPP leadership. The bureau proudly implicated themselves and even took credit for the insensate violence between the two organizations. In an FBI Memorandum from San Diego field office to FBI Headquarters-dated 1-16-70 in the words of an FBI official the actions that they'd taken "resulted in shootings, beatings and a high degree of unrest in the area of southeast San Diego.

On January 17,1969 two members of the BPP Apprentice "Bunchy" Carter and John Huggins were killed by US members on the UCLA campus after a meeting between the two organizations and university student. One month later the FBI San Diego field office requested permission from headquarters to mail derogatory cartoons to local BPP offices and to the homes of prominent BPP leaders around the country. The purpose was pellucidly stated: "The purpose of the caricatures is to indicate to the BPP that the US organization feels that they are ineffectual, inadequate and riddled with graft and corruption," according to memorandums from the FBI San Diego office to FBI Headquarters dated 1-20-69 and 2-20-69. Agent bolds had unwittingly, under the auspices of serving the interest of the government, furnished the Intel of that meeting to his superiors and had even attended the meeting under the premise of being a concerned UCLA student. It was only in 1976 when internal memos documenting the bureaus cointelpro activities were made public did he realize the intrinsic role that he played in this heavy drama and he sought atonement for his actions. It was his hopes that this new target of the bureau was in fact working for the poor and not exploiting the poor. "Uhali gani brotha" Kisasi said reaching across himself, extending his right hand to the man with the familiar face, "My name is Kisasi." Agent Bolds too extended his right hand and as they shook stated, "My name is Joseph Bolds please to meet you." "Likewise," Kisasi stated as he released his grip and returned to his forward position in his seat. They remained silent for about five minutes, but since they were the only two black men on the flight Kisasi engaged him in discourse. They talked the whole flight discussing everything from sports, diet, to the plight of black people, a subject that Kisasi was willing to discuss with anybody-any-time-anywhere.

Agent Bolds found Kisasi engaging, charismatic, eloquent and knowledgeable, all qualities that made him the target of the bureau. "He possessed the charisma of Malcolm the fortitude of Huey P. Newton the compassion of Dr. King the eloquence of Farrakhan and the street grit of Tookie Williams. This man was 25-26 years old exchanging sound philosophy and ideological concepts with a man twice his age. His political acumen was incredible yet he'd not been taught in any of the prestigious Colleges as I have." He thought to himself. Being a west point alum he was impressed with Kisasi's intellect and knowledge of urban communities, but this fact acted as a double edged sword, on the one hand, he was impressed, and on the other hand, he was suspicious. This was his training kicking in. He'd been trained to be suspicious of charismatic black men that posited their concern for the poor in general and the black community in particular, for the vast majority of them turned out to be parasites that exploited the poor while they lived in luxury.

At the other end of the spectrum, Kisasi was too impressed by the knowledge of the man that had introduced himself as Joseph Bolds but, he too had been trained and his training told him that it was more to this man than he knew and that it was not fortuity that placed him on the same flight, both to and from, as it applied to this trip. Kisasi being the child of revolutionary parents could smell an agent from a mile away. Their dress- their dialect- their gestures were indicative to the trained eye. When Mr. Bolds got up to use the restroom Kisasi searched his waistline, not to see if he had a gun, but to see if his leather belt was worn from wearing a gun holster and when he saw that it was, he smiled out loud and silently thanked his father Vitani for teaching him this counterintelligence technique.

The flight landed at PDX and the two men exchanged farewells "Kwaheri" Kisasi said. "Kwaheri" Agent Bolds replied. They shook hands and parted ways but, Kisasi knew that this was not the last time that he would see Joseph Bolds. As Kisasi replayed the whole encounter in his mind Myisha appeared in the distance smiling from ear to ear coruscate, inviting. Kisasi flashed a smile and quickened his pace in anticipation of the welcoming. As she approached he could see that she had a newspaper folded in hand "Uhali gani sweetheart" she exclaimed "Mimi sijambo sistah.

He retorted as they fell into intimate embrace. she abruptly broke the embrace and stated, "You made the paper" opened it up and handed it to him for inspection. Kisasi took the paper and begin reading the article out loud, "The gang problem in Portland has grown exponentially. As residents clamor for more police patrols, president of the nonprofit "Diamonds In The Rough" tells a packed house that "First we must recognize that gangs are in fact a culture, then we must address the trauma that spurns violence by addressing the thought process out of which violent behavior emanates." The Portland gang taskforce leader Sgt. Greg Fox sated in reply, "I don't subscribe to that hug a thug ideology, what needs to be done is that all of these terrorists be locked up and the key be thrown away." Kisasi folded the newspaper and pushed it into the trash can as they egressed the airport.

CHAPTER 46

On their way back to headquarters Myisha informed Kisasi that Askari had been missing in action, since he'd went to Texas. "Sweetheart he's so caught up in these random women that he's ineffective in your absence," she stated. "I'll deal with Askari when we get to Headquarters" Kisasi said and cleverly changed the subject as if there was no problem when deep inside he'd been calculating recent moves that Askari had been making. He didn't want to openly express his concerns with Myisha, for he wanted her opinion of Askari to be her own not tainted by his observations. There would come a time when Askari's loyalty to the organization would come into question and when that happened on an organizational level discipline would be swift without obfuscation, without favor, and without yielding to interpersonal affinities or lack thereof.

Myisha interrupted Kisasi's rumination "Now the good news, there is a foundation in Seattle Washington called, Save The Youth started by this billionaire named Jim Tate, that has donated $5,000.000.00 to our organization," Kisasi couldn't believe what he was hearing "Five mill?" he questioned "Five Million" Myisha reassured with a smile. "I vetted his foundation and found that he himself is worth 50 Billion and that he does a lot of work in impoverished countries across the world. He's at the forefront of technology and sincerely cares about the youth. He likes to remain anonymous and make these kinds of donations to grass roots organizations once a year. I accepted his donation on behalf of the organization by phone. He'd also donated computers and cell phones to the organization with the promise that every year he will update the technology that we may remain competitive." "The ancestors have blessed this work and we must make sure that everything that we do is above the board." Listen sweetheart I don't want you to think that five mill. solves the problems that our people are faced with for he could donate the whole 50 billion and we would be faced with another problem unique to our circumstance tomorrow. No amount of money can change the condition of our people for if it could the change would have already occurred. We as a people account for almost a trillion dollars of this economy yet we still endure issues that date back to slavery "Kisasi said then through a smile added, "But the five mill helps" "O.K." Myisha exclaimed through an elevated inflection of her voice then added "Don't look a gift horse in the mouth!" They both laughed as they pulled up to headquarters parked and ingressed the house.

As they walked through the door Chantel stood in the kitchen making Kisasi's favorite meal "Uhali gani comrades" she greeted both Kisasi and Myisha "Uhali gani comrade" they both returned the greeting in unison looked at each other and said "Don't pinch me." Kisasi walked into the living room, sat his Louis Vuitton bag on the floor and sunk into the cushions of the couch.

"How was your trip brotha" Chantel asked. "It was cool" Kisasi replied. "How is Lana?" Myisha asked more out of duty than genuine concern "She has her degree in law now" Kisasi answered without elaboration or affection. Myisha caught the gesture and smiled inside. "You guys hungry?" Chantel asked "As a mad Russian" Kisasi answered. "I'm cool, I have to go and handle some business for the organization, but I won't be long," Myisha said-shot a glance at Chantel and left the house. Chantel smiled mischievously and continued cooking

After she was sure that Myisha had left Chantel came into the living room, plate in hand and sat down next to Kisasi. "Here's your food sweetheart" Chantel said. "Asante sana sistah" Kisasi replied, accepted the food and began eating. Between mastication Kisasi inquired, "How have you been sistah and how has the organization been treating you?" "Everything is cool. I missed the hell out of you" Chantel answered coquettishly. "The sentiment is mutual sistah. I appreciate you cooking for me, I needed a home cooked meal. I couldn't eat that hotel food" Kisasi replied.

Kisasi sat in wait for Chantel to initiate the conversation that he'd promised they'd have upon his return, instead she spoke of the organization and how she could be of better service. Kisasi was intrigued by Chantel's desire to play a more active and professional role within the organization and her rationale and reasoning concerning the result of social stratification and the reality of what Kisasi had termed "The benefit of complexion" was spot on.

Chantel advanced a well known reality which allowed those of a lighter complexion to advance in arenas wherein those of a darker complexion was proscribed. This was an intricate part of the ideology employed on the plantation by the slave master to separate and control the slaves. On the plantation the slave master would rape and impregnate a slave and when the child of this brutal rape was born, if the child was of light complexion the child, though still a slave, would serve in the home of the slave master-rather than in the field with the darker slaves. This gave the slave of a lighter complexion a false sense of exclusivity and favor when in all reality they were still in fact a slave. The tactic proved effective and caused the darker slave to hate the lighter slave and the lighter slave to feel that they were better than the darker slave because they were closer at least in complexion, to the slave master. Chantel rationale that she could get into places based on her complexion easier than Myisha could was based on this reality. Kisasi listened and searched the connotations and intonations of Chantel's voice in an attempt to gauge whether she believed that the complexion of her skin made her more efficient, or if she truly overstood the ideology that she described and was merely offering herself to take advantage of the reality.

Kisasi listened intently then questioned Chantel to verify his conclusions, "Do you think your education would permit you to be more effective in this endeavor than Myisha's?" "No as a matter of fact Myisha's education far surpasses mine and she is better qualified but we live in a world that makes exceptions for the color of one's skin and since that is the reality I think that we should use me and capitalize off of their misconception or attempt to keep us separate" Chantel answered. Kisasi smiled out loud. It was obvious that Chantel both overstood the dynamics of complexion and was willing to exploit the psychological malady of white supremacy that perpetuates this maladaptive mentality." I have an associate's degree in business management and I'm willing to go back to school to further my education" Chantel stated. "I agree" Kisasi replied.

Askari ingressed the house "Uhali gani!" they could hear him say from where they were "Uhali gani brotha" both Chantel and Kisasi replied. Askari came into the den extended his hand to Kisasi. Kisasi took his hand and pulled Askari into his embrace –momentarily, released his hand–then sat back down on the plush loveseat. In that brief embrace Kisasi read Askari and concluded that something wasn't right. He didn't exude the camaraderie that he once exuded. Kisasi remembered his mother once saying that "Some people enter this struggle and maintain intensity for a while but eventually become disenchanted, frustrated by the slow pace of the people becoming conscious, accepting their circumstance, and moving to ameliorate their condition."

Had this happened with Askari? Had he become so disappointed in the slow progress of the people that he'd simply abandoned the struggle? Or was it something more? Kisasi thought to himself while conscious not to reveal his thoughts through his facial expressions.

There was a tried and proven way to ascertain an individual's commitment to any organization and its Principles. Kisasi had assiduously studied the successes and failures of the Black Organizations in general but, those of the Nation of Islam in particular-not because he believed in their doctrine for he had no faith in the institution of religion, but because he was fascinated with Malcolm X- his rise and fall and the dynamics between him and Elijah Muhammad. In his studies he found that the Nation of Islam had accomplished in America, at a time of overwhelming opposition, that which no other black organization had accomplished. Not only were they successful in business, building an independent economy but they successfully rehabilitated the prostitute, drug dealer, pimp-videlicet the criminal mentality. Malcolm revered Elijah and publicly credited Elijah for teaching him a truth that was the catalyst for his redemption and success but when Elijah disciplined Malcolm for not adhering to an order that was given to all of his ministers pertaining to making any comments concerning the assassination of President Kennedy, their relationship began to deteriorate. So it was the introduction of loss of position or status which spurs the thought that someone is doing something to you, when in all reality they may be doing something for you, that exposes ones true veracity or lack thereof as it applies to organization. Kisasi's father once said "We as black people have been devalued, vitiated in our

American sojourn to the point where when we get a position of status or title within an organization we think that it is the position-status-title that validates us. We experience a certain exclusivity, affinity for the title, to the detriment of the organization. If you want to ascertain an individual's commitment to the organization, take away his title."

"I need both of you to have a seat so I can bring you up to speed on our new strategy for the organization." Kisasi said to Askari and Chantel. After they were both sitting Kisasi continued, "The save the youth foundation, in Seattle has donated five mill to our organization" Kisasi said taking into account the coruscate eyes of both Askari and Chantel, Then he continued. "We have to make sure that this money reaches the hood. Every dime of this money has to benefit our youth by enhancing their quality of life. I want to open a tutoring process within the Diamonds In The Rough building, where the youths progress can be protected, encouraged and documented. We'll start an internship wherein college students can earn extra credits for their courses and when necessary we'll employ professionals to tender services to the youth.

Kisasi watched as they listened intensely, then he dropped the bomb "Askari I've decided to remove you as vice president" "For what! I've been with you from day one and now that we got these millions you're going to switch up on me?" Askari exclaimed. "Its not about switching up on you brotha, it's about doing what's best for the organization and lets be real you've been neglecting your duties to the organization" Kisasi said in a raised tone while looking directly into Askari's eyes. Chantel measuring the animosity in the texture of Kisasi's voice became tense, anticipating violence. After a moment of intense eye contact Askari said, "You act as if you're better than me brotha." "I act like your comrade brotha and, if you'd step back from your internal issues and view my actions through the prism of intellect, rather than emotion you'd be able to properly decipher not only my demonstration but your own, or lack thereof" Kisasi replied. "What are you trying to say?" Askari asked. "I am saying exactly what I mean brotha there's no esoteric interpretation of what I'm saying," Kisasi replied.

Chantel intervened, "I think that we should table this discussion for now and focus on Kisasi's vision for the organization, after all he is the leader." Chantel words rang in Askari's ears like an indictment. The fact that Kisasi was revered in this manner effected him twofold. First he sought the same reverence to no avail, secondly he was envious of the fact that the relationship between Kisasi and himself was deteriorating and in his mind it was due to both Kisasi's successes and the presence of these females.

Weighing the validity of what Chantel said, Askari said. "If you don't have anything that you need me to do right now, I'll catch you later brotha." Seeing that Kisasi wasn't going to reply he spinned and egressed the house. After Chantel was sure that Askari was out of earshot she turned to Kisasi and said, "He bears watching." Not wanting to make evident his thinking concerning Askari, Kisasi stated "He'll be alright sistah, he just needs some time to recalibrate.

CHAPTER 47

Kisasi and Councilwoman, Naomi Gaston had been playing phone tag for the last month. Between her shoring up her constituency for the next election and him relocating and remodeling the Diamonds In The Rough building that it may hold 20 students and computer stations for each student, it seemed as though their communication had been reduced to mere messages. Before anyone was aware it was mid January 1991. Askari, in light of the last discussion that he and Kisasi had–had began to get more involved in the everyday functions of the organization and though this pleased Kisasi the fact that Askari would be incommunicado at times caused him to perceive his activities through raised eyebrow.

Chantel had enrolled in college to further her education in business management and Myisha, along with her role of Chief Financial Officer, acted as principle agent for the organization. She was forced to cut back her hours at the hospital in preparation of handling the day to day functions of the organization and though she loved working at the hospital she was willing to abandon that work to further the plight of "in risk" youth.

It was 1:00 pm on a Tuesday afternoon as Myisha and Kisasi sat in the den going over the costs of the renovations, Kisasi's cell phone rang "D.I.T.R" how can I help you?" "Don't ask me that question if you're not willing to grant my request" the councilwoman stated coquettishly through a smile. Kisasi got up and signaling Myisha with his index finger, stepped out of her earshot to take the call. Sistah Gaston how are you doing?" "I'm fine brotha but call me Naomi. It seems as though we've been playing phone tag but I'm glad that I caught you." she said. "Yes I've been busy trying to get this building ready before April." Kisasi said.

I heard about your new building and the problems that you were having concerning zoning and the type of organizational activities that you will be conducting out of this building." Naomi stated. At that moment Kisasi realized what had transpired and why all of a sudden his permits were instantaneously granted. Naomi had intervened and called in some favors to get the building up to code and running. Realizing this fact Kisasi stated. "Thank you for the assistance sistah I'm forever in your debt." "Thank you brotha," but I only did what I was supposed to do as a black woman who is concerned with the viability of our youth. I want to get together, have dinner and discuss some things with you" Naomi suggested, "Name the time and place I'm all yours" Kisasi advanced flirtatiously as he ingressed the den to write down the time and place "How about Divanni's at 8:00pm" Naomi suggested "I'll be there with bells on" Kisasi stated and hung up the phone.

"You'll be where with bells on?" Myisha asked catching the end of the phone call. "Do you remember we were having those issues concerning zoning and permits, and all of a sudden those issues disappeared?" I just found out that it was the councilwoman that made those issues disappear and she wants me to meet her for dinner to discuss some business. I'm going to need you to drop me off at Divanni's tonight at about 7:30 pm" Kisasi replied. "Well I'd better get these bills paid now" Myisha stated, gathered up the documents that they'd been going over, put them in her brief case and headed towards the front door. As she reach for the door knob Myisha hollered back over her shoulder "Kwaheri baby" "Kwaheri sistah" Kisasi said as he ascended the stairs. When Myisha returned to headquarters it was 6:30pm. she stopped at Chantel's room and greeted her before ascending the stairs to Kisasi's room. She then gently rapped on the closed door, but there was no answer.

When she opened the door she could hear the shower running. She walked to the restroom opened the door and announced her presence. "How did everything go sistah?" Kisasi asked through the sounds of the cascading water "Everything is handled. I'm going to get cleaned up so I can drop you off" Myisha said turned and egressed the restroom. After Kisasi had gotten dressed he descended the stairs and walked into the den where he found Chantel sitting watching television "Uhali gani daddy where are you going?" Chantel asked "I'm on my way to meet with the councilwoman" Kisasi replied then asked "How was school?" "It was good not as hard as I'd expected it to be" Chantel answered.

Kisasi could hear Myisha coming down the stairs he then checked his watch, it was 7:20 pm. perfect timing he thought. They both extended goodbyes to Chantel as they egressed the house. The ride to Divanni's in downtown Portland was serene. Myisha overstood that Kisasi liked to gather his thoughts before meeting with people of this magnitude. She could hear him saying in her mind, "In order to give these kind of meetings the attention that they deserve you must still yourself for one wrong sentence could obstruct the goal of the meeting." She respected his philosophy and remained as quiet as he did. They pulled up to the five star restaurant equipped with dance floor and bar. As Kisasi got out of the car he stated "I'll call you when I'm ready for you to pick me up." "O.k. I'll be ready" Myisha replied and pulled off from the entrance of the establishment. As Kisasi walked towards the entrance he took stock of his appearance through the reflection of the glass doors. He wore a black Armani velour jacket with matching dress shirt and silk tie, a pair of royal blue Le'Taxione Urban Couture jeans with black gator shoes and matching belt. He smiled at his reflection and ingressed the restaurant. He was met by a waiter who after receiving his name escorted him to his table. After settling in at the luxurious table he checked his watch. He was approximately 20 minutes early. The waiter returned and asked if he could get anything for him. Kisasi ordered a shot of cognac and sat quietly observing his surroundings.

The waiter returned with his drink just as Naomi sauntered towards him. Kisasi accepted the drink then rose as Naomi arrived. He first extended his hand but Naomi opened her arms and he obliged her embrace. After breaking her embrace and exchanging pleasantries Kisasi moved to her side of the table, pulled out the chair, and after Naomi had sat down scooted her chair up to the table and returned to his seat. After he'd sat down Kisasi took a drink of the cognac then asked "Can I get you a drink?" "After dinner" Naomi replied, then complimented the exquisitely dressed young black man across from her. Kisasi thanked the beautiful wise black woman through a smile. The waiter returned and asked. "Can I take your order?" Kisasi yielded to Naomi forcing the waiter to recognize the sistah before himself. "I'll have the sushi," Naomi stated "And you sir" the waiter asked. "I'll have the sirloin steak and asparagus" Kisasi replied and they both handed their menu's back to the waiter. Kisasi broke the silence "I want to thank you again sistah for your help with those permits." "Don't mention it brotha it's my duty. I wanted to meet with you to discuss your organization and how we can assist each other in working with our people. That being said understand that I, as you, will soon be experiencing opposition to my uncompromising position when it comes to our youth and the refurbishing of our community. Now this opposition comes in many forms but its fundamentally based in systemic racism which impedes funding in urban communities as you are now privy to" Naomi said through a half smile.

"Sistah it was this opposition that acquainted us so regardless of how they attempt to impede our progress, water seeks its own level and they will never be able to destroy what you and I are-as of now, building" Kisasi replied "That's what I wanted to hear sweetheart. You don't know how many brothas that allow the promise of inconsequential amenities-play on their inhere venality to cause them to abandon their principles and even offer up those who are truly trying to effectuate change. Here's my proposition that we work behind the veil in tandem, in order to serve our community. I'll do all in my power to facilitate your needs and you do the same for me" she stated. "I want you to know that you have my word as a black man that I will extend to you not only my resources but my loyalty and integrity because this cause is greater that both of us but, it needs both of us to thrive" Kisasi replied.

The waiter walked up and Kisasi fell silent. She observed his every move. She not only respected his mannerisms but she was smitten by him. The fact that a young black man was this industrious, intelligent and serious about his people was titillating, enticing. She wanted him and entertained prurient thoughts as they discoursed. After they'd finished the meal Naomi suggested they move to the bar, have some drinks, listen to some music, and learn more about one another. He agreed, paid the check and escorted Naomi to the bar.

Lost in the music and now a little tipsy they lost track of the time. Kisasi looked at his watch it was 10:35 pm. "It's 10:35 sistah" Kisasi said. "Do you have somewhere else that you need to be," Naomi asked "No I don't" Kisasi replied."

"Then lets just enjoy the moment" Naomi said leaned in and kissed him full on the lips. Kisasi held her tight returning the gesture. They exchanged tongues blind to the fact that they'd become the center of attention, lost in each other's embrace, lust abound. Realizing that they'd expressed these sentiments in public, they broke the kiss, Naomi smiled eyes coruscate-coquettish-feminine.

"Let's move sistah" Kisasi suggested "Where to?" Naomi asked rhetorically. She knew where she wanted to go, not to engage in the act of copulation, but to learn more about this very interesting intriguing young brotha. When she saw that Kisasi advanced no destination she stated. "I live up in those hills not far from here." Kisasi remembered when he was younger going downtown, looking up into those hills at the community and houses that lined the landscape, wondering how life was up there, now he would find out first hand. "Sounds like a plan" Kisasi agreed and they left the restaurant hand in hand. Kisasi silently marveled at the scenery as they traversed winding roads punctuated by grand houses, manicured lawns and expensive vehicles. They pulled up to Naomi's house. It too was grand. The garage door opened and she pulled her 1989 Jaguar in. They ingressed the house through the garage and there it was exquisite granite kitchen tops, cherry wood cabinets, stainless steel appliances and that was just her kitchen. Her living room had plush leather couches, glass tables, bronze Egyptian statues, velvet curtains, hard wood floors, high vaulted ceilings, sky lights, chandeliers. But what intrigued him the most was her vast collection of literature held in a six foot tall wall to wall book shelf. "I could come here and just read all day" Kisasi said. "Have a seat brotha there are some things I want to discuss with you." Naomi said. Kisasi sat down on the plush couch. Naomi disappeared down the hallway, "Do you want anything to drink brotha?" Naomi 'yelled from down the hallway, then continued before Kisasi could answer "The bar is in the den, help yourself." Kisasi rose from the couch went into the den, poured two glasses of cognac, returned to the living room and sat down. Naomi returned to the living room clad in a satin robe loosely tied at the waist. It was obvious that she was very health conscious, physically fit, toned and her skin was like silk.

"Thank you for pouring me a drink sweetie" She purred. This wasn't the first time that she referred to Kisasi in that manner, he made a mental note of that fact. She sat on the couch right next to him, so close that he could feel the electricity that her body emitted. She took a drink then turned full to Kisasi and began to speak. "I want to be perfectly candid with you brotha, your name has come across my desk several times. It was no coincidence that I was at the function where you spoke. I attended not only for the cause but to also hear you speak. Brotha you are exactly what white people fear in a black man and what black people envy. You and your organization will be put under a microscope, and if there are any in-proprieties, disgruntled associates, jealous exes, they will find it and exploit it in order to impede your progress. There are politicians that get elected by exploiting the conditions in our communities and the amelioration of those conditions eliminates campaign talking points" Naomi expressed. "I'm well versed on these tactics of misinformation, propaganda and the distrust created in our people that they employ to stop the rise of effective leadership among our people, Kisasi said. "Do you know that they've already begun investigating you and are watching how you'll spend that 5 million that was donated to your organization by the save the youth foundation?" Naomi asked. "No I didn't know that but I suspected it." Kisasi replied. "Look sweetie, I just want you to be successful. There is no doubt that you have the youths ear and that you have the integrity needed to procure change but that's not enough, you must also have the right people in the right places to watch out for your best interest," "and are you the right people in the right place that has my best interest in mind?" Kisasi asked. Naomi smiled and leaned in to Kisasi, and said, "Sweetie I'm the right woman with a group of people in the right place that has your best interest in mind."

Kisasi leaned in to Naomi and pressed his lips against hers. She moaned as they exchanged tongues. He reached into her satin robe, she gave him no resistance. He lifted the bottom of her bra her 38d breast fell firm from it. She spread her thighs and raised her hips inviting him to explore her secret. After gently rubbing, measuring her breast, squeezing her erect nipples, he moved his hand slowly down her firm torso into her panties, his fingers finding her wet and wanting, she let out a controlled passionate scream as soft as just releasing air from her mouth, writhing, pushing her hips towards his hand. Her body began to convulse, as Kisasi gently touched her there, she clasped her firm caramel thighs together holding his hand in place as her orgasm rushed and her eyes rolled back in ecstasy. She held his hand, fingers hostage between her legs for about 3 minutes, body shaking. When she let go her breaths were labored, short. She looked into his eyes, Thank you sweetie she said softly. "You're welcome baby" he replied. They lay on the couch and fell asleep in each other's arms.

CHAPTER 48

Kisasi was the first to awaken. On his way to the restroom he stood for a moment and marveled at the beauty of the 54year old sistah that he'd just spent the night with. As Naomi began to stir and awaken Kisasi spun and walked down the hallway to the restroom. He was washing his face when Naomi walked in and greeted him "Habari ya asubuhi" then wrapped her arms around his waist from the back and kissed him gently on his upper right shoulder. Kisasi reached back with his right hand, palmed her firm ass and replied, "Nzuri Asali-do you have an extra toothbrush?"

Naomi opened a cabinet, retrieved a toothbrush and gave it to Kisasi, "Asante sana" "You're welcome sweetie, do you want to take a shower?" Naomi said with a smile. "I would love to take a shower Asali" "Samahani?" Naomi said "Asali means honey, your complexion reminds me of honey" Kisasi explained "What about the taste of my lips?" Naomi asked through a smile, "Pure Asali" Kisasi answered.

After taking a shower and getting dressed he joined Naomi in the den where she sat in a business suit, her briefcase on the floor beside her and a cup of coffee on the table in front of her. "Would you like a cup?" she asked. Kisasi didn't like the taste of coffee but he would drink it before his workouts for the burst of energy that he got from it, he obliged her hospitality and accepted the offer. While pouring a cup for him Naomi asked "Where do we go from here?" we both know that we must be careful that we don't cause unwanted scrutiny to our positions and to this cause." "We continue to do what two mature intelligent, politically active people do, we stay pushing the agenda aiding and assisting one another and cherishing these stolen moments from behind the veil of confidentiality" Kisasi stated. "I want to be clear brotha I've developed some strong feelings for you and I want to explore that, but in a manner that does not render us impotent in the cause so what I'm really asking is how do we do that? how do we continue to enjoy these moments without scrutiny and the perception of impropriety that comes with it?" she asked pointedly. He thought for a moment. He knew what she was asking and implying, which was how do we remain intimate without allowing our intimacy to be cast as some tawdry relationship that undermines our integrity as community reformers and paint us as enemies of the struggle. "You can act in the capacity of consultant to the organization that would cure the issue of proximity and deter impropriety on our part, this way we can enjoy, explore these stolen, intimate moments when needed while simultaneously addressing the urgent issues that our youth are faced with" Kisasi suggested.

Kisasi's phone rang "DITR" Kisasi speaking how can I help you?" he listened intently then replied, "I'll be there in about 30 minutes," then he returned to his conversation with Naomi. "I've never met a brotha your age that thinks and navigates as you do. You are a testimony to how our young brotha's can rise above their circumstances and be productive and successful," she said. "My mother and father came from the struggle and taught me well," he replied. "Well lets get out of here," she said picking up her keys. "Can you drop me off at the DITR building? They have some documents prepared that need my signature." "Of course sweetie." Naomi replied. She pulled the jag up to the curb of the DITR building. As they pulled up she noticed the thin light skinned sistah standing out front and asked "Does she work for the organization?" "Yes" Kisasi said without offering any more information. "How well do you know her?" Naomi asked. "I don't know much about her personal life but she's about the cause" Kisasi replied. She reached across Kisasi opened her glove compartment took out a pad and pen then said, "Give me her full name and I'll run a check on her" "Her name is Chantel Criglar" Kisasi said, he made a mental note of the fact that the sistah has the ability to access this kind of intel and egressed the car. As he approached Chantel, Kisasi asked "Uhali gani? They have some forms that needed the signature of a board member and since I'm not a board member I couldn't sign." Chantel answered with playful sarcasm. "Where's Myisha?" Kisasi asked. "She was on her way to the bank and instructed me to come and show organizational presence as she put it, until you made it here" Chantel answered with pure sarcasm. "She did the right thing and you were the right person to handle this job" Kisasi said through a big smile.

Chantel realizing the playful banter, lightly punched Kisasi in the arm as they walked into the building. Once inside Kisasi couldn't believe the finished interior of the building. There were offices, a library, weight room, child care room, computers in the classroom, front desk/lobby and a dining area with full kitchen. Kisasi had planned to employ the students to maintain and sustain the daily operations of the building and though their activity would be supervised by licensed professionals, they would participate in order to learn work ethic. "What do you think?" Chantel asked. "It's just what I envisioned it to be." Kisasi stated as they walked through the building inspecting each area for efficiency. The workers had did an excellent job bringing Kisasi's vision to fruition and as he inspected each area he could hear the youth in the classroom working on their computers to complete assignments. His mother and father will be proud of him and he would employ their degrees in political science and criminal justice by allowing them to teach at the center. After completing the walk through and signing the necessary documents, Chantel and Kisasi returned to headquarters to celebrate the unexpected progress on the newly dubbed ----Diamonds In The Rough Center.

CHAPTER 49

Kisasi sat at his desk consumed by his deepest, truest ruminations. Things were moving at space shuttle speed but this is what he was born to do. His father had always stressed that "When a people are lost in a circumstance or under seemingly unbearable conditions the collective vibratory frequency of their pain, despair, suffering and loss are emitted into the universe, which then shapes, fashions that one that will be the answer to their cries." Though Kisasi didn't see himself in that light, he did see himself as an effective proponent of change. He also overstood the position that he was placing himself in by shouldering the responsibility of educating the youth, for those in the past that had taken on this responsibility were maligned, discredited and or assassinated and most of the time, though unseen forces pulled the strings, it was at the hands of their own people.

It becomes a fragile balancing act that places one in a position to subject himself to a socialized venal psyche And the concomitant genocidal, homicidal manifestation of said psyche. There would certainly be an all out assault launched on the organization, his character, and the character of those that are in positions of authority within the organization and when that happened, some would fold like a summer lawn chair, becoming complicit to the plot to dismantle the organization. They'd sell their souls and the future of the youth for inconsequential trinkets, amenities, immunity. If it is my destiny to spend and relinquish my life in this struggle I readily, wholeheartedly offer my life today!" Kisasi thought out loud. I have no other purpose on this earth but to give my life willingly to perpetuate life, he reasoned. And what about these four sistahs that have exhibited varying degrees of loyalty to either him or the struggle? All having inhere qualities imperative to this demonstration. All beautiful in their own right and bring a different quality to the cause. Lana-Kisasi's first love and a brilliant legal mind, Myisha the strong independent sistah versed in the medical field loyal to the cause and even more to him. Chantel, though the cause is secondary for her, her loyalty to him is beyond reproach and has been demonstrated by facilitating the cessation of human breath on two occasions and Naomi whose love for the youth, community, people, is inestimable, unquestionable and whose value continues to unfurl daily. One whose political savvy is as imperative as oxygen in this theater.

Then there is Askari a brother who has in the past shown loyalty that was unquestionable. It was Askari that aided and assisted Kisasi in the embryonic stages, formative period of the organization, inviting him into his home sharing with him his wealth and when the memory of his parents that was attached to the $375,000. dollar home that they'd left to him became too unbearable, sold it to Kisasi after making him part owner. It was Askari that helped orchestrate the Christmas day murder's in the interest of the organization, but since he'd sold the house to Kisasi he'd become distant and his constant womanizing could prove detrimental to the organization.

He tilted his head back, the wind blowing through his dreadlocks, looking into the sky he whispered may the ancestors stand with me on this journey and may they be pleased with me. At that moment he felt light, as if his spirit had left his body. He didn't fight the experience he just relaxed and embraced what was transpiring. His spirit ascended into the ethers and he looked back down on the earth. Fear crept into his consciousness like a thief, he quickly admonished it, sending it fleeing, descending from the heights, screeching like a wounded eagle. He then saw himself sitting in a high backed chair as familiar faces reach for it, it's arms, legs and though they extended their arms fully he remained outside of their touch, their fingertips. A man flashed across his vision, he wore a star on his chest a scowl on his face. He saw Askari pointing the .40 cal kept in the den at a figure standing in the den and Chantel screaming, terror on her face.

Then Myisha walked up and stood at his right as he sat in the chair. He heard Lana's tearful voice cutting through the silence, then Naomi walked up and pressed her lips against his left ear and began to whisper. At that moment he heard "Uhali gani daddy" he returned to his physical, turned back to his room and saw Chantel standing there "Are you alright?" she asked. Kisasi walked back through the sliding doors into his room past Chantel into his restroom, turned on the water, bent at the waist over the sink, cupped his hands letting the water fill his palms then splashed his face. Chantel followed him into the restroom, "What's wrong daddy?" She asked unable to hide her concern. Kisasi stood water running down his face, took her into his embrace held her close and said "Mimi sijambo" "What!" Chantel asked Kisasi broke the embrace, smiled and said, "I'm good sistah."

Kisasi after drying his face returned to his desk, Chantel in tow. He sat down at his computer, glaring at its terminal, yet lost in thought. What did this vision mean? What was the ancestors trying to tell him about the people in his cipher? Deep in thought he was returned to the present moment at the intonation of Chantel's voice. "Are you alright?" she asked again. "I'm good sistah" Kisasi replied. Kisasi's phone rang saving him from Chantel's interrogation. "D.I.T.R Kisasi speaking." he said. The voice that returned was familiar, it was Myisha, but the texture of her voice was unfamiliar. He'd never heard this level of concern in her voice. "We have an issue baby" Myisha said then continued. "I was pulled over by the cops under the premise that I had a dysfunctional tail light. After my information was ran the police returned to the car with my I.D., handed me the I.D.

and stated "You're with that Diamonds In The Rough group huh? Is that some kind of Black Power group." "I told him no, it's a Black empowerment group" Myisha said and Kisasi smiled out loud.

Myisha was one of Kisasi's best students. She could espouse the socio-political and economic ideology and philosophy of both DITR and Almasi without hesitation or flaw. She'd been taught strait from Kisasi's mouth and by watching his demonstration of the principles that he veraciously expounded upon in public as well as in the privacy of headquarters without reticence. "But that wasn't the part that concerned me, as the cop walked away he stated "We'll soon find out." Myisha explained. At that moment Kisasi replayed in his mind the vision wherein the brotha Joseph Bolds wore a star on his chest. The vision in an instant began to make sense and the pace at which it began to unveil itself, informed Kisasi that what he thought may have been a representation of distant, future events, was in fact a representation of the immediate present. This amplified the urgency in which he had to interpret the vision. "Where are you sistah" Kisasi asked. "I'm on my way to you" Myisha replied. "I'll see you when you get here" Kisasi said and hung up the phone. He thought about the statement that the police made and smiled out loud. He knew what the next move would be and he put a strategy in motion. "Isn't your mother white sistah?" he turned to Chantel and asked. "Yea but I'm black" Chantel stated proudly. "What about your younger brother" he asked. "Well after my father and mother separated she went back to her high school sweetheart, who is a white man" Chantel said defensively.

Noticing that the questions had given Chantel the wrong impression, Kisasi explained his position. "I'm not questioning your blackness sistah, Myisha was just pulled over by the police and the questions and statements that he made gave me a glimpse into the angle that they are going to use to discredit the organization, so we're going to need to use your little brother to stave off their advances." "What do you think they are going to try to do." Chantel's concerns now relaxed asked, "Their going to try to paint us as this evil black militant organization that operates to the exclusion of non-black youth.

This was an old tactic used against the panthers but it was effective. Kisasi marveled at the fact that they'd not changed their tactics in all of these years, but if it's not broke don't fix it, he reasoned. "I need your little brother front row at the opening of our building." Kisasi said. "No problem, he'll love to just get out of the house, they are smothering him." Chantel replied.

CHAPTER 50

Kisasi decided to prolong the opening of the Diamonds In The Rough Center until June 2, 1991. He had to make sure that the right people attended, politicians, law enforcement, social workers, community activists, members of the community and news reporters that were in favor of youth violence prevention. Of course there would be in attendance the Nay Sayers, saboteurs and those who fed their families by exploiting and perpetuating the existing conditions.

He wanted the opening to be a grand production and when that day came that's exactly what it was. One could not underestimate the power of theater and the visual impact of its suggestive nature. Kisasi overstood the dynamics of a great visual imagery and he didn't disappoint. In the audience were people from all walks of life and social standing. As he stood on the fabricated stage behind the rostrum flanked by Autumn Tate-vice president of the Save the Youth Foundation, Council Woman Gaston and other community activists who'd all spoken before him and Chantel's little brother there at her side he began his didactic:

"Today marks the beginning of a new opportunity to address the results made manifest in our youths behavior by a social construct that denies, marginalizes and impedes the social economic, academic growth of our youth. The Diamonds In The Rough Center will provide our youth with the life skills, conflict resolution, tutoring, entrepreneurial training and structure that they need to be productive members of the community. It is your duty, those of you who want change in our communities, to assist these efforts. They say that it takes a village to raise a child, but lately, all it has taken is a villain. It is my hopes that our village supersedes our villains. The success of this endeavor must be a concerted effort. "Join me!" Kisasi implored. The crowd erupted in applause. He panned the audience and noticed that Snip Snap and some of his homeboys were in attendance and made a mental note to try to catch him before the day was over. The crowd then moved to the front of the building for the ceremonial cutting of the ribbon.

Instead of Kisasi being the one who cut the ribbon he yielded to Council Woman Gaston. This afforded her a photo op and an opportunity to campaign. Once the cameras and microphones were thrust into her face, Naomi smiled at the political savvy of Kisasi and began answering questions,

"Do you support the Diamonds In The Rough Center, Council Woman" one reporter asked. "I support any organization that wants to eradicate violence and drugs in our communities." Naomi answered. The consummate politician fielded questions in raw political form, videlicet she answered every question without giving an answer to any of them. In the midst, behind the veil of the media blitz, Kisasi quietly slipped away and caught up with Snip Snap as he was egressing the event. "Snap!" Kisasi yelled after his circumstantial comrade. Snap spun on his heels to face Kisasi. "West up cuzz?" he answered. As he approached he extended his hand as did Snap. Their hands met and a firm shake was exchanged-followed by a hug and a pat on the back.

They both genuinely happy to see one another. Though they were from different aspects of the struggle-different ideologies- different methods they shared a camaraderie based on objective. 'Uhali gani comrade" Kisasi asked after they broke the embrace. "Mimi sijambo kiwe" Snap replied then continued "I see that life has been treating you good cuzz." "In reality I've been treating life good, what about you?" Kisasi asked. "You know chicken one day feathers the next. I saw your boy Askari. Did you know that he was under the influence of that shit" Snap replied.

Kisasi's mind began to race. He couldn't believe what he was hearing but at the same time he knew that Snap wasn't the kind of brotha that advanced conjecture. He was a serious banger that adhered to the Crip constitution and had served time back in Cali where if you made a false statement about someone's character without evidence of the charge you would be disciplined severely, and depending on the severity of the charge there were a range of disciplinary actions from a physical beating to what they described as a California smile, where the culprits throat was cut ear to ear. As Kisasi processed the information that had just been tendered to him Snap said "I can't tell you how to run your squad but cuzz is going to fuck up everything that you're trying to build. You need to snatch cuzz out the huddle and leave him in a puddle."

Kisasi's thoughts returned to the moment and he said, "He needs help, not killing brotha, I'll take care of him." The utility of this statement was two-fold. He informed Snap that Askari's life was of his concern and that it wasn't his desire to have any harm come to him and that one must give black men the benefit of the doubt. It showed Snap how to show compassion to his people. Snap smiled and said "If you need me give me a call" he then spun and began to walk away. Kisasi, knowing that Snap had just offered to kill Askari caught him in mid stride and yelled, "Snap!" when Snap turned back to face him he stated unequivocally, "I'll take care of that" Snap yelled back "I know you will" and walked off, his homeboys on his heels. Kisasi returned to the group of people gathered for the grand opening. He was met in mid stride by Myisha who was smiling from ear to ear. "We did it baby." she said and extended her hand, a tactic that Kisasi had taught her to veil the extent of their interaction while remaining professional at all times. Chantel then approached and did the same thing, "The plan to use my little brotha was on point. Now they can't misrepresent the intentions of the organization." she said. Myisha shot a glance at her then at Kisasi as if to imply that they intentionally excluded her from the plan, then she smiled to take the sting out of her accusatory glances but Kisasi was still reeling from the information that he'd just received from Snap.

The Council Woman approached and asked that she have a word with Kisasi privately. They walked out of earshot and she stated "Remember I told you that the donation of the five million would cause them to place you under a microscope? Well I was just informed by one of my sources in law enforcement that there is a special FBI agent that has worked to discredit Black Organizations in the past, that has been brought in to look into your activities. That being expressed I've already looked deeply into your activities and know for sure that you are clean, so it's nothing to worry about but, a word to the wise is sufficient."

Kisasi thought about aspects of his vision then silently thanked the ancestors for blessing him with the foresight. "When can we get together sistah?" Kisasi asked Naomi. "I'm free this weekend" she replied. "Excellent I'll call you this weekend" I think we should meet at your house. "I'll catch a cab" Kisasi said. "It's a date," Naomi replied through a seductive smile and walked away, got into her jag and pulled off honking the horn twice. Kisasi returned and told Myisha and Chantel that he needed to speak with them at headquarters. As they walked to separate cars a reporter approached Kisasi. He recognized her face from previous years, it was investigative reporter Nacita Ugalde. She had, in the past, covered the Christmas Day Murders and the killing of BK Blue in room 28 of the Copper Penny Motel. "Can I have a word with you?" Nacita Ugalde asked as she pushed the microphone towards Kisasi. "No comment!"

Kisasi replied, got in his black BMW, pointed it in the direction of headquarters and pulled away from curb.

CHAPTER 51

Lana, after Graduation was immediately offered a job in Seattle, Washington with The King County Dept. of Human Resources. What she didn't know was that the job offer wasn't based purely on her talents. Seattle, to the naked eye, looked like a melting pot of racial tolerance yet, the African American population was under represented in the job market, disenfranchised in the business sector and disproportionately incarcerated for similar crimes committed by their white counterparts.

There was no doubt that she was qualified for the job, maybe over qualified, but she was hired to make a quota a token. Seattle had been experiencing civil unrest led by Troy Mc Millen or "Mac" as he was called, President of the local

CHAPTER of the NAACP. Mac was a very light skinned brother born of an interracial sexual tryst. He was very outspoken, articulate, courageous, flamboyant born with an intense love of both his people and justice.

It was his demonstrative demonstrations for equality that forced the Seattle government to employ new hiring practices, a fact that facilitated the hiring of Lana. She worked directly under Ron Allen, the executive director of human resources. Mr. Allen, though a black man, did not identify with black people or their issues. He'd worked hard to get where he was and blamed black people for the conditions that they found themselves in. He could be caught at any time laughing aloud at the stereotypical racist joke told by his white counterparts about black people and their conditions. He thoroughly orientated Lana into this mind-set upon her arrival. "I know that you are fresh out of college and that you might think that it is your duty to save the world but we have it good here and that kind of agitation is frowned upon. We are team players here so don't rock the boat and you'll achieve longevity here" Ron Allen said to Lana behind the closed doors of his plush office located in downtown Seattle. Lana overstood what her supervisor was saying and agreed wholeheartedly with his ideology. It was not her job to make waves. She was not the savior of black people, all she wanted to do was make money and enjoy life. She sank herself into her work, did what she was asked to do, defended the government's position regardless of the blatant injustices that were perpetuated. She became an asset to her white superiors who would wield her like a sword against her own people, which in turn eradicated their argument of racism and discrimination.

She fought the unions victoriously becoming so efficient that her pay was increased and promises of upward mobility was tendered to her though, every time supervisory positions came open they were given to white, less qualified employees. She silenced her inner angst concerning this fact by reasoning that she was making more money than she'd ever made, which allowed her to live in a suburban community, drive a new Cadillac and rub elbows with prominent white people. She'd made it out of the ghetto and though she lost touch with self, the struggle, which birthed her ambitions, she'd arrived and no one could take that from her.

Lana endured the open and at times blatant disrespect of her intellect, womanhood and ingenuity. In one incident her supervisor Richard Pittman, a white man, sat in on an arbitration meeting between the king county jail sheriffs union representative and herself, in which Mr. Pittmans voice, becoming timbre, told her to shut up! She coward at his authority accepting the disrespect. The union representative smiled and nodded at Mr. Pittman for putting his token in her place. She began to resent black men for not only the hell that she had to endure at the hands of her uncle Carl and others that took advantage of her at her church, but also for their lack of presence in the business sector. She became bitter, resentful, cold, histrionic and barren. This too she laid at the doorstep of black men. She became a member of the Colgate Christ Church in an attempt to find solace, the scripture out of context becoming a crutch and justification for her loneliness. From the outside looking in, one would think her to be a devout follower of Christ, for she did not entertain men but this fact was due to the std that she'd contracted from being raped. Lana closed herself off from the world. She refused to watch television and poured herself into her work on the weekdays and church on Sundays attempting, like most people duped by the false "interpretation" of the teachings of Jesus, to tithe her way to heaven, the road most traveled.

CHAPTER 52

Myisha, Chantel and Kisasi pulled up into the driveway at headquarters simultaneously, got out of their respective cars, ingressed the house and went straight to the den where Myisha poured them all a shot of cognac. Kisasi took a long deep drink before he spoke, "listen ...the word is that Askari is using and I don't have to explain how detrimental this could be to our organizational goals." At the same time that he was speaking Kisasi was trying to figure out his course of action and how he could insulate himself from any repercussions that may emanate from his actions. He'd thought that this part of the demonstration where people would have to be disappeared was over after Carl.

This new issue would be a logistical nightmare and could result in the destruction of the organization if not handled properly, not to mention that the bureau was now dusting his every conversation for fingerprints. "How could he jeopardize all that we've built" Myisha said. "That's not cool" Chantel added.

"We've come too far to let this brotha destroy all that we've done, not to mention he knows too much to allow him to become this kind of threat" Myisha advanced. "Nobody's above this organization, nobody's more important than this organization! This is the only family that I have and now this buster is putting me in the position to lose that," Chantel said as the tears welled up in her eyes, voice tremulous. Kisasi for the first time saw Chantel's loyalty to the cause. She was truly affected by the possibility of the organization being destroyed, to the point where her body language indicated distress. He looked over at Myisha who too were gauging Chantel's reaction. Myisha, in that moment, felt a sisterhood between Chantel and herself that she'd not felt before. She walked over to Chantel and wrapped her arms around her, enveloping her in her embrace, "Nobody is going to take this family from you" Myisha assured her while simultaneously thinking, I'm still going to watch you around my man. "There's nothing to worry about. I don't think that the comrade would ever become a confidential informant and even if he did he could not implicate us in anything without implicating himself. I definitely need to address this issue with him and we'll go from there" Kisasi said in an attempt to ease any concerns, but he wasn't naïve in the least. He knew that Askari could be offered immunity to help the feds build a Rico Act case against him and the fact that they'd recently been verbally sparring and the contempt which was made evident by Askari could inform or even perpetuate treachery.

Kisasi immediately began to insulate himself just in case he would be charged with the task of disappearing Askari, "Remember...this is our comrade who was there for me from the beginning. He helped me build Diamonds In The Rough and we owe him a debt of gratitude. I love this brotha and we have to help him in any way that is beneficial" Kisasi entreated. Myisha shot a glance at Kisasi. She caught the "we have to help him in any way that is beneficial." She knew how Kisasi thought and took this to mean exactly what he'd always advanced and that was "If anybody gets in the way of this movement he must be eliminated by any means mandatory." Myisha smiled inwardly at her familiarity with this man. She knew that Chantel had no inkling of what Kisasi was truly saying and this made her feel even closer to him. No one else enjoyed this proximity with Kisasi, except for Lana, and she, for all intents and purposes, was out of the scene.

Kisasi's phone rang interrupting his conversation "DITR Kisasi speaking" he answered. Though Myisha could not hear who was on the other end of the call she could tell by Kisasi's expression that it was important. "I'll come through tonight" Kisasi said and ended the call. "Kuna matatizo gani baby?" Myisha asked conveying her concern. "I have to meet with the Councilwoman tonight, it appears that she has some important Intel for me." Kisasi replied.

Kisasi egressed the den, ascended the staircase, ingressed his room and sat at his desk in front of the computer where he done his best thinking. After having dinner with Naomi and returning to her house the last time that they'd met, he'd decided to change his diet and become a vegetarian, this fact, though it had enhanced his senses on every level, had made him easily irritable. He enhanced his work out regiment to address this fact doing calisthenics both morning and night, yet he was irritated at the news concerning Askari and dreading the possibility that he would have to disappear him for the cause. As he sat, lost in thought, a knock came at his bedroom door. He spun in his high black leather diamond tucked office chair, "come in," he said. Myisha ingressed his room, she could see the concern on his face so instead of walking over to him she took a seat in the recliner that sat in the corner of his room.

"For real baby…Uhali gani?" Myisha asked. "I'm just trying to wrap my mind around the fact that my comrade has fell prey to that substance…again, knowing the ramifications and repercussions that it has rained on our people, on himself, on our cause. This is what has created the distance between us. That drug has arrested his developmental process causing not only separation between us but also suspicion and we both know that suspicion is the mother of hypocrisy" Kisasi answered. "It's the reason why a 40 day journey took the Israelites 40 years to make …they followed Moses in doubt and suspicion" Myisha said drawing from her Christian upbringing offering solace. Kisasi spun in his chair faced his computer and turned it on. He began searching documents concerning DITR, its finances and its activities to make sure that everything that concerned the organization was above board and defendable.

Myisha rose from the recliner walked over to Kisasi, kissed him on the cheek and said, "Whatever decision that you make overstand that there is no doubt or suspicion on my behalf" then she egressed the room. She wanted Kisasi to know that not only did she catch what he was saying in the den concerning Askari, but also that she would support any decision that he made to address any threat against the organization or the cause, Kisasi smiled out loud.

CHAPTER 53

As the cab pulled up through Naomi's long cobblestone driveway, Kisasi could see her silhouette standing in her large picture window. He watched as she obviously saw the Cab and moved towards her front door to greet him. He egressed the cab, approached her door, it flung open to Naomi standing, drink in hand, with a beautiful coruscating smile complimenting her beautiful face.

"Hello sweetie" Naomi greeted Kisasi and extended the drink to him. As he took it she walked into the living room swinging her hips. Kisasi followed marveling at her physique. She sat on the love seat, he sat next to her, drank the contents of his glass at once, set it down on the glass table and sank back into the comfort of the love seat.

Though he had not spoke a word he communicated to Naomi through his body language. She knew that the information that she was about to impart on him would not ease his tension, not in the least. "It looks like you've had a lot on your mind lately." She said in an attempt to gauge his disposition. He looked into her eyes and flashed a smile. He found the texture of her voice dulcet, every intonation sultry, titillating, woman. "Yea I was informed that one of my comrades was under the influence of that poison and it presents me with a twofold issue…first I have to remove him from his post then I have to find a way to motivate him to transcend the circumstance, which will be a complicated task after he experience the loss of a position he'd held since the organization was formed." Kisasi said. Naomi sensing the need, took Kisasi's empty glass from the table and said, "Let me refresh your drink" and walked towards the bar, looked over her shoulder and said. "Lets move into the den." Kisasi followed sensing that the information that he was about to receive would be sensitive and maybe even distressing but, imperative. He sat on the couch in the den and waited for Naomi to return. When she joined she had two glasses and a pint of Hennessy. She sat both of the glasses and the liquor on the table as not to evidence presumption of how much Kisasi wanted to partake in the spirits. This allowed him to not only pour his own drink but to also pour hers, after all, she poured the first drink and fair exchange ain't no robbery. It was only proper etiquette that he returned the gesture.

Asante sana sistah" Kisasi stated as he took the bottle poured her a drink and then poured one for himself. Naomi lifted the glass to toast "To us, authenticity and the cause"

"Here-here" Kisasi replied and they both drained their glasses then cleared their throats. Kisasi refreshed their glasses then asked. "What's the demonstration sistah?" raised the refreshed drink to his lips and drained the glass again. Naomi followed suit, let out a guttural grunt, then began to speak. "As I told you there has been an agent brought in and assigned to investigate you and the organization. Well, I did my research on the agent and though he was essential in dismantling the BPP, he has since developed a conscience due to his reassignment to desk duties after he'd helped the bureau in their racist agenda. His name is Agent Joseph Bolds."

"Joseph Bolds?" Kisasi repeated the name out loud. His mind raced to place a face-time and circumstance with this familiar name then, it hit him, this was the brotha that he'd met on the flight back from Texas, "I know that brotha!" He blurted out. "Where do you know him from?" Naomi inquisitively asked. He was on the flight with me back from Texas. We talked for a moment after I'd realized that he'd also been on the flight with me from Portland to Texas. This cat has been following me for a while now." Kisasi reasoned out loud.

"That's good" She stated and begin to explain her reasoning when she saw the perplexed look on Kisasi's face. "He's been on you for a while and he's yet to visit you in his official capacity. That being said, I know for a fact that there is someone in your organization that is envious and out of that envy is willing to say or do whatever is necessary to displace you. I say envious because I've searched your organizational documentation and everything is in accord. I also listened to what the streets have to say about you and though you're not liked in all social circles, no one accuses you of being insincere in the cause or corrupt. This leaves no other reason but envy. Naomi's reasoning resonated with Kisasi. Though he knew that the organization and its activities were beyond reproach he knew that this inquiry could expose the clandestine activity of Almasi-activity that not even Naomi knew about, so he thought. He had to find out who it was that was complicit with this investigation and silence him or her. He was lost in thought when his mind was brought back to Naomi, who had obviously been watching, as the wheels turned in his head. They locked eyes and She said, "I know more than you think I do sweetie and though we don't have to discuss the details let me say this, I know that your intentions are pure and I know that you love our people and I'm not going to allow myself to be dissuaded by any methods that you've employed in the past to achieve the objective.

Kisasi searched her face waiting with bated breath for her to divulge what she knew about his activities, Naomi continued, "There are things that I've done, methods that I've employed that everybody would not agree with but the objective was achieved. This game called life is not always pretty but it's always real and in full session. It's like the making of sausage, everybody likes the taste of the finished product, but if they could only see the process and the contents that go into the making of the sausage they wouldn't eat it" Naomi smiled out loud and coquettishly, touched Kisasi on the forearm, then closed the distance on the couch between them. Kisasi placed his left arm up and over the back of the couch, opening his embrace, then turning towards Naomi. She slid into his physical invitation, he tempered his delivery and said "Overstand that I'm not ashamed of my past activities, nor do I blush at the fact that circumstances may one day again call for drastic actions, and I will oblige for the advancement of the cause, upward mobility for my people, for our circumstance in this social construct is too dire to take anything off of the table as a remedy, except venality, which would only serve to compromise our position in this struggle."

Naomi leaned in and kissed Kisasi deeply, passionately. No man has ever made her feel as he did. His kiss was electric and her mouth acted as a conduit that transferred that electricity throughout the extremities of her body and yes, even to her secret spot. The spot that no man has ever touched, her guarded special place that coexisted with and through the emotions of her heart. That spot she protected from immature boys that sought to explore without responsibility, without accountability. She'd longed for a man like Kisasi for most of her adult life and she held dear her every stolen moment with him. She needed to feel him inside of her, sharing himself with her, a fusion of their quintessential selves on another plane of existence where masculinity and femininity become one, euphoric, nostalgic, resulting in orgasm, the opiate of sexual satiety. She placed her left hand between his legs, she was having the same effect on him, his erection bearing witness. She unzipped his designer jeans her hand seeking to embrace his erection. He reached between her legs and pulled her laced panties down over her knees, she stepped out of them, one leg at a time. Kisasi broke the kiss and stood abruptly, she stood with him. He pulled her skirt over her head and threw it on the floor exposing her body, visualizing her curves for a moment, then reengaging in the kiss. He kissed down her body until he was on his knees before her, kissing her navel. As he moved further down she sat on the couch, thighs spread wide.

Kisasi stood up between her thighs, removed his pants, then his boxers, exposing his full erection before kneeling back down between Naomi's thighs, "Make love to me Kisasi" she whispered through barely parted lips, consumed by desire, sultry, erotic. Kisasi rubbed his erection up and down the length of her moist mound then in a circular motion around her clit. He plunged himself into her fully, she met him with every stroke, synchronized penetration deeper, more intense, familiarizing himself with every aspect of her inner sanctuary, every wall breached, every angle explored, then orgasm. They exploded simultaneously, then resumed going well into the night.

CHAPTER 54

1992 came in with a bang! Lana had played her part so well that she'd been promoted and given her own office, staff included. She'd gained the confidence of not only her supervisor Ron Allen but she'd proven to her white counterparts, as Ron had, that not only was she not a threat but she was willing to persecute her own people for the Seattle Governments, veiled agenda. This fact was made clear when African Americans held in the King County Jail brought forth a claim of racial discrimination and excessive force when an officer, after calling one of the black prisoners a "crack head nigger" attacked and began to pummel him. This caused other black prisoners to intercede on the 50 yr. olds behalf, a riot ensued and 10 prisoners sustained injuries, 5 officers sustained minor scrapes and bruises.

Lana not only suppressed evidence for the sheriff's department but she also negotiated in bad faith ascertaining an outcome that benefitted the sheriff's union to the detriment of the black prisoners. She rationalized this act of treason by telling herself that "since the brothas were in prison they were obviously predisposed to violence beyond the pale of "justice and equity." As a matter of fact they were less than men, for their mistakes were an indictment of their character and statistically they would never amount to anything. Most of them were abusers, drug attics, gang bangers, pimps and rapist, society was better off without them. She'd, for the sole purpose of easing her own conscience, adopted the stereotype that was arbitrarily super imposed upon black men.

After a long day she sat back in her recliner located in a corner of her condo in downtown Seattle overlooking the city as the crime rate sky rocketed just beneath her in the very same streets that she traversed everyday to get to work. Her phone rang….."Hello she stated into the receiver. A voice that had become familiar to her came over the phone, "How are you doing Miss Xavier?" the voice asked. I'm fine….."How are you?" Lana replied "I'm well I wanted to know when could we get together and discuss in greater detail all that you know concerning the target?" the voice replied. Lana thought for a moment. She was ambivalent concerning her role in this "target" but she'd been suppressing her conscience for so long that the voice of righteousness inside of her had dissipated. At first when she'd began closely interacting with Kisasi and the movement the voice inside of her screamed into her ears at every injustice! Those screams had now become soft whispers. "We can meet this weekend" she replied. "I'll see you then." the voice replied and hung up the phone. She sat back again "I don't owe anybody anything she said rationalizing her betrayal. She had began a relationship with an older white man named Richard Hagen who acted as a liaison between Ron Allen and herself. It was an open secret that Richard used Ron as a ventriloquist uses his dummy, videlicet, Richard called the shots. Lana had started this relationship out of her fear to reject his advances, then quickly thought "this interaction could mean upward mobility" and decided to entertain the possibilities. They'd never been intimate, how could they? That would mean that she'd have to disclose the fact that she has herpes, instead she kept that interaction to touching, or in Richards case, groping her whenever he felt like it. She didn't care that Richard was a bigot who held, in the least, a biased opinion of black people. The fact that he was married kept the relationship from growing or advancing into full blown coitus. He would never leave his wife, especially for a black woman and, though these facts played in Lana's conscience she'd grown to entertain emotions for him. She often daydreamed about being married to him and the benefits that came with being married to a white man. In her mind this would garner her status and was the litmus test by which one measures success. Her delusions of grandeur was interrupted by the reality that Richard didn't feel the same about her and where-in her mind being married to a white man was the measure of success, in his mind being married to a black woman was just the opposite. In his social circles, it would be a badge of shame for him to openly be sexually involved with a black woman and his duplicitous actions made this fact pellucid to her....yes it was titillating for him that he grope and molest the figure of a black woman but he saw her as nothing but an exertion of his power and prowess, his control over his environment and as long as it was exciting he would indulge.

Once she uttered words of endearment, made evident emotions for him, he would strongly admonish her, put her in her place or if the situation called for it, terminate her employment, so she played her role as most women did in the white male dominated job market. Lana realizing the time abruptly rose from her recliner. It was Wednesday night and she, as always, would attend a scheduled bible study. She loved going to bible study for there she found solace-repented for her treachery as if through her attendance she made everything good between herself and her fabricated concept of who, what and where god was.

In all reality bible study was another tactic employed by charlatans to extort tithes from the women in the congregation. Pastor Eugene Caldwell mastered the techniques of, massaging, the women in his congregation through his bastardized versions of scriptures, out of their money. He taught the women that they didn't need a man they were women of Christ, baptized in his blood, which purified them to be married to the Christ. This served a twofold purpose. It created a standard that men could not reach and without men in the household he, by proxy became the authority in the women's household. The church was full of unsuspecting victims. Awash, mesmerized by his blasphemous, spiritual penis that penetrated them in places wherein they yearned to be touched. The pastor in the black church is seen as the intermediate between God and the congregation. So in the congregations mind, duty to the pastor is duty to God. This fact is exploited by charlatans who not only exploit the congregation financially but often times emotionally and sexually. Pastor Eugene Caldwell conducted himself in this vein. He was more of a pimp, than the congregation was willing to acknowledge, but they needed someone to believe in, someone who would not judge them, someone who at lease acted as if he had their best interest at heart for this relieved them of responsibility. Pastor Caldwell reveled in being that person....for a price.

CHAPTER 55

Kisasi had set up a meeting between Askari and himself to address Askari's evident drug use and give him an ultimatum to either go to rehab and get clean, or be placed outside of the organization. As he sat in the den visualizing what the conversation between Askari and himself would entail and its resultant ramifications, both Myisha and Chantel ingressed the den. "Uhali gani sweetheart?" Myisha inquired, "Sijambo" Kisasi answered. "What's up with you, it looks like you got a lot on your mind?" Chantel said. Kisasi pondered her question for a moment noting her intuition and evident familiarity with him. It was obvious that her close proximity had given her greater insight into him and he enjoyed that fact. He wanted her to be familiar with him. To a certain extent, this was necessary he reasoned that she may make decisions in his absence yet influenced by his ideology.

"I called Askari and set up a meeting that we may address this issue of him using drugs and how it jeopardizes the cause. I'm going to give him an ultimatum, either go to an inpatient rehab and get clean, or back away from the organization." Kisasi stated. "How do you think he's going to take that?" Myisha asked. "I don't know how he'll take it but what's for sure is that's the posture that I'm taking on this issue and there's absolutely no room for negotiation." Kisasi emphatically stated. At that moment they heard Askari come through the front door and yell. "Uhali gani!" "Here in the den comrade" Kisasi answered. "Do you want us to leave?" Myisha asked. "This affects all of us sistah, it's better if both of you stay so you can present the feminine aspect of the ultimatum." Kisasi said.

Askari ingressed the den where he found Chantel, Myisha and Kisasi, sitting, all had a drink sitting in front of them. "What's this?" Askari sarcastically asked. "Pour our comrade a drink" Kisasi stated to no one in particular in hopes of easing Askari's evident concern. Chantel moved over to the bar and began pouring a glass of cognac. "Have a seat comrade." Kisasi said and waited until Chantel tendered the drink to Askari before resuming the discourse. Askari took the drink form Chantel. "Asante sana" he replied, then took a long drink, draining the glass. "Listen comrade it's been brought to my attention that you've been smoking crack, I don't have to explain the position that places us in or, the scrutiny that it subjects us to. You know that not only violates the bylaws of the organization but, also violates the principle and code of ethics that we adhere to, I can't allow you to, not only jeopardize the organization but, also the integrity of our camaraderie which is the substratum of the organization" Kisasi said before he was rudely interrupted by Askari. "See that's your problem brotha you act like you're the only one that has a voice in this organization, you can't let me do shit! I'm a grown man!"

"And what is it that makes you a grown man brotha? is it the fact that you place the cause in a precarious position by using drugs? is it because you can run through these sistahs like you run through underwear? What part of being a grown man is you using the night as a veil for your suspicious impulses that exact retribution upon self?" Kisasi asked. At that moment Askari stood up, Kisasi followed suit, what transpired next took everyone by surprise. Askari began his next paragraph with "Nigga!" but before he could finish the sentence, Kisasi swung and caught him on the right side of his face. The right hook was so crisp and precise that Askari absorbed it's full impact which sent him to the floor with a loud thud. Before Myisha could express her protest, Kisasi was on top of Askari pummeling him with cascading blows to his face. Chantel quickly noticed that Kisasi, as usual, had his 44 snub nosed bulldog in a belt holster at the small of his back. Thinking that Askari could perhaps grab it during the scuffle, she reached down and grabbed Kisasi around his waist and said to Myisha, "Kisasi is strapped." Upon hearing this Myisha joined in to help her get Kisasi off of Askari.

As they pulled Kisasi up he swung again connecting to Askari's left eye, causing blood to gush out of the brow above his eye. Askari fell under Kisasi's relentless blows reached under the entertainment center where they kept the .40 glock to protect the house. Both Chantel and Myisha now stood between Askari and Kisasi, obstructing the latter's view. When Askari got to his feet he had the .40 glock in his right hand, extended towards Kisasi. Chantel was the first to notice this and screamed "Put the gun down Askari." "Move! I'm gonna kill this nigga!" Askari ordered. Kisasi knew that he'd disarmed the .40 the last time that he and Askari had a heated disagreement in the den concerning the sistahs. He reached back and took the .44 from its holster at the small of his back and said to himself "regardless of the fact that the .40 is not loaded, if I hear the click of the hammer that means he wants to kill me and I'm going to let his ass have it."

Kisasi hoped that Askari would not pull the trigger. They'd been comrades for years and he genuinely loved Askari but love is not a noun, it's a verb that demands reciprocation to effloresce. He used his left hand to move both Myisha and Chantel from in front of him. There they stood, both with weapons drawn. A real Mexican standoff. Silence permeated the room, I mean it was so quiet that one could hear a church mouse pissing on cotton, then came the click of the hammer from the .40 glock that Askari held trained on Kisasi, Chantel screamed in terror. Askari's eyes widened with surprise but before he could fully grasp what had happened a loud boom from Kisasi's .44 filled the empty space in the den. The projectile entered his right shoulder, it's impact spinning him first to his right then threw him on the floor. Kisasi walked over to him straddled his body and pointed the gun right at his face "I should kill you right where you lay, but this is how it goes down, you're going to get dropped off at Emmanuel Hospital and you're going to tell them that you were shot in a drive by shooting-umefahamu?!"

He then turned to Myisha and said "You drop him off at the hospital and stay with him until he's stabilized. If he utters a word about what happened call me on the cell phone." Then he turned to Chantel and said. "I need you to make it look like nothing happened in here." Chantel helped Myisha get Askari to the car and by the time she returned to the den Kisasi was on the phone saying "I need you to meet Myisha at Emmanuel and make sure that she gets back to headquarters safely." then he got off the phone.

As Chantel cleaned the blood as best as she could from the carpet and wall she asked. "Why did you let him bust first?" "I knew there was no bullets in the gun because I disarmed it after the last verbal altercation that we had." Kisasi answered, "Then why did you blast him?" Chantel asked. "Because the Fact that he pulled the trigger informed me that at that moment he wanted to kill me...it was mandatory that I return the gesture. As paradoxical a this may sound I had to blast him to save his life." Kisasi replied.

CHAPTER 56

Snap was around the corner from Emmanuel Hospital when his cell phone rang. "West up?' he answered Kisasi's voice came from the other end of the phone "Without a doubt" Snap replied, clicked off, pointed his six duce drop top, royal blue Chevy towards the hospital and mashed the gas pedal. He didn't know what had jumped off but he knew that the brotha that he deemed his comrade needed him. He blew through the light swung the six duce into the parking lot of the hospital, tires screeching, parked and jumped out head on a swivel as he approached the emergency entrance.

Moments later Myisha's BMW pulled up to the emergency entrance, she jumped out "Get this buster up out of my car" she said urgently. Snap looked to the passenger's seat and there he saw Askari holding his shoulder wincing, writhing in pain. He moved, opened the passenger's side door, "Get your ass up out of here cuzz!" he demanded. Askari fell out of the car, regained his balance, and as he stumbled towards the emergency entrance, Snap kicked him square in his ass quickening his pace. "Snap, wait for me out here I'm going to go in and make sure this dude tell these people what he's supposed to tell them." As they approached the nurses' station one of the nurses noticing that this man had been shot, abruptly stood and asked what happened. "He got shot in a drive by" Myisha injected before Askari could answer. "Is that what happened sir?" the nurse asked. "Yea" Askari said through the pain. Myisha egressed the hospital where Snap stood waiting for her. As she approached, Snap said. "You got blood all over your passengers seat, take the Chevy and I'll take the beamer and get it detailed" Myisha agreed.

CHAPTER 57

Months had passed since the incident with Askari. After being discharged from the hospital, he checked himself into an inpatient treatment facility in Arizona, where he'd spend the next eighteen months fighting his addiction. Kisasi had been given the Community Service Award by the House of Emoja, the Redirection House, and the Camp Fire Gang Peace Program in a ceremony that celebrates the work of non-profit organizations in north and northeast Portland.

After Snap had her car detailed to remove the evidence Askari left in it, Myisha sold the BMW and bought an infinity. Chantel was working hard on her MBA and would have it by the end of the year. It was November of 91 as Kisasi, Chantel and Myisha sat in the den going over projections for DITR the regular programming was interrupted, Breaking news flashed across the television screen and reporter Nacita Ugalde's face appeared, a close up for effect. "At 10:22 tonight Governor Walter Gossett was arrested for the death of a young teenager whose body was discovered by his wife Madison Gossett, upon her return from a vacation at her parents' home in San Diego, California. It is unclear how long the body had been there but, the coroner estimates that the time of death was within the past 24-36 hours. The camera then cut to the Governor being escorted out of the Governor's mansion, hands cuffed in front of him with a blazer draped over the handcuffs. The camera then cut back to Nacita Ugalde who was walking stride for stride with the Governors wife, who was being whisked away by plain clothed police officers. "Where was the governor when you came home?" the savvy reporter asked then pushed her mic. towards Madison Gossett. "In the shower" she stated before an officer covered the lens of the camera and yelled "Move those cameras asshole."

"These are the people that they have running the government" Kisasi said as he dialed his cell phone and egressed the den for privacy. "Did you see this?" he asked the person on the other end of the phone. "His term was up next year and I don't think that he would have been re-elected. There was a report coming out, documenting his sexual philandering" Naomi stated. "You should run sistah" Kisasi stated. There was a long pause,-empty air. "You there sistah?" "Yes I'm here....I was pondering your statement" Naomi answered. "Well?" Kisasi asked "If you'll help me get the youth vote I'll run" Naomi challenged.

There was no doubt in Naomi's mind that she could win. Her record was stellar. She'd made all the right connections, greased the right palms, kept the secrets of very powerful people within the government, but she also knew how dirty politics were. She weighed her interest and asked herself what dirt would be slung at her in such an intense campaign. The only indiscretion that could possibly be used against her was her public support of Kisasi, which was not as bad on paper as it was in perception. Kisasi had no police record, not even a traffic violation, but he was being investigated by the FBI, which up until now had produced nothing but innuendo, conjecture, assumptions that could not be substantiated.

He was working hard in the community and Having success among the youth. Crime, though prevalent was down in the north and northeast Portland and she was fully prepared to attribute some of the success to the work that he was doing with gang affected youth if they questioned her ties with him. She could even get out in front of this line of questioning by using her council position to publicly award Kisasi, on behalf of the City council, for his exceptional work and dedication to substantially reduce youth gang violence and even credit him for the statistical reduction of drive by shootings. Yea...why not. "Listen sweetie I'm going to get an award ceremony for DITR and the work that you're doing in the community. They'll try to use my support of you against me because that's all they have on me, so we must negate that angle before I announce that I'm going to run. It'll take me about a week to contact the right people to appear-place you in the frame with these very influential people, and because I've kept their secrets they will speak highly of you, one by one, then I'll present you with the award. Let us get busy and I'll get back with you regarding the details," Naomi said. Just before they hung up the phone she stated "I want to see you after the event" her voice seductive, laced with innuendos. "I'm looking forward to it sistah." Kisasi replied, then they hung up the phone.

CHAPTER 58

After meeting with the voice, Lana felt ill an unexplainable tingling in her extremities-exhausted. She'd been experiencing these and other physical abnormalities for the past eighteen months but, had attributed them to stress and the countless hours she poured into her work and career. This latest tingling was different and she decided to see a doctor. After being given a full physical including blood work, Lana sat in an exam room at Swedish Hospital anxiously anticipating her diagnosis. She'd hoped the doctor would inform her that she was just suffering from extreme exhaustion and prescribe her something that would facilitate a restful night. Dr. Singh. came into the exam room with folder in hand. "How are you doing Ms. Xavier?" he asked rhetorically while preparing the proper words in his mind to give his Patient, news that would not be easily acceptable. "I'm fine doctor" she replied. "Well, we think that we discovered why you are experiencing the symptoms that you have described. Of course we'll need further testing to be sure." The doctor said. Lana's anticipation grew exponentially at the fact that he'd stated that there would be further testing. Was the issue this complex? And if so this could not be good news. A myriad of thoughts raced through Lana's mind simultaneously, neither yielding to the other, each overlapping – crowding the others space not allowing it to fully mature. She searched the Doctors face for a hint, his features, no answer, no explanation then he took her hand into his as to console her and stated "Our preliminary test leads us to believe that you have multiple sclerosis." She cringed and pulled her hand out of his. Her mind exploded, thoughts ranging from disbelief to rage. "What the fuck do you mean?" Lana yelled. Before she could complete a thought, her mind immediately imagined the worst case scenario. All she could see is herself crippled in some wheel chair without the ability to take care of herself. Her mind returned to the Doctor. "What do I do from here?" She asked.

"Well, first we get a second opinion and if it confirms our tests we explore the best treatment for you. Ms. Xavier this does not equal a life of immobility, there has been great strides in this field and though we still don't know what causes MS we've developed better drugs for the treatment of this disease." Lana watched as the Drs lips moved but she'd already checked out On the conversation. All she could think of was her career and all that she'd been through to get where she was. All that she had to endure and at 27 she'd now been diagnosed with MS. After discussing the possibilities with Dr. Singh, she returned to her condo, fell down on her living room couch and cried uncontrollably. She cried all night long to herself. Monday morning presented itself in regular fashion and work beckoned. She pulled herself together, put on her best suit and presented herself in the office as if nothing had transpired. She'd grown adept at hiding herself-deceiving the world and she now employed this tactic in every facet of her life-her every interpersonal interaction and though this fact proscribe intimate interaction, it made her efficient in the workplace. She poured herself into her job and became the immoral-unethical-ruthless individual that it required in order to be successful- achieve upward mobility.

Lana's second opinion came only weeks after the first and verified that she in fact had MS "Why was all of this happening to her?" she asked herself, why could this not have happened to one of those little bitches that pined for Kisasi's attention?" It was them that this should have happened to, not her. She had a career that she'd worked hard to effectuate, actualize, while they, Chantel and Myisha merely fell into the graces of Kisasi by accident. Lana's resentment for Kisasi grew more vehement, pointed. She'd already resented the fact that not only had he been successful in her absence-without her assistance but these ghetto bitches seemed to have his affection which was rightfully and should have been exclusively hers. In the throes of her emotional tsunami Lana's ability to reason failed her. Not once did she acquiesce to the fact that she'd entertained men outside of Kisasi-intimately betraying the bond that they once had. Months had passed since her diagnosis and the effects of spasticity were evident to her as she stood naked in front of the full body mirror in her bedroom. Though she had been injecting herself once a day to stave off the effects of the MS, it was evident that she'd began to lose muscle tone in her thighs which resulted in indentations in the muscle. As she stood in front of the full body mirror in her bedroom, injecting medication into her stomach, she cried uncontrollably. She felt like less than a woman for she would never know the joy of bearing a child and her body, it seemed, was atrophying. Everyday Lana reported to work no one knowing her most personal trials and tribulations.

She became an introvert guarding her personal secrets while simultaneously presenting to the world an air of perfectionism. At work she could bury her sorrows and become someone else. At work her personal trials did not exist. She took her work home with her, in an attempt to proscribe thoughts of her disposition, working well into the night, then arising early only to resume the charade-the façade that gave others the perception that everything was alright as she died a little every day. In the cultish environ of her church she was the quintessential Christian taking part in fundraisers-active in the women's group –but her vehemence, bitterness, selfishness was far from Jesus-a fact she attempted to tithe away.

As Lana numbed herself emotionally, she turned to food for Comfort and the fact that she began to gain weight depressed her, causing her to up her dosage of her anti-depressants and occasionally smoke. While she excelled in her career she was spiraling out of control personally. After a long days work arbitrating disputes between her office and unions,

Lana laid her head on her ostrich feathered pillow and replayed the events of the day. This was the part of the day wherein one had to address oneself, ones triumphs, failures, ambitions, activities or lack thereof and the steps that one has taken to either advance or remain stagnant. She lye in her queen sized bed, deep in thought, conversing, questioning herself mentally. In the midst of this psychological question and answer period. Her pettiness and bitterness became self evident and it's motivations pellucid. Her disdain of both Myisha and Chantel in reality was fed by her illogical resentment of Kisasi and though he'd always treated her like a queen, acted in their best interest, honored their bond, she found a way to blame him for her misfortunes-her barrenness. This is how she justified-rationalized the thoughts of sophistry and subterfuge, making valid through deceptive reasoning the gutepans she entertained.

CHAPTER 59

November 1992 Kisasi, Myisha and Chantel and a Caucasian female named Denise Cheri all sat in the den glued to the television when a knock at the door broke the silence. Myisha sat her drink down and rushed to the door hurriedly in order to answer it and get back to the televised governor's race that had them all entranced. Naomi Gaston was engaged in a hard fought neck to neck race with Lester Stomsvich an unsavory attorney that acted as Governor Gossets handler during the scandal. "Who is it?" Myisha asked through the closed door "Snip Snap" the voice returned. She opened the door greeted Snap and moved quickly back to the den, Snap on her heels. As they ingressed the den, Kisasi greeted Snap, shook his hand, introduced him to Denise and returned his attention to the television.

"Pleased to meet you" Denise said to Snap-coquettishly smiling extending her hand. Snap first looked at her hand then into her face and merely said "West up cuzz?" Denise was a friend of Chantel who she attended college with and had brought to headquarters to meet Kisasi in hopes of her skills being employed with DITR. She was a red head, blue eyed, pale skinned female with a sharp aquiline nose but it was her politics that had caught Kisasi's attention and the fact that she was Caucasian could be used to benefit the organization, if she exhibited the requisite integrity-loyalty-dedication not to him but to the cause of fighting injustice and social stratification. Denise was what is described as a bleeding heart liberal who, through activism, sought to right the wrongs that she'd witnessed only through the college experience. It was on the college campus where she'd met Chantel-befriended her and became conscious of the work that she held so dearly. She could remember the first time that her and Chantel met. At first she'd mistaken Chantel to be a white woman, a notion that was quickly abandoned after the first minute of their conversation. Chantel spoke so passionately about the organization, it's leadership and the work that they were doing in the community- amongst the youth, Denise saw a way to purge herself of the guilt she experienced concerning the injustices perpetuated against people of color by her people and asked if she could assist. Now she stood in the den at headquarters in the presence of Kisasi the leader of this magnanimous movement and she was captivated. The votes were in and though the race was close Naomi won the Governor's race and thunderous applause rang throughout headquarters. Kisasi popped the bottle of Louis Roederer 1955 Champagne, poured everyone a glass, then offered a toast "To our sistah Naomi Gaston –

DITR, our success and the upliftment of our youth." Glasses were raised contents drained as genuine good cheer permeated the room. Kisasi panned the room only to catch Denise casting furtive glances at him. He smiled out loud turned his attention to Snap and started to speak when his cell phone rang "This is Kisasi" he stated. A loud scream came through the receiver then a voice "We did it sweetie" Naomi screamed, the back ground noise so loud and festive he barely made out her voice, "It was the youth vote that did it. I can't thank you enough for that, though I have an idea on how to try" Naomi intimated, Kisasi smiled out loud "Call me when you get home" he stated, exchanged good byes, then disengaged.

"You needed to see me?" Kisasi asked Snap then egressed the den and ascended the staircase, Snap in tow. Kisasi egressed his room then sat at his desk and motioned for Snap to have a seat. Snap sat, positioned himself for comfort, then spoke "I got a homeboy that just fell for assault with a deadly weapon and I don't have the paper to bail him out." "How much do you need?" Kisasi asked. "They're asking for $750,000 Snap replied then searched Kisasi's face for any discomfort. "Ten percent is 75,000 is your homeboy worth that?" Kisasi asked. "Every bit of it kiwe" Snap replied. Kisasi turned in his chair, picked up his pen, and as he wrote on a piece of paper stated "I have a bail bondsman located across the street from the Justice Center contact him and tell him this is for Almasi, he'll take care of this." he tore the paper from the notebook tablet and extended it to Snap. Snap took the piece of paper from Kisasi's hand. "I owe you kiwe" he said "You don't owe me nothing comrade, your loyalty is appreciated" Kisasi said they rose and returned to the den, where they found the women engaged in political discourse. "Myisha I need you to call Trumans Bail bonds and let them know that a comrade will be calling within the next thirty minutes and to assist him with anything that he needs." Kisasi said. Myisha quickly made the call, Kisasi and Snap egressed the den, walked to the front door, exchanged goodbyes, and Snap disappeared into the night.

Kisasi returned to the den to find that dialectic had not subsided. He was impressed with the savvy that Denise displayed and the way she expressed herself though her ideology was slanted by white privilege, she could definitely be of assistance for it was not necessary that she shared every nuance of his philosophy-only that she intrinsically wanted to fight against inequality. It was getting late Kisasi decided to go upstairs and rest leaving the women downstairs. He checked his Rolex it was 1:30 am. He had not heard back from Naomi "I'll catch her tomorrow" he reasoned. His head embraced the pillow and he rested.

Early the next morning Kisasi arose from a dream that alarmed him. The issue concerning him being investigated still tugged at him. The fact that he was no closer in 1992 than he was in 1990 to finding out who the informant was made him somewhat uneasy. Not because he was doing anything wrong, for his demonstration, at this stage of the rotation, was beyond reproach, but he knew the strategy and methodology that had to be employed to get where he was and hoped that it would not come back to haunt him. I've done all that I could do to ensure silence on behalf of those that were privy to intimate details." he reasoned as he walked into his bathroom, turned the shower on, took off his boxers and got in. Halfway through his ritualistic cleansing he heard a light rap at his bathroom door. Quickly assessing the possibility of personnel that could have been in his room he stated "Come in." "You left your phone downstairs last night so I answered the ring" the mellifluous voice of Chantel distinguished itself from the sound of the cascading water. "Asante sana –who is it sistah?" Kisasi asked. "It's Governor Gaston." Chantel answered. Naomi on the other end of the phone listened to the exchange –ascertaining the fact that Kisasi was in the shower and that sistah Chantel had accessed him at such an intimate time-felt a twinge of envy but quickly checked her emotions.

Kisasi stated "Tell her to give me a second." As he turned off the shower, took the large terry cloth towel from its place and took the phone from Chantal's extended hand. "How can I help you Governor" Kisasi said with a smile. "Stop it, I'm sorry that I didn't get back to you last night. I got caught up in the celebratory atmosphere, and couldn't get away but I thought about you all night in the midst of the distractions" Naomi said. "No problem sistah we too celebrated your victory here at headquarters." Kisasi answered. "When can I see you?" Naomi asked. "After breakfast I'll be in my office at DITR. I have a meeting with the president of Mycap, but I'll be free for a work lunch if you can make that happen." Kisasi stated. "Let's schedule it for ..what...12:30 at Alfa Omea's downtown? Naomi asked. "Nimefahamu-tutaonana" Kisasi replied, and after Naomi stated "Kwaheri" they disengaged. Chantel who stood-leaned back against the sink during Kisasi's brief discourse quipped "When are we going to get the opportunity to spend some quality time together?"

"Every moment that we interact is quality time sistah." Kisasi stated through a mechanical smile. "You know what I'm talking about daddy." Chantel replied, words dissipating at her pouting lips for effect. "Soon sistah, as a matter of fact let me take you to an early dinner tonight, we need to discuss the potential viability of your friend Denise working for the organization."

Kisasi stated-kissed Chantel gently on the forehead then walked back into his bedroom and, started getting dressed. Chantel followed him back into the bedroom longing to touch his half naked muscular body, longing to be touched by him. After he pulled on his boxers and began applying lotion to his upper body she moved in close and wrapped her arms around him. Now enveloped in his embrace she looked up into his piercing grey eyes beckoning his lips-and he accommodated her. As they exchanged tongues her breast rose and fell with passion, she then reached down into his boxers and finding him erect, moaned softly without breaking the kiss. Kisasi pulled away. "Sistah I have to go to work we'll talk tonight." Chantel reluctantly relinquished and stated "I'm going to hold you to that." turned and egressed the bedroom. Kisasi, now dressed in his Le'Taxione urban couture jeans-David Eden Alligator shoes-midnight blue-a white silk t-shirt- and a midnight blue Armani blazer, descended the stairs to find both Chantel and Denise sitting in the den and took the opportunity to enact his plan. "Ladies" he greeted then continued "would you like to accompany me to the DITR building?" He requested that Chantel drive knowing that he had a lunch appointment with Naomi that way they could part company when the need arose without either one hindering the others plans. When they arrived at DITR he instructed Chantel to give Denise a tour of the facility as he ingressed his office to conduct business. Mr. Williams-President of Mycap had left a message confirming his appointment; he returned his call to inform him that he was now in the office and looking forward to their meeting. Fifteen minutes later Mr. James Williams sat in his office discussing the desire to have Kisasi come in to speak to the youth at Mycap. "I have a more robust idea Mr. Williams, why don't we organize all the youth groups, go out into the business Community and solicit their support for a process in which gang Affected youth can be paid to work at their establishment for a month at a time earning a check for that month and also being exposed to a skill that could be parlayed into part time employment." Kisasi suggested after an almost two hour meeting. Mr. Williams and Kisasi stood shook hands and agreed on a strategy to solicit employment for gang affiliated youth in the communities in which they lived. On their way to the campus both Chantel and Denise stopped by Kisasi's office to inform him they were on their way out "What do you think about our organization Ms. Cheri" Kisasi asked. "I can't believe that a black man your age has accomplished so much." Denise answered. Kisasi almost took offense to her answer but reasoned that this is the attitude socialized-orientated into individuals by parents and social constructs. It is not the norm that black men exact any measure of success considering the forces of poverty –social stratification, institutional racism- inequality in health care-education and a judicial system plagued by intrinsic racism aimed against them. "How would you like to be a part of the solution to injustice and work for DITR?" Kisasi asked. "I would love to work here." Denise answered. "Chantel will mentor you and familiarize you with the expectations here at DITR." Kisasi said. "When does she start?" Chantel asked. "When you say so." Kisasi answered with a half smile. After Chantel and Denise egressed his office Kisasi called a cab and in moments he was on his way to meet the Governor for lunch. As he rode in the back seat of the cab his mind mused, "I'm going to have lunch with the governor of the state of Oregon." he then smiled out loud.

The Taxi pulled up at Alfa Omea's a five star restaurant located in downtown Portland, Oregon. Kisasi ingressed the restaurant and was escorted to a reserved table, seated and given water. "Your guest is running late, I was told to inform you that she would be here within 15 minutes." the waiter said. Not even 5 minutes passed when he saw Naomi sauntering in his direction escorted by security. She arrived at the table –offered her apologies for being late and dismissed her security who sat three tables away, keeping her in sight. "I didn't plan on the security that came with this gig." Naomi said half joking, frustration permeating the texture of her voice, "The price we pay to serve the under-served," Kisasi attempted to massage Naomi verbally. "First things first Naomi started, re-shifted in her seat, then continued. "My new position has afforded me the clearance to obtain otherwise sensitive information and though I'm not cleared to obtain intimate details, I can access information pertaining to cases that would otherwise be considered high profile. He repositioned himself in his seat then stated, "Please continue." The waiter approached the table to refresh the water supply and give menus to the patrons. "Let me preface what I'm about to say with this, as I've told you before, I know more about you than you think I do, but it's not about what one know's, it's about what one can prove." she-noticing that Kisasi's brow was now furrowed, his grey eyes piercing-searching her soul for any display of sophistry or subterfuge- reassured him that her position remained the same and that she too had resorted to methods that may seem to the untrained eye as subversive, but that the cause sometimes called for drastic actions for we live in drastic times. Only after Kisasi relaxed his posture did she continue. "Kwame Odoms and Antoine McCray two years ago drove over an overpass on Jensen Ave. in Fresno, California. Upon further investigation it was determined that the car they were driving had been tampered with. The brake line had been cut, it was also determined that alcohol played a significant role in the accident, the investigation was closed. Both were from Portland, Oregon, from what the investigation ascertained they were involved in some clandestine gang wherein death before dishonor means that one will take his own life before jeopardizing the gang. Because they had no ties to Fresno their activity in Portland has been the subject of intense investigation which in one way or another led to the suspicion of them being involved in the Christmas Day Murder's. Fast forward-the FBI agent that I told you about has been interviewing an informant who has little knowledge of, but a whole lot of accusations about the murder's. "And how does this affect me?" Kisasi asked. "This Person has mentioned your name as one who had such a group –that being expressed this informant has agreed to wear a wire in an attempt to get you to incriminate yourself. Without a confession-explicit or tacit you can't be touched. Now as I told you before I'm not interested in your methodology, but sweetie sanitize your cipher." Naomi implored. Kisasi's thoughts raced.

Twenty-four billion miles per second, but he flashed a smile at Naomi and stated "The cup which they seek to press to my lips will be forced to their own." Naomi felt a cold chill behind what Kisasi said and instinctively knew that someone would pay for this betrayal and she almost felt sympathy for the culprit-but quickly mused "fuck um and feed um fish." Naomi informed Kisasi that she'd had a house rented wherein they could meet and share stolen moments. "I'm tempted Asali but until this inquiry is over I think it best that you and I meet in public-perception is everything." Kisasi stated. Naomi knew that he was right but she longed to feel him next to her, inside of her, she reluctantly agreed. "I'll give you a rain check this time but I'm looking forward, with anticipation, to having you alone" Naomi intimated. They ended their lunch, shook hands for the security and onlookers, then parted ways. As Kisasi rode in the cab he wrestled with the fact that someone he'd placed his trust in would now be aimed at him like a loaded weapon. He refused to entertain who it could be, he resigned himself to whoever it was they'd unknowingly reveal themselves through their ambition to cross him and collect their thirty pieces of silver.

CHAPTER 60

The Sky had darkened from primrose to purple when Chantel called Kisasi to inform him that, though she was late she still wanted to have that dinner that he'd promised her. She'd allowed time to elapse purposefully, for she wanted to capture the intimacy of night in order to seduce Kisasi. She made reservations ahead of time at the Hyatt along with a suite that would facilitate her plan. "This is Kisasi" the voice came on the other end of the phone "Uhali gani daddy, I'm sorry I'm late. I had some things to take care of at DITR after classes. I'm getting ready to leave the office, I've made reservations at the Hyatt Hotel for dinner if you're still down" Chantel said, voice both Mellifluous and specious. Kisasi smiled out loud at her ingenuity. He perceived the move hours earlier when he'd not heard from Chantel and though he didn't want to put himself in a position to be alone with her in an intimate setting, he had to, in order to ascertain if she was the mole leaking information. "No problem sistah I'm looking forward to our interaction." Kisasi replied, exchanged goodbyes and hung up the phone.

He then called the Hyatt hotel and massaged the female at the front desk out of the time that Ms. Chantel Criglar made reservations, and just as he thought, the reservation had been made at 10:30am that morning, meaning that either Chantel was setting him up to entrap him or she was setting him up for a night of intimate exchange-the latter preferred. Chantel pulled up outside of headquarters and blew the horn. She didn't want to run into Myisha tonight for that would kill the vibe. Her looking into the rearview mirror inspecting her makeup was immediately abandoned when she saw Kisasi egress headquarters, closing the door behind him. Kisasi got in the car with Chantel, he complimented the Blue Donna Karen dress, white pearl necklace with white Le'Taxione Femm Fatale Couture 8 inch heels with blue bottoms, she was beautiful. Chantel, redolent with fragrance, thanked Kisasi for the compliment, pointed the car towards their destination and pulled off from the curb. It had begun to rain, as he initiated small talk the vehicle's headlights parted the rain and the wipers collected water at the corners of the windshields. "Did you finish what you went to DITR to handle?" Kisasi asked. "Yea, it wasn't much just some projections that need to be included in our DITR 990 form due at the beginning of the year," she replied. Then, minutes later they pulled up to the Hyatt Hotel, had the car parked by the valet attendant, and entered the lobby. They were escorted to their table and sat, she ordered Louis Roederer

1955, Caviar on paper thin slices of white toast-endive salad and strawberry whipped cream, Kisasi, frowning at the menu ordered the meatless chef salad. As they discussed DITR, it's projections and then Kisasi's vision of DITR'S ten year plan he glanced at his watch, it was 11:00pm. Chantel's words had begun to slightly slur then she informed him that she'd reserved a suite for them. "Brilliant idea lets go see what it looks like," Kisasi stated as if he wasn't already aware of the fact.

The suite worked to Kisasi's advantage for he needed to get her undressed to see if she was wearing a wire. Once in the suite Chantel went into the restroom, turned on the shower, came back out, asked Kisasi to join her and sauntered back to the restroom, Kisasi in tow.

Upon arriving in the restroom he took her into his embrace, he kissed her passionately, deeply, reverently his hands explored every contour of her petite anatomy. Unzipping her dress, unsnapping her bra, all without breaking the exchange of tongues, she moaned lightly ever so soft. When anticipation became more than they could bear, they removed their clothing and got into the shower, oblivious to the cascading water, re-engaged in cutaneous stimulation, bodies wet and wanting. Kisasi held her so tight that he could feel the increased palpitations of her heart, her nipples pressed against his chest. They egressed the shower without toweling their bodies, laid on the thousand thread sheets of the king size bed. Kisasi now explored Chantel's body with his tongue, he started at the nape of her neck then moved slowly down to her breast, first taking one nipple then the other between his lips, lightly nibbling on each before tracing down her stomach with his tongue.

Chantel spread her thighs, her pheromone enticing, beckoning, exciting Kisasi procuring erection, titillating. He stood, moved to the nightstand, retrieved a condom, applied it, then moved back to the bed. He positioned his body over hers took his erection in his right hand and with his left elbow supporting his weight begin sliding his erection up and down the length of her mound. Chantel's green eye's fixated on his as she pushed her hips upward in an attempt to force his entrance. Kisasi using his hand moved his erection in circular motions between the lips around the entrance of Chantel's mound, then without warning pushed the head inside of her, she gasped- then moaned out loud. In mid-stroke Kisasi stopped-placed Chantel's legs on his shoulders-positioned on his knees upright staring down into her face then plunged his erection into her, angling himself that he touched every wall inside of her. Chantel experiencing both pleasure and pain matched his every stroke with synchronized motion "Shit! Don't stop daddy?" she said voice tremulous. Thirty minutes had passed before Chantel exclaimed harder daddy I'm cumming please don't stop." The headboard tempering and measuring the rhythm and force of Kisasi's penetration beckoned him to go deeper, harder, enthralled by the sound of its banging up against the wall he subconsciously obeyed it's instructions until her body convulsed and shook uncontrollably beneath his. She wrapped her thighs around his muscular torso as he buried himself all the way in her, causing her to scream aloud. After her orgasm had subsided he turned her over placing her on her hands and knees. Then placing his left palm between her shoulder blades-he pressed her down to the bed- breast and face flat, with her ass up in the air. Chantel while keeping her breast flat on the bed reach back with both hands and spread her lips for full access. Kisasi pushed his erection in her and after every seventh stroke-slapped her on her ass as she pushed backwards into him until he exploded.

Now ensconced after being enveloped by the throes of passion, ecstasy. Kisasi and Chantel laid in each other's embrace, recounting what had just taken place. Was this love?" Or just an hour and a half of sex?" Chantel's mind admonished her, only to relent to satiety-washed with pleasure.

Kisasi knowing that a woman's life is influenced by her historical emotional experiences and affection overstood that it is within her heart that the true issues of life are shaped, fashioned and pour forth, It is in the heart, the seat of emotions where ones ambitions strive and ones avarice mines for hidden treasures. That being said "It is in ones heart where deception and treachery are given expression." so he tugged at her heart strings "I will spend my life to preserve yours," he stated, and her reply was as the sound of a well strummed harp. "And I will give my life that yours may be furthered," she stated. Kisasi measured the veracity of her response, She's not the mole" His mind admonished him, but who is? that question would be answered sooner than he thought. Night submitted to the judgment of dawn and Kisasi knew that Returning to headquarters with Chantel, in the same clothes that he'd worn the night before would draw the ire of Myisha and though he would eventually inform her that he'd had sex with Chantel, he wanted to choose the time when that conversation would take place. "I'll catch a cab to headquarters sistah." he stated. Chantel knowing the reasoning behind his decision agreed but stated, "Myisha is going to have to overstand that we all have positions to play in this demonstration and accept the fact, as I have, that we can accomplish more as an intimate unit."

"I love both of you as comrades and intimate companions" Kisasi ventured in the most soothing sonorous texture. He wished that he could give them both the world wrapped in a blue satin ribbon, bow and all but he'd witnessed what the struggle had done to the BLA up close and personal, he knew their struggle may not yield results in their lifetime, so all he could do is cherish the stolen moments, respect and revere them equally and hope that was enough. It was clear that he would have to now sit both of them down for this conversation that is if Myisha wasn't the mole.

CHAPTER 61

Kisasi, Myisha and Chantel sat in the den sipping cognac listening to Luther Vandross. Kisasi had requested they meet and insisted they cancel any plans that they made prior, his statement. "It's imperative that we meet and discuss new developments that effect us as individuals and an organization." Chantel had asked if she could bring Denise, but Kisasi didn't think that would be a good idea at the time so Chantel dropped her off at her place before arriving at headquarters. Kisasi couldn't imagine sabotage on the part of Myisha but he'd witnessed his parents and the BLA undermined by those who'd previously pledged their allegiance to the cause only to break weak under the scrutiny and divisive tactics employed by the bureau used to destroy organizations that dared to question government policy.

Their self alienation, coupled with their desires to be relevant, their need to possess the social constructs manufactured, fabricated symbols and outward appearances of success, created and perpetuated a personality disorder that rationalized their self- defeatist dog eat dog mentality, which in turn facilitated intra communal-intra-personal-sabotage that if awarded with trinkets, the trappings of a material marketed social construct was not only excusable but encouraged. "First and foremost I want to thank both of you for the loyalty and tenacity that you exhibit, not only in the cause but in the camaraderie that you make evident to me on a personal level. Next year I am scheduled to speak in Washington D.C in commemoration of our American sojourn, Civil Rights Leaders and the benefits of their guidance and work. This speech will place us and our organization on the national and maybe the world stage. That means the scrutiny of our activity is about to intensify-tenfold.

The speech that I will deliver will not be what they expect from a guy that they've pigeon holed as a "concrete activist." This speech will be socio-political-economic and will take the social construct to task concerning black people immersed in it. After this speech we will become the target of "negroes" that, through their complicity-support perpetuate the status quo. This will be a dangerous position to be in for they've eaten off of the plate of oppression for so long that they've now become, by proxy, the oppressors of self and their own people. They've adopted, to the detriment of the whole-a distorted form of capitalism wherein they work against their own body politic and the sacrifice of those who look like themselves is rationalized as self preservation.

I need to know are both of you ready for this?" Kisasi stated. After receiving a harmonious, simultaneous "Hell yea!" Kisasi pivoted to the personal aspects of their interaction. "Listen I've found myself loving both of you, individually as well as collectively, it wasn't and isn't my intentions to Hurt-betray or deceive anyone of you nor did I plan to be intimate with either one of you, but proximity and our shared desire and activity within the struggle has placed us within an exclusive cipher of intimacy-wherein I've been intimate with both of you. That being advanced, you both are assets to the demonstration and bring to the table different ideologies, experiences and qualities that are paramount to the cause none more valuable than the other, neither of greater import than the other and to lose either one of you would be a travesty." Kisasi panned their faces as both sat quietly waiting for the other shoe to drop.

Myisha being the more assertive asked, "So what are you saying baby?" because I'm not going anywhere." "And neither am I," Chantel chimed in. "I'm saying that I care deeply for both of you, if you two decide that in order for us to stay in perpetual motion, the intimate interaction between us must cease, then I will refrain from that activity in order to not only protect and preserve the integrity of DITR and this struggle that we've chosen to engage but also to protect and preserve our camaraderie, for I cherish what we have as individuals also, I would hate to lose that."Kisasi explained. "I overstand your position baby, I too would hate to lose our personal relationship as well as our professional demonstration, as long as there is respect and rules to our activity, I can and will handle it." Myisha stated. then turned to Chantel for her response. "I agree, as long as we are not devalued, and what we both bring to the table is respected and recognized, I can deal with it." Chantel agreed then asked Myisha, "What's the rule?" "The rule is that we continue to work hard for the organization, protect each other with our lives and never undermine the authority of the general." Myisha said through a genuine smile, "I'll drink to that." Chantel added, they raised their glasses then drained the contents.

Kisasi set his glass down egressed the den-ascended the staircase then sat at his desk. As he thought about the speech he would make, Myisha appeared at the entrance of his room, tapped lightly on the door. Kisasi turned in his chair to see Myisha standing there, "Come in sistah." he stated. Myisha ingressed the room and sat on his bed, "What 's on your mind baby." she asked. Kisasi not wanting to divulge any sensitive information stated, "This speech is going to put us under the microscope, though I'm conflicted, I know that it must be delivered." Myisha walked over to the desk and sat on Kisasi's lap. "It's better to tell the people the truth, even in their ignorance, lest they become aware and condemn you as a liar, I think Elijah said." Myisha stated as she wrapped her arm around Kisasi, who returned her affection while simultaneously searching for a body wire.

CHAPTER 62

It was July, 1993 8 months after Kisasi was informed by Governor Naomi Gaston that someone with intimate knowledge of his activities would be fitted with a wire aimed at him to incriminate himself. He'd vetted both Chantel and Myisha, at this point they both were clean as the board of health, yet, he remained hypervigilant. He'd had Naomi vett Denise Cheri and found, that her family came from old money who'd made their fortune in both cotton and the tobacco industry, both ventures inextricably bound to slavery. Naomi informed him that Cheri was not her true last name, her true last name is Spingarn, a name attached to the founding of the NAACP.

In a conversation with Denise, Kisasi asked why she'd chosen to change her last name. her reply was "I wanted to separate myself from the legacy of chattel slavery that made my family wealthy and destroyed so many human beings." Kisasi had intimate knowledge of Spingarn and his ties to the NAACP, which were unsavory at best but through the blessing of God that organization was at the forefront of the movement for equality in America's crimogenic social construct. The national news had been advertising the Washington DC event as a march, when in fact the youth's circumstance had become so dire that this was a rally in which prominent leaders, community organizations were gathering to speak directly to the youth and share ideas on how that circumstance could be turned around giving the youth a chance to have access at the American dream. July 16, 1993 arrived the day of the rally. Kisasi sat on the stage carefully listening to the politicians, activist, lawyers, social workers, law enforcement, legislators and clergy pontificate and espouse their positions, slanted by the ideology of those who sign their checks, he realized that no one addressed the substratum of the youth issue. Lost in thought and disgust his attention was brought back to the moment when he heard his name announced, coupled with the complimentary applause, he deliberately approached the rostrum, panned the sea of faces fixated on him in anticipation. He could hear cameras flashing, then silence prevail; He began.

"I want to first thank those who have spoken, tendering to me, a man with no degree, no letters behind my name, one who's from the streets, a platform wherein I could speak directly to you without deception, pretense or inhibition. Here's what's real in twenty years at the rate that this country is moving the unemployment rate for black people will be 14 percent, one in every 15 black men will be incarcerated, the wealth gap between black and whites will be so wide that white Americans will have 22 times more wealth than black Americans. There will be 49 million people, 16 percent of the American population in poverty, 11 million of which will be black-yet it seems as though you think that you have the luxury of eliminating yourself at an alarming rate in a misguided manufactured attempt to access the American value system of power-wealth and prestige not knowing that the same social construct that you seek to access, to integrate, has socialized, orientated you for failure. They speak of you using descriptive terms such as endangered, irresponsible, maladaptive and they've successfully applied the label criminals to your color, existence and activity. According to Freud "Criminality is a maladaptive compromise between two or more conflicting forces within a special or societal personality which have not yet been completely integrated." Crime in itself finds its origins in an inequitable distribution of power so the criminal is a socially created reality that reflects disparity between groups-wherein a caste group is created and the opprobrious label have been attached, which not only prescribes ones thinking process, but also informs ones activity. Out of this state of powerlessness and impotence you seek to establish self-esteem, self-worth, and affirmation in order to be, so you use the only tool or vehicle available to you and that is violence. This is how you protest your impotence, your insignificance, but in this superimposed rage you're like Sampson pushing down the columns, only to have the building collapse upon you, destroy your own communities and they will collapse on you. You've accepted and actualize the projected images-superimposed upon you by the nefarious oppression to the point that the self fulfilling prophecy of self destruction and being endangered is becoming true. You enter into proxy alliances with the forces that oppress you and your own black hand is used vicariously to plunge the dagger into the collective hearts of your own communities viability. Relinquishing control of self-you become a thrall to your impulses, raw emotions and desires. Through the transference of your internalized self hate, you externalize your pain, hopelessness, acting in accord with those who have shaped-fashioned and formed your oppression. You seek to established your self-esteem through an insensate violence against those who display the characteristics that you hate in self.

This externalizing of pain is a form of suicide, for to kill one who bares the same characteristics is to kill the physiological-biological, genetic reproduction of self and ethnicity while simultaneously, superciliously rationalizing the act as self preservation. Your desires, needs and drives are socio-politically fabricated and manufactured by a ruling class that profits from your violence financially-egoistically and narcissistically. A ruling class that created your circumstance as a function of market economy. Then you're placed within the belly of the beast-the prison industrial complex wherein Corporations can exploit you as slave labor and because slavery, though outlawed, was written into the 13th amendment of the constitution in these words "neither slavery nor involuntary servitude, except as punishment for a crime where of the party shall have been duly convicted, shall exist in the United States etc. no one can argue your renewed enslavement."

The crowd erupted in applause that lasted for two minutes-before Kisasi was given the chance to finish "It's time that you shed the skin of adolescence, define your own reality, and stop attempting to be accepted under the auspices of who you were socialized-orientated to be. Be your beautiful black selves and eradicate, eviscerate the alienated personality identity that has been surreptitiously, diabolically manufactured and marketed to you." The crowd again erupted as Kisasi left the rostrum. As he attempted to egress, the youth in attendance crowded him shouting agreement and accolades. Out of his peripheral vision he saw clean cut, suited white men who were taking photos of him, this was the Bureau he reasoned. Myisha and Chantel immediately appeared at his side to help guide him out of the crowd to the limousine. Kisasi saluted the crowd then ingressed the limo where they sat dissecting his speech on their way back to the hotel suite. "Where did all that come from?" Chantel asked "You grow more and more every time you speak Myisha stated. Kisasi knowing the repercussions of the speech he'd just made merely stated, "There can be no growth without pain."

CHAPTER 63

Upon arriving at the hotel suite Myisha, Chantel and Kisasi relaxed in the living area discussing the speakers and their agenda. "Did you hear law enforcement attempting to advance the idea that more intense suppression tactics, police manpower, and legislation that allows them to stop and search anyone that looks suspicious as a way to reduce youth crime?" Myisha asked disgust permeating her intonation.

"They just want to put these young brothers back on the new plantation-prison," Chantel said expressing the same disgust. "Both of you are right but it's even deeper than that, they know that any and all sustainable change comes from the life blood of the community and that is the youth. They are the black oil that lubricates the wheels of change. They also possess the rebellious spirit to demand change. Through incarceration they disenfranchise and immobilize the youth, for the prison experience strips one of the Constitutional rights of voting-the right to bear arms-the right to equal protection in the job market-the right to equal housing-health care, and in some instances parental rights." Kisasi expressed. The phone rang and a knock came at the door simultaneously. Myisha moved to answer the door as Kisasi answered the phone. "DITR Kisasi speaking." he said as he looked toward the door to see who was on the other side. For a moment Myisha blocked the silhouette of the person on the other side but the voice was distinctively female. "Excellent speech sweetie" Naomi's voice emphatically stated into Kisasi's ear. He didn't know she attended the rally, and stated such. "You didn't think that I would not be here to support my favorite revolutionary did you" Naomi asked through playful banter.

"Not for a moment sistah, I'm glad that you were here," Kisasi reciprocated the gesture still looking towards the door to finally see Lana ingress the suite. As she brushed pass Myisha, Kisasi could clearly see that she'd gained a significant amount of weight, her skin dry, her eyes dim, her smile half hearted, though she was dressed in the best raiment, Manolo shoes, Vera Wang dress, diamond necklace with matching bracelet. "Let me call you back sistah, I have a visitor." Kisasi stated, exchanged goodbyes and hung up the phone. He walked towards Lana, arms extended-anxious to embrace his first love. They stood in the middle of the room holding each other as Myisha and Chantel watched-indifferent to the display of affection. "How have you been Malika?" Kisasi asked after breaking the embrace, Lana

326

stepped back spun and asked "Can't you tell?" Kisasi immediately noticing the attempt to sidestep his question stated, "I didn't ask about your finances sistah, I asked about you...money has never been the litmus test by which we measure our disposition." Lana had long ago abandoned the struggle and settled for matriculation into the status quo, rationalizing her treason she resented those who exhibited the integrity and testicular fortitude to remain in resistance to marginalization of their existence and now viewed the cause as one that was a relic of the past-engaged by dreamers that had not the intelligence to accept society as it was and act in the role designated for them. She adopted the fabricated ideology that one's inability to pull himself up from his bootstraps as an intrinsic defect devoid of social influence or coercion.

"Well the jury is still out on that issue." Lana quipped then asked "When are you leaving the capital?" "Our flight leaves tomorrow night." Kisasi answered. "Good we can meet for dinner tonight, is 8:00 o-clock good for you?" "8:00 o-clock it is sistah." Kisasi replied. 'I'll call from downstairs when my cab pulls up." Lana said as she spun and egressed the suite. Kisasi, not wanting to discuss what had just transpired, flashed a mechanical smile and said "excuse me" then returned Naomi's call. Both Myisha and Chantel Looked at each other in disbelief. It was clear to them that Lana had fell prey to the trappings of the social construct that was guilty of creating a circumstance wherein equal opportunity was denied, while the seductive charade called democracy was espoused. "Alright sistah "I'm back Kisasi said into the phone. "Listen sweetie I have family here, I would like to meet you sometime tomorrow before your flight leaves."

Naomi said. "My flight doesn't leave until tomorrow night, so lets get together about 12:00 or 1:00pm."

Kisasi suggested. "1:00 o-clock would be best for me." Naomi replied, gave Kisasi an address, exchanged goodbyes then hung up the phone. Night advanced quickly, before he knew it Lana's call came from the downstairs lobby. "I'm on my way down," Kisasi said. As he reached the door, he yelled back over his Shoulder to Myisha and Chantel who were both listening to the news reports of the rally "I'll be back later," as he egressed the suite and headed towards the elevator.

As soon as the elevator opened to the lobby, Kisasi saw Lana Sitting at a table waiting. They shared another brief embrace then got in a cab. She'd made reservations at an Italian restaurant, they arrived and were seated before Kisasi stated that he wasn't hungry, Lana followed suit. They ordered a bottle of wine, reminisced for a moment, which brought smiles to both of their faces, before Lana decided to challenge him concerning the effectiveness of his plight, "I hope you know that the majority of these people forget everything that you say soon after you've said it. Kisasi looked deep into the windows of her soul and said. "You sound like those bourgeoisie negroes that you used to disdain." Lana shifted in her seat preparing to defend her position," All I'm saying is that you keep putting yourself in a position for people that are not trying to change their own circumstance, we can't keep blaming white people for our own laziness, and lack of desire to work hard so that we can achieve. Look at me. I went to school got an education and am successful." "Yes you went to school, got a degree and are experiencing some fruits, but successful? That's subjective, for your definition of success may be another's definition of capitulation. As for blaming white people, I agree, though they created the circumstance, a belief system that gave birth to an attitude towards black people then enacted laws like Jim Cow to effectuate those attitudes, it is us that perpetuate our condition. That being expressed don't misoverstand my sentiments. I love this country, not for what it is but for what it has the potential to be for all that resides here." Kisasi said. "It doesn't sound like you love it, it sounds like you've bought into the back to Africa philosophy." Lana replied. "Back to Africa for what? My people built this country, blood, sweat, and tears, fought in every war, why should I invest in a back to Africa philosophy?" I want my piece of this country, this body politic-this economic system, this social construct and I refuse to capitulate to obtain it." Kisasi shot back. "And how are you going to obtain it Kisasi? Through violence? Through murder? How are you going to stop our own people from killing our opportunity through the drug trade? Are you going to kill the drug dealers?" Lana asked sarcastically. Kisasi searched her face for betrayal, why would she make a statement like that? He asked himself, was she the informant? If so Kisasi could seize this opportunity to disseminate a sanitized version of the posture that he'd taken in this struggle "I'll kill the mindset out of which the behavior emanates thereby modifying the sphere of activity." Lana, discouraged sat back in her seat pondered her rebuttal then spoke. "How will you kill the mindset Kisasi?" A mindset that is so ingrained that the same people that you are trying to help may end up killing you?" Lana asked. "The so called criminal behavior that we are witnessing in our blighted communities are the symptoms of an insidious social stratification, a diabolical marginalization, it's substratum is access denied, so to kill the mindset we must raise the consciousness, empower the disempowered and effectuate access at this social constructs value system changing self image and self concept which in turn enhances self value and once one values self, the love of self negates self destruction and will by proxy be attributed to others that share the same characteristics of self." Kisasi replied. Kisasi then looked at his watch "I got to get going sistah I have a lunch appointment tomorrow afternoon. I haven't had much rest since arriving in Washington." In reality Kisasi had become irritated with who Lana had become. He hadn't paid for her education that she may abandon the struggle. He'd paid for her education that she could garner a degree that would be employed in the struggle. He knew the temptation to resist the alien capitalistic ideology that lye just beneath the surface of curriculum, would be great, but he was sure that Lana could not be swayed by such pellucid contradiction of the American mantra. Though it was a bitter pill to swallow, Kisasi accepted the truth for what it was, instead of going against the machine, Lana had chosen to maintain and sustain the functionality of the status quo. He took this personally and vowed to effectuate reciprocation through Mrs. Cheri.

CHAPTER 64

Kisasi's cab pulled up to the address given to him by Naomi, a two story house in an affluent D.C. community. As he paid the cab driver Naomi egressed the house and stood on the front steps, flashing a coruscate, genuine smile. "Hey sweetie" she greeted him upon approach in case they were being photographed. Kisasi, overstanding the gesture took her hand shook and ingressed the residence. After the door was closed, Naomi wrapped her arms around him and kissed him full on the lips. Kisasi returned the gesture in spades.

They ingressed the exquisite dining room clad with original art-fine china display and a board room cherry wood table accented by matching chairs with a crystal chandelier suspended over it. "Have a seat brotha, do you want anything to drink?" Naomi asked while simultaneously egressing the room. "Ndio ndada–konyagi tafadhali- asante sana." Kisasi replied. "I watched the event from the crowd, so that I could get a feel for the reaction to what you said and also inventory the expressions of those who represent the status quo and brotha, as far as the status quo, you've ruffled some feathers but the youth felt what you were saying," Naomi said from the adjacent kitchen, when she ingressed the dining room both hands had drinks in them. She extended to Kisasi his drink, as he stood and pulled out a chair for her to sit, his cell phone rang. After seating Naomi, he answered his phone. "Uhali gani ndugu?" the voice on the other end asked. "Mimi sijambo." Kisasi replied then asked. "Jina lakonani?" "Askari," the voice answered Unatoka nchi gani?" Kisasi asked "Ninatoka almasi." Askari answered. After quizzing Askari in Swahili in order to ascertain his state of mind, Kisasi stated "How are you doing brotha?" "I'm good comrade I called to congratulate you on the speech you gave at the rally. As I watched the clip on the news I realized what I'd jeopardize under the influence of that poison. I wanted to personally ask for your forgiveness." Kisasi remained silent, Askari continued, "I know that it's going to be hard to rebuild the camaraderie that we once shared but if you give me the chance brotha you'll see that I'm still down with the struggle." Kisasi pondered what Askari had said. "Comrade you were the one that believed in me when this was nothing but an idea, you'll always have a seat at the table, but I need you healthy mentally, physically, spiritually and morally." Kisasi overstood the dynamics behind what had transpired between Askari and himself the dynamics that play themselves out within every black organization. He also knew the science behind the crack cocaine pandemic. It pained him that his camaraderie fell subject to this reality. If this interaction could be repaired that's what he wanted. Though his mind suggested that Askari too could be the informant, he'd still embrace him but, keep him at arm's length. "I only have a couple of months left in rehab. After I've completed treatment I want to return." Askari said. "We'll cross that bridge when we come to it brotha you just get healthy. I'm in the middle of a meeting at this moment, it was good to hear your voice we'll talk soon, shem hotep." Kisasi said. Askari returned the greeting, then they clicked off. "Samahani sistah" Kisasi apologized for the interruption, sat down and drained his glass. "Would you like me to refresh that?" Naomi asked. "I'm good sistah." Kisasi replied through a mechanical smile. "As I was saying the youth felt everything that you said, but the expression on the face of those that shared the rostrum was indignation and envy, at least on behalf of the men, the women hung on every word measuring the plausibility, then nodding their heads in agreement. That being said you're going to have to insulate yourself from this day forward. I saw those same looks on the faces of black men that opposed Malcolm and Huey whether it be the prison yard or the graveyard, they'll do whatever is necessary to silence you because in their minds you're infringing upon their delusional position of importance which funds their aberrant lifestyle. My suggestion is that you put together a security team of about five people trained in hand to hand combat and weaponry." Naomi said.

Kisasi hearing every nuance in Naomi's voice stated. "I agree, But if I arm my squad, outwardly I'd only be furnishing my opposition with the narrative needed to kill me openly like they did the Panthers. I can't put my people in that position. I must make it public knowledge that we don't carry weapons, that doesn't' prohibit me from possessing an arsenal to secure headquarters." Kisasi replied. "Also, Denise is active politically as it applies to legislation. She actively pushes legislation that empowers blighted communities and opposes legislation that behind the veil of its language-disproportionately targets individuals in blighted communities. She mastered the petition process and is actively sought by organizations to help them get favorable legislation passed. It would benefit our communities and DITR to give her the language needed to combat this civil injunction legislation that is being put forth, that would allow law enforcement to not only designate what a gang member is but, also give them the authority to take that identification process to the courts and have our brothas barred from the communities that they grew up in-bifurcating the family," Naomi said. Kisasi looked at his watch. They'd been talking for hours and he needed to get back to the suite and prepare for his return to Portland. He stood and said. "like always sistah, I've thoroughly enjoyed our discourse. I want to thank you again for all of your support." he extended his hand but Naomi walked into his embrace and kissed him passionately. After breaking the kiss she said. "Don't worry you'll get the opportunity to thank me for real." "I can't wait." Kisasi said, flashing a smile.

As Myisha, Chantel and himself sat quietly on the plane he thought about who he could trust to be security and the first name that came to thought Was Snip Snap. He then smiled out loud and leaned back into his seat.

CHAPTER 65

January 1,1994 Myisha, Chantel, Denise and Kisasi sat in his office at the DITR Center discussing the contract that Denise had negotiated with the judicial system wherein Kisasi was granted access to their juvenile and adult facilities to facilitate incarcerated peoples endeavor to transform their lives and return to their respective communities in an attempt to change the conditions from the inside out. She'd negotiated a yearly, fifty thousand dollar contract that Kisasi donated to the DITR Prison Reform Fund, which was used to fund transportation to and from institutions for family members and initial clothing upon release. Kisasi knew that transformation started with the reformation of family values, mores, and norms promoting the familial bond that governs interpersonal interactions which in turn informs societal interactions and dictate community responsibility. He took the opportunity to make pellucid his intentions as they applied to the capacity in which Denise would be employed.

"Before Denise came on board I'd been using Chantel to infiltrate boardrooms, corporate interests, judicial systems, political circles, financial institutions etc. because in reality her complexion opened doors that would have been closed to me as a black man and Myisha as a dark skinned black woman, that's the nature of the social construct that we are immersed in and though we've had successes across ethnic lines, the reality is that Denise is not only Caucasian but her family has strong governmental ties, wealth opens doors that have been historically closed to our people. There is no doubt in my mind that her families influence played a major role in us getting the contract with the judicial system, that fact must be and will be exploited and used to the advantage of those who languish behind the steel curtains of the prison industrial complex, regardless of their ethnicity, for justice is greater than race. Dr. Martin Luther King stated, "Injustice anywhere is a threat to justice everywhere." This statement being both profound and true we aid and assist any and everyone who truly seeks change. Overstand that the age old tactic of metaphrasing will be employed to render us impotent. For those who don't overstand what metaphrasing is-metaphrasing is when negative connotation are attached to positive activity to render said activity impotent or when positive connotations are attached to negative activity to make said activity palatable. Case and point when the word revolution was interpreted by government, law enforcement, and parroted by the media to mean a bloody overthrow of the government, the Panther Party was targeted for extinction, when in reality their interpretation of the word revolution was political and social change. Though their activity was positive, they were, through metaphrasing, painted negatively. They will also attempt to entice those inside of this organization with false promises of upward mobility, finances, and other trinkets to effectuate betrayal and dissension within the ranks and those that can't be enticed will be threatened to offer up the leadership. These tactics will be executed in black face. This is the reality of pursuing social justice, so our every move must be deliberate and distinct." Kisasi said searching Denise's eyes for any hint of inhibition, fear or sabotage.

Then he spoke directly to Denise. "Though we must use your white privilege you must be willing to sacrifice white privilege in order to be successful in executing the mitigating strategies that I will instruct you to employ that we ameliorate the circumstances, conditions, that our youths are faced with. Are you willing to do that?" "Of Course!" Denise stated empathically. "I'm going to use you, for anyone that can't be used, is useless, but I promise not to misuse you." Kisasi stated. Denise smiled coquettishly Kisasi knew that the only way to use Denise was to use her with her consent and now that he had it, it would be all gas, no brake-perpetual motion. Kisasi concluded that it was necessary that he re-define the sphere of activity in which each individual would operate that there would be no confusion which would cause anyone to inadvertently step on anyone else's toes hindering the functionality of the organization. "Denise you will be in charge of contractual agreements, Chantel will be in charge of running the everyday DITR scheduling and publicity and Myisha will act as chief financial officer and personal assistant. I'll do all the field work, speaking engagements television appearances, motivational speaking, institutional work Kisasi stated.

Myisha knew that her role would place her in Kisasi's presence at all times but she would keep her eyes peeled. She didn't trust Denise not because she exhibited any traits of subterfuge, but because of her life's experiences that she'd had with Caucasians. "Something that she would have to work on," she reasoned in an attempt to quiet her suspicions. One thing was for sure though, she would take advantage of every moment that she had with Kisasi. Chantel on the other hand saw how Denise would coo and pine for Kisasi's attention and approval. She knew that Denise saw the struggle through a rose tinted, rainbow hued prism and that her affections for Kisasi were based in that perception, but the struggle had a way of becoming so visceral that it had the capacity to turn affection into resentment. Changing ones furtive glances, ones unctuous whispers into scowls and slander.

Denise, smitten with and attracted to what she deemed as brilliance, reasoned that her meeting Kisasi was destined and that destiny could and would be all that she made it. She burned for the fight against injustice, yearned for the weapon that the creator had chosen to use to exact justice-Kisasi.

CHAPTER 66

It wasn't long before Denise made her feeling s for Kisasi known. The discourse between Chantel and herself began innocuously, "What's going on between you and Kisasi?" she asked. Chantel, measuring her response said. "He's my mentor, my comrade, the guy I feel can help the youth out of this condition that they are in, why do you ask?" "I asked because I'm interested in him." Denise answered.

"Just days after their meeting at DITR, this female tells me that she, in essence, has designs on the man that I not only love but am already engaged in a fight for, with Myisha, Chantel thought. I just wanted to be up front with you so that There would be no friction between us, and now that I know that you guys are not intimate I can pursue him in good conscience." Denise stated through a smile as they sat going over the schedule for Kisasi's speaking engagements.

The phone rang Denise answered "DITR how may I help you?" No he's not here can I take a message and have him contact you? Chantel knew that someone was inquiring about Kisasi and trained her ear on the telephone conversation that was taking place a few feet from her. "Yes Chantel is here, just a moment I'll transfer you," Denise said. The phone at Chantel's desk rang, she picked up "DITR Chantel speaking, how may help you?" The voice on the other end was familiar...it was Lana. "He's probably too busy to take your call, but I can take your message and make sure he gets it." Chantel said sarcastically after Lana, in an attempt to flaunt her familiarity with Kisasi, said that she'd been calling him on his private number to no avail. Denise took note of the catty back and forth between Chantel and Lana and though she was not privy to the history between them, she could tell that it wasn't all pleasant and hostility existed. "Listen sistah I'll relay your message, if that's all I have some work to take care of, you have a nice day, do take care of your health." Chantel ended the conversation with a backhanded comment. Lana now furious hung up the phone. Had Kisasi told this bitch About her health issue? He had to have she reasoned, and though he had not, Lana, out of her need to rationalize her abandonment of the struggle and to ameliorate the guilt that she felt concerning her capitulation and genuflecting in her work environment, settled on the idea that Kisasi had betrayed her trust and at that moment envy and venality took refuge in her heart. As the day wound down just before Denise and Chantel were to close the office for the day, Chantel turned to Denise and said. "I can't tell you what to do as far as it goes with Kisasi but overstand that if you pursue him you're going to have to deal with Myisha, she is no punk." Chantel, though she was taken aback by Denise's intentions to pursue Kisasi, took no issue with the fact, but she knew Myisha's experiences with white people and knew that Myisha would take issue with this. Denise gathering her personal effects from the office smiled and stated "May the best woman win."

Lana alone in her hotel room fumed with anger. How could Kisasi do this to her? He was the one that always propagated Loyalty- integrity. How could he divulge such personal information about her, to these little bitches, and this is why they'd been treating her in her opinion, with such antipathy? In light of this information why should she remain loyal to him, fuck him! Her mind screamed.

Le'Taxione

Concrete Roses

ABOUT THE AUTHOR

Le'Taxione is a student of the human condition and a specialist in the Structural Gang Culture © ideology. A scholar of a wide array of various discipline's including psychology – sociology – political science - physiology and grass roots organizations. He brings to bear his extensive studies and his own life experiences in his works to give the reader a glance into worlds that for the most part remain hidden behind the veil of night.

Concrete Roses

Le'Taxione was nurtured by relationships forged with other members of the diamond boys, and those relationships made possible his journey towards wholeness. He works to eradicate the violence of gang life, or racism and oppression, but treasure the gang and relationships between his members.

- Barbara Bennet, PH.D.

Concrete Roses

For years we have tried to address the violent behavior present in the structural gang culture © with recreational escapism-legislation and incarceration. N'S.T.E.P.™ addresses the violent gang psychology.

Concrete Roses

Gangology 101 is a holistic approach which identifies and addresses both the psychological and sociological aspects of gangs and gang violence prevalent in Post Traumatic Gang syndrome (PTGS) ©

Cover Art by Le'Taxione ™ for Diamond Culture Art

Concrete Roses

x

COMING SOON

Original Diamond Boy Part 2

This is the second part of a gripping memoire by Le'Taxione that takes the reader inside the insidious penological ideology – littered with authentic – official documentation that illuminates the surreptitious use of confidential informants in an attempt to thwart the pen of La'Taxione.

Concrete Roses

Cali draws from the principles and code of ethics taught to him by his Big Homie "Oso." His ban on the sell of crack cocaine, causes conflict, deception, disloyalty and splits the hood.